Embers and Sparks

Amy Allen

Other Bella Books by Amy Allen

A Sheep in Wolf's Clothing

About the Author

Amy is a trans woman who lives in Virginia with her brother and their two cats. When she isn't writing—or thinking about writing—she plays tabletop RPGs with her friends and devours far too many indie video games. Occasionally, she even remembers to do a little reading, from time to time.

Embers and Sparks

Amy Allen

BELLA
BOOKS

Acknowledgments

I must once again thank Evy, my trusty beta reader, on whose sharp teeth and claws I can always depend to rip and tear my work so that I can build it back stronger than before. Even when I throw a genre at her that she's not familiar with, she gives it her all.

I would also be remiss if I did not give a proper thank-you to the editor for my previous work, *A Sheep in Wolf's Clothing*, Heather Flournoy. I neglected to offer up the praise last time that she is most definitely due. Heather seemed to immediately and intuitively understand the spirit of the book and provided some really amazing ideas for how to make it sing. It was also a treat to receive the occasional infodump about why certain grammatical rules work the way they do. Getting to team up on another book has been an absolute delight.

After the outpouring of support, I owe a huge debt of gratitude to all of my friends, family, and coworkers who bought my book, read it, and perhaps even enjoyed it. That means the world to me.

And finally, thank you to Bella Books for taking a chance on me in the first (and second) place.

Dedications

For Matty and Nancy. Any similarities to any siblings present or absent is entirely coincidental and unintentional, except where noted otherwise by the author in canonical or supplementary material.

Love you.

PROLOGUE

Penny

Someone is trying to break down the front door of our apartment.

The sound is intense enough to jolt me out of my deep sleep. A shotgun blast, I think at first, or maybe some kind of battering ram threatening to burst through the cheap wood separating us from the chaos just outside.

But with each strike, it sounds less like an invading force and more like steady hammering.

I piece things together slowly. It takes a lot of brainpower, which is currently in short supply, but I finally finish processing it. What my poor, hungover mind had taken for cataclysmic danger is merely someone trying to get one of us to answer the apartment door.

I groan dramatically from where I'm sprawled out on the living room couch and look around for someone more lucid to put a stop to it. I attempt to say something coherent, like "Ah, I believe we have a visitor, but it would seem that I am presently indisposed! I should very much like to show them the socially acceptable level of warmth, to greet them with a smile, but to move from my current situation would no doubt cause me undue pain and stress. Please, could someone check on them, perhaps ask them to return at a later time such that we might be able to host them properly?"

What comes out is a pathetic, garbled noise, something between a groan and a whine.

From the floor next to me, with his head resting on a balled-up sweatshirt, comes a similar noise. My poor twin brother, Theo, is in much the same state as me. He'll be no help either.

I see our roommate Kai walk past to answer the door. My friend. My savior. There's a good lad. A sweet, young boy of twenty-and-nine, with his dark tousled hair and his almond eyes. He'll know just what to do.

"Mr. Callahan, hey, what can I do for you?"

"You can pay me the rest of your rent."

Ah. Crap.

Kai is silent for a few moments. "Sure thing. Let me rouse the troops and see what we can do. Uh, what's our…timeline?"

I hear our landlord give a beleaguered sigh. "Friday, end of the business day. After that, well…" He lets the unspoken threat hang silent for a moment.

"Yeah, I got you. Don't worry, you'll have it."

"That's what they always say. But you'd be surprised."

The door shuts—another noise that feels apocalyptically loud. Kai walks into the living room and looks down at me and my brother in our sorry states and lets out a sigh of his own. "Penny, Theo. You two were out getting plastered while we're on the edge of eviction? Real classy."

"In our defense," I reply groggily, my voice coming out like gravel, "most of our drinks were courtesy of other people. Birthday libations. Gifts from friends."

"Pretty sure that's not the point he's trying to make, Penny," my brother says from the floor, sounding equally gravelly.

"He's right, it's not. I feel like we go through this every month." Kai moves over to the recliner and slumps into it. "Are we screwed, or can you two cover your half of the rent?"

Kai is so good at just saying this stuff outright. It's not a skill Theo or I ever really learned. Growing up, it just wasn't the Hartwell way to talk things out. You could talk around things, tiptoe daintily in a circle about them. But having A Talk was a thing that required a great deal of buildup, pomp, and circumstance. We're at even more of a disadvantage because he's the only one in the room who isn't hungover.

"My next paycheck drops Thursday, and I've got some commissions I'm finishing up in the next few days," I say, already knowing it's not that easy but trying to offer something so Kai won't give us that pitying look.

Theo somehow manages to push himself up to a seated position. "Mm. I'll move some funds around. Besides, the band was gonna do some busking this week. The leech will get his share of lifeblood."

It's not much, but it's enough to put a relieved smile on our friend's face. "Cool. Thank you." He looks both of us over for a moment. "Sorry, I know this stuff isn't fun, and doing it on your birthday stings worse. Just…y'know. None of us can really afford to get evicted. Meagan and I could probably crash with family for a bit, but you two—"

He leaves it at that, thankfully letting the rest go unsaid. That we could never find a place as cheap as this one without moving into a shadier neighborhood. That we'd probably be forced to move back home. That moving back home would be monumentally traumatic. We're already having one hard conversation, better not segue into family shit.

With no small amount of effort, I manage to get myself off the couch and onto my feet. The room only spins a tiny bit, so that's probably good enough for now. "Water. Meds. Art."

"Hell yeah," Theo says weakly, doing his best to cheer me on.

I go into the hall bathroom and grab my pill divider, carefully removing the small collection of medication from the Monday slot and tossing them into my mouth, chasing it with water from the tap. Then, very hesitantly, I take a look in the mirror to survey the damage.

Frankly, it's not as bad as I feared. I feel worse than I look— though I definitely *look* thirty. My eyes have noticeable bags underneath, and they're a tiny bit bloodshot. The green of my irises seems like it's faded over the years, but that's probably just me being dramatic. Once upon a time, my black hair had been a pretty decent fringe bob, but now it's growing out weird and uneven. And I didn't do it—or my spine—any favors crashing on the couch like I'm still in college. I'm going to be feeling this particularly stupid decision for the next few days—or, more realistically, weeks.

All in all, could be worse. Could be a lot better, granted, but you get out what you put into it, and I haven't exactly been taking the best care of it. Her. Me.

That's probably just about all the self-examination I can do before the dysphoria sets in, so I leave the bathroom and swing through the kitchen. I grab two bottles of water and the painkillers from the top of the fridge, and go back to join Theo.

Kai has already disappeared back into his bedroom, and my brother is sitting on the couch cradling his face in his hands. "I feel like an asshole."

"Ditto," I say, popping two pills before passing two more over to him with the other bottle of water.

"We gotta do better, Penny," he mutters, taking them with a large glug.

"How?"

"Terra Vertebrae is taking some more gigs, and like I said, we'll try to play more in the stations downtown, or out at Boston Common. The battle is coming up, and we have a really good shot of getting in this year. First prize would be a big deal—we could get some actual studio time, maybe put out a real album." He looks at me with a shrug. "And you've always got your commissions and shit. You could take on a few extras. I know you can knock them out in no time."

Like it's all so easy. I can do them when I'm not exhausted from work. And the only way I can get people to buy my art is by charging a fraction of what it's worth, drawing the things they want, not my own stuff.

Besides, I remember us having this same conversation five years ago. Has anything really changed? We've just been coasting by. Debt and late rent are enough to light a fire of desperation under you. But they're not really conducive to making good art. It's all just…getting by. Cinders by comparison.

It's enough to make a woman wonder if mumsy and papá were right. Being a starving artist is all fun and games when you're a twenty-something, but it doesn't have quite the same ring to it when you hit the next decade marker. "So we just do…more?"

"Art harder," he says with a serious nod.

"Art smarter?"

"Art like the wind."

"Fart out that art."

There's a beat, and then we're both laughing like it's the funniest thing in the world, even knowing that we're just hungover and loopy. We slump back on the couch and continue to giggle together like we're kids again. All these years later and it's still the really stupid stuff that gets us going.

Only after we've gotten out all of our giggles and we're only occasionally bubbling with light chuckles do I finally relent. "Okay."

"Okay?"

"Okay. We got this."

"The only other option is—" He stops and shakes his head. "Well, it's not an option."

With another herculean push, I manage to get myself up to my feet. My task is before me, my path laid clear.

Time to fart out that art.

Anthea

I'm awoken by the shrill ring of my phone, and I strongly consider not answering it. I already know who is on the other end of the call, and I already know what she's going to say.

But because of that, I also know a third, much more important thing. She will not stop. She's been waiting ten years, to the day, for this. And despite the fact that we quite literally have all the time in the world, she won't wait another minute.

Family, right?

Finally, I relent and answer. "Hello, Matilde."

She's several hours behind me, which means it's even earlier for her. And yet her voice is so bright and chipper you'd never know. "Anthea, darling! It's a bright, beautiful world outside and my sister is going back to work!"

"Exactly. I'm going back to work. You're not my warden, surely you trust that I won't shirk my sacred duty."

I can almost picture her—towering high with that mane of golden locks, making her trademark little pout, checking her nails as though they aren't already perfectly manicured and painted. "I most certainly am not your warden. I'm your loving, older sister."

She's never once let me live down the fact that she has a few decades on me. As if that's not the equivalent of a few seconds by comparison, in the grand scheme of things. We can't all be lucky enough to have been born from a song. Some of us had to wait for the discovery of fire. "And as such, I am personally invested in your well-being. It was perfectly understandable that you needed to take a constitutional, all things considered. I supported that."

"You put a time limit on it."

"Because the Work is important, Anthea. Because it gives us life and fills our hearts with song. You've spent ten long years denying that." She's quiet for a surprisingly long time. Matilde doesn't normally go in for long silences, unless she's being dramatic, in which case she can go quite a while without speaking. "How was your time away? Any grand discoveries? Any earth-shattering revelations?"

There's a *tone* in her voice, because she already knows the answer to that. Or she thinks she knows. In her world, the two are one and the same. "No, I'm afraid I did not live, laugh, nor love my way into some kind of nirvana. But it was a pleasant distraction after—" I stop myself, not ready to say any of it out loud. It was a good vacation, but it didn't actually heal any of my wounds. "Well.

After everything. So I hope you'll temper your expectations for the foreseeable future until I've found my sea legs again, yes?"

"Absolutely! I'm not suggesting you jump into the deep end, to muddy metaphors here somewhat. No, no, find yourself something easy—some*one* easy. Get your feet wet—oh dear, there I go again—until you're ready to buckle down and inspire something truly great again."

It's not a bad idea, really. Start small. Follow the ebb and flow of the city until I find someone worthwhile and give an experimental little push. Simple as that. After all, that's the saying, isn't it? All it takes is a spark.

For all my exasperated eye-rolling, I have to give Matilde her due. Most of our siblings would have ignored my pain and encouraged me to get right back out there and play the field again. Matilde was more measured, more understanding, even if she did force me to limit myself to only a decade free from responsibility. Again, seconds on the grand scale of the universe. But hopefully it was enough to clear my head and give me what I needed.

"I can do that. Hmm, I hope I'm not too rusty." While inspiring art might be our natural inclination, that doesn't mean it's easy to do it right. The ideal balance is difficult to find, and it's different for each artist.

"There isn't a lick of doubt in my heart. You'll find your stride again in time, dear sister. Like riding a bike. Oh! No, no, like a duck to water. There, I've brought it back around to aquatic theming."

I just can't help it. When you get past all her ridiculous posturing, Matilde still knows how to bring a smile to my face, and I begin to chuckle. "Quack quack, darling. I promise I'll give it my all."

"You needn't give it one hundred percent immediately. A solid effort is all I ask. Now get to it! Or I'll have to catch the next flight out to the East Coast and show you how it's done."

Still laughing, I perch on the edge of my bed and ready myself to start my first day back on the clock, so to speak. "I'll update you soon, I promise. Now don't let me keep you. I'm sure you have a full day ahead of you." Matilde is a busy woman. She runs her own talent agency in Los Angeles, ensuring she has no end of performers she can shower with her gifts. She never could be tied down to one human at a time. Not like me.

Perhaps that's why she never developed a complex. Not like me.

"That line could wrap around the block three times over and I would still make space for you, Anthea." From anyone else, that would just be a bit of familial hyperbole to sound pretty, but I know she means it.

"Love you."

"Love you too. Ta."

As I finally hang up, I think for just a moment about crawling back under my fluffy comforter for a few more hours. Maybe a few more days. I could potentially get away with it. Lie about how things are going the next time she checks in. But I also know she'd see right through me. Matilde knows me too well. And while I'm loath to admit it, for all my fears, some part of me is eager to finally try again.

If I'm going to do this, then I'll do it right. Start slow. Put on the armor. Keep a healthy distance until I'm ready for the real thing.

First things first, I need to get cleaned up. I head for the bathroom to get in a proper shower. But I stop long enough to examine myself in the mirror first. I've had this particular face for several decades now, with the occasional tweak to account for "aging," so to speak. For those of us who have taken on physical forms, we've long since learned all the necessary tricks for staying incognito. Either move around a great deal, or alter your appearance enough to avoid getting noticed. Or, do what Matilde does and lie through your teeth about coming from extremely sturdy stock where all the women look shockingly youthful and similar. It takes confidence to pull off, and she's got that in spades.

I suppose I could do a full reconstruction in honor of my big return. But I find I've grown fond of this version of me. Anthea Corey is a woman who might be in her midforties and probably comes from somewhere vaguely Mediterranean. She has striking features, with just enough imperfections to avoid the uncanny valley—the nose is just ever so slightly crooked in a way that I feel extremely proud of.

But enough self-congratulatory preening. It's time for me to get ready and hit the scene. There's a city full of people outside my window. Surely one of them will be a safe bet, a quick and easy job for a muse who's maybe a little out of practice.

STEP ONE: SKETCH

CHAPTER ONE

Penny

There's something particularly infuriating about the inability to create. Art is so very human, and when you find yourself running into a wall, it makes you worry. Am I less human now? Have I lost my connection to the past and the present and the future because I'm in a rut? Is there some essential thing that I am no longer a part of just because my brain refuses to play along?

I tap my stylus against my tablet and stare at my computer screen, watching as a series of dots form. Tap. Dot. Tap. Dot. If I put down enough dots, it'll make a line. Get some more lines, and baby, that's art. But I'm stuck on the dots. It doesn't matter that I've got this commission staring me down with a looming due date. The music pumping through my headphones does nothing for the process.

Create, you asshole. Make something. They want fan art of an anime you know inside and out. You should be able to draw these two characters smooching in your sleep. Your room and board are riding on this. It'd be really nice to not have to eat rice and beans for every meal. And this tiny bedroom in our tiny Boston apartment costs ten times what it should. Callahan is breathing down our necks demanding rent, and we don't really have the luxury of sitting around bemoaning the nature of capitalism.

I shot myself in the foot thinking I could make a living being an artist. All I had to do at some point was look at the world around me, or at the long history of actors and painters who spent their lives struggling and suffering. It would have saved me a lot of time and heartache.

Oh, who am I kidding? I'm a creator. I make things. It's what I've always done, and what I always want to do. Not even a visit from present-me via time machine would have stopped baby Penny from making the choices she did. All theories about alternate universes aside, there was really only one path that this version of me could have gone down.

None of that ontological assurance does much good in the face of overwhelming artist's block, though. I can tap this stylus against my tablet until the nib is pulverized, but it's not going to make an image magically appear. I'm working full shifts the next two days, and that many hours on my feet is enough to kill pretty much any artistic drive I might otherwise have. So if I want to earn the extra scratch from these commissions, then this needs to happen now. I'm desperate. I need a change of scenery and some fresh air—or as fresh as the air gets around here.

I put the stylus down with a dramatic sigh and stand up from my creaky chair, stretching out my creaky body. As my back muscles protest, I bemoan my stupid, drunken decision to crash on the couch only to spend several hours hunched over a tablet. Dammit, Penny, you're not a young doe anymore. Welcome to your thirties, idiot.

I grab my backpack and throw in some of my crappier art supplies. No point in wasting the good stuff right now, I'm just going hunting for inspiration. So a cheap spiral sketchbook and mechanical pencils will do the job fine.

Next, I check my phone to figure out how many layers I'm going to need. It's early March in New England, which means the weather is completely unpredictable. Thanks, climate change. According to the app—once I suffer through the unskippable ad—I can confirm that it's, scientifically speaking, "cold as balls" out there. So I throw on a hoodie and my heaviest coat and leave my room.

Theo's still out in the living room, though he's now busted out his bass and I can hear him working on something funky. As I walk past, he looks at me curiously. "What's up?"

"Cabin fever. Or, apartment fever, I guess? I'm having trouble really making anything worthwhile, so I'm gonna run out for a bit and see if I can't jump-start my brain a little."

"Hell yeah. Get out there and find something beautiful. That's what I'm talking about."

From behind me, I hear the door to Kai's bedroom open, and our friend pokes his head out. "I'm making dinner for everyone later. Partially because I do feel kind of crappy getting on your cases about stuff." He gives me an apologetic smile. "Can you grab paper towels while you're out?"

I do some quick mental math. I've at least got enough in my bank account to grab a roll of the shitty stuff. It'll have to do. "Yeah, no problem. Be back in a few hours."

He gives me a grateful thumbs-up before disappearing back inside, returning to his latest project. I'm pretty sure he mentioned writing code for some new app that will inevitably crash and burn. But he got a massive advance, so he's kept his complaining to a minimum.

As always, there is silence from Meagan's room down the back hallway. Her bartending job keeps her on a different schedule from the rest of us. Last night was the first time any of us have really sat down and hung out in a while, and she still spent half the time behind the bar. But she's cool and she pays her portion of the rent on time. Kai will make sure there's a Tupperware container of leftovers in the fridge for her. It's not much, but it's something.

Be it ever so humble, there's no place like home.

It's four flights down from our apartment to the ground floor and I'm already a little winded—yup, definitely getting older. I used to justify it to myself, that it's good exercise to be forced to take all these stairs constantly. But I know the truth is just that we're a little too settled to look for somewhere with a functioning elevator. Places with functioning elevators are for people with deeper pockets than us.

The second I step through the door, I'm hit with a wave of frigid air made all the more biting by the breeze blowing in off the harbor. In the late spring and summer that airflow is a blessing. But in winter, it makes a manageable twenty degrees Fahrenheit feel subzero. Regardless, I've made my decision to go wandering, and I don't feel like climbing back up those stairs. So I bury my hands in my pockets, grit my teeth, and trek off into the day.

Only as the T stop comes into view does it occur to me that I haven't actually picked a destination yet. If the day were nicer, I might go over to Boston Common or out toward Boston College to soak in the scenery. But I need somewhere that's inspiring and, more importantly, *warm.*

I suppose I could always hit up one of the half-dozen different coffee shops nearby. But the thought of being that cliché hurts, and there's always the risk of the place being unexpectedly swarmed by college kids.

I update the list of things I need: inspiring, warm, and *quiet.* Finally, it comes to me—the library.

For my first few years in the city, I made the mistake of assuming that the Boston Public Library would be big but otherwise unimpressive. Everyone knows what a library is. It's got books and desks and computers and an unhealthy obsession with some guy named Dewey. But then Kai dragged me along to a concert there, and my eyes were opened. It's opulent and gorgeous inside, as much a museum or wedding hall as it is a repository of knowledge.

I don't go as often as I'd like, but whenever I do, I find myself filled with something special. And if I'm very lucky, it might give me what I need.

I retrieve my trusty pair of battered headphones from around my neck and slip them over my ears, plugging the fraying wire into my phone. With weather like this, and considering my slump, a melancholy vibe feels appropriate. So I put on some shoe-gazing hipster music and make the trek down the sloping hill toward Commonwealth Avenue.

The T stop closest to our apartment is a sad little above-ground affair, with a meager handful of people waiting around for the next train to pull through. We all stand around awkwardly, shifting and stamping our feet to build up a little heat against the cold air. And while my dour tunes match the weather, they also make me that much more aware of the chill fighting my jacket.

By the time a train does finally pass through, I'm eager to push through the doors and find a seat where I can curl up and soak in the heat for a while.

It's not until I climb the stairs up out of Copley station that I remember why coming downtown on a cold, blustery day is a terrible idea. That breeze from the harbor picks up between the buildings and you're shot through with razor winds. I move as fast as my weak noodle legs will carry me and rush into the massive gray stone building.

There's a small crowd in the lobby enjoying a guided tour, and I carefully step my way around them. Still, I can't help but move slowly through the space and admire everything. I don't know much about architecture, but I know what I like, as they say. The soft pink of the marble is so uncanny and yet so inviting, you feel like you're entering some ancient temple. But then you see these iron lampposts topped with glowing globes, and the juxtaposition is wonderfully striking. It gives the foyer this feeling that you're in a dream, a mash-up of two vastly different places that still, inexplicably, seems so right.

Moving up the Grand Staircase, I pause beside one of the two marble lions guarding the threshold. Almost reverently, I pull the headphones down from my ears and drape them back in place around my neck, then reach out to stroke it gently on the tail, like so many visitors before me. "Keep up the good work, buddy," I mutter softly to him.

I'm vaguely aware of someone entering my periphery to join me in admiring the noble beast. "You do realize they can't hear you, right? Please tell me you understand that."

My cheeks start to burn. Caught in the act, indulging in a silly rite of passage. I glance nervously in their direction and am almost bowled over by what I see.

The lions look like living creatures turned into stone. And this woman, she's their counterpart—a work of art turned flesh and blood. She's got maybe an inch or two of height on me, and I'm not exactly short myself. Her skin is warm and golden-beige, and she's wearing an olive-green dress with a chunky knit scarf. Her curled, deep-brown hair is pinned back, decorated with a faux-laurel headband. There's something almost classical about her face—the aquiline nose, the solid jawline, the full lips in a puckish smile. A face this striking demands to be drawn, and I can feel my hand practically twitching.

Alas, *Sweet Mother, I cannot weave...*

All I can do is stammer for a moment, caught between my embarrassment and my admiration. "Of course. It's just a stupid ritual I started a few years ago."

She studies me for just a moment, until that playful look shifts into one of genuine warmth. "Sorry, I'm only teasing you. I think that's sweet. This place *is* pretty special, and for all we know, these two could be fending off any number of unseen threats. Maybe they really do deserve a little recognition." That sounds like another joke, but there's something steady in her tone that sounds sincere.

"You don't get into my line of work without allowing for the occasional flight of fancy or bizarre superstition."

"Oh? And what line of work is that...?" She trails off and gestures toward me. It takes me a moment to realize she's asking for my name, rank, and file.

"Penny. Artist. You?"

"Ah, that'll do it. I'm Anthea." The name has a fanciful, musical quality to it—An-*thay*-uh. She hesitates before providing her second answer, like she really has to think about it. "I suppose you could say I'm between jobs at the moment. I just came out of retirement and I'm looking for something new."

Gauging how old Anthea is feels like a monumental task. She's youthful, but I don't think she's young. Not to mention, even if she's just a damn good-looking fifty, that's still a pretty early retirement. "Wow. What'd you do before?"

"I'd tell you, but then I'd have to kill you," she says with a little wink. It's charming, as far as evasive threats go.

Not wanting to press my luck with a relative stranger, I let it go with a light chuckle. Besides, I still have my mission. Operation: Don't Get Evicted, Idiot. "Say no more. Anyway, I don't want to keep you." I turn and start making my way up the stairs toward the reading room so I can set up shop and try to make some magic happen.

After a beat, Anthea turns and heads up the stairs after me. I laugh softly and pause on the landing at the top of the stairs. "We're going the same way, aren't we?"

"That all depends on where you're headed," she says with that same playful tone.

"I was planning on grabbing a table up in Bates Hall."

"It would seem you are correct, then. A classic social bungle. Shall I continue awkwardly following a few steps behind?"

"Eh, that seems like an unnecessary complication. We're both adults. I think we can survive this embarrassment together."

Anthea laughs too. Just like her name, it's got a musical quality to it that lands nicely on the ear. She slots herself in next to me and we continue on our way together. "As long as we're taking our journey side by side, do you mind if I ask why you came out here? Hunting down some elusive tome?"

"Nah, just…needed to get out of my apartment for a while. And out of my head. Go somewhere beautiful, find a little inspiration."

"Hmm." It's not even a word. Barely a syllable. Just an exhalation and a thoughtful noise. I don't think I've ever heard a single sound that was so weighty before. "Well. Boston's got its fair share of inspiring locales, and you've chosen a fine one indeed."

"I really hope so." For a split second, I find myself compelled to dump everything in this woman's lap. But the feeling passes just as quickly as it struck me, and I manage to hold it all in. "I could use the spark."

We finally pass through the doors into Bates Hall, the library's grand reading room. It's a cavernous space with a high, barrel vault ceiling. The bookshelves that line the walls, the tables with their classic green-shade bankers lamps, and more of those beautiful iron lamps built into the walls—some of this stuff has been here for nearly one hundred and fifty years. This place has a history that infuses every single inch of it. It's one of the benefits of living in a city that's been around since the colonial period. You get to see some truly awesome monuments to the beauty humans can create.

I take in a deep breath, and I'm hit with the wonderfully calming smell of aged paper. Away from the tour groups and the chatting visitors, the silence in here is palpable and visceral, punctuated occasionally by the rustle of a page being turned or fingers tapping away at laptop keys.

This could be another world, a million miles away from our claustrophobic apartment and my lack of inspiration and my cloying sense of inadequacy. Here and now, I just might be able to do this.

Anthea leans over, dropping her voice to a respectful whisper and patting me on the shoulder. "I think it's safe to say this will get you where you need to go. Good luck, Penny." She steps away and over to a row of bookshelves along the wall, walking her fingertips along the spines in search of something.

Our interaction, however small, has done a lot to ease the tension that had been building up all day. Between the rude awakening and all the heavy conversations before running headlong into my own art block, my thirtieth year wasn't off to a great start. But now, there's a kind of eagerness as I pick an empty table and sit down. I'm feeling, dare I say it, hopeful as I set down my bag and start retrieving everything I need—lay out the notebook, flip to the next open page, brandish one of my cheap mechanical pencils, put my headphones back in their rightful place.

I switch to something bluesy and nod in approval. Yes, this is good, this is right. I can definitely make some magic happen now. I bring the tip of the pencil to the page and just…stare at it, instrument still and motionless. The pure, white page stares right back, begging me to use it, daring me.

Sorry, bud. Art block is a real bitch. I thought we had it this time.

I consider packing it in now. Even if I don't get any commissions knocked out in the next few days, my paycheck should be enough to cover rent. And there's always Thursday to get caught up, drop the money from PayPal to my account on Friday and maybe get groceries or whatever. Things suck, yeah, but they could be a lot worse. I can muddle through somehow. I'm only a temporary failure.

As I glance around, I see Anthea with a book in her hands walking closer. I think perhaps she's going to grab one of the empty tables around me. The library's not particularly busy on this otherwise nondescript day. But, to my surprise, she comes right over to where I'm sitting and occupies the opposite corner. As she sits down and cracks open the book she's grabbed—a beautiful, weathered hardcover copy of *The Wonderful Wizard of Oz*—she gives me a supportive nod.

Okay, Penny, this random stranger you talked to for five minutes apparently believes in you. That's good enough. That's your lifeline. Try it again. One more attempt, for real. And if it's just not happening, then we'll go home and lick our wounds, and we'll try again tomorrow.

I turn my eyes back to the page, and my pencil is already moving. It's flying. Like magic.

CHAPTER TWO

Anthea

I have to admit, this feels *good*. And Matilde was right: You never really forget the fundamentals.

Stepping out of my apartment building earlier this morning, I clutched my coat tighter around me as the chill threatened to seep into my core. Whether it was the lingering winter or the strength of this woman's potential, I found her warmth almost instantly. I closed my eyes and saw her in the distance like a candle illuminating a pitch-black cave. I felt that gnawing desire to offer up my spark and turn her into a blazing bonfire. She was close, too, barely a few blocks away.

That warmth, that desire, called to me so intensely that I lost all sense of the world around me. Not even the blaring horn from the car that nearly hit me was enough to snap me out of my trancelike state. There was one thing, and one thing only, that I cared about.

And as we talked, however briefly, I found myself surprised by this curious woman who had pulled me here so powerfully. There was no real way of knowing what to expect, of course. An artist's energy doesn't come attached with a dossier, just a sense for how big the inevitable bonfire might become. But that didn't quite prepare me, not for this one. There have been so many over the millennia. But there was a pattern to them, especially during the last century or two. Brilliant but eccentric. Incredibly self-assured yet achingly dramatic in their failures. More than a few narcissistic nepotists.

I never said it was a pleasant pattern.

Penny feels different in a very visceral way that I'm still sifting through. Less confident, but with a deep well of potential that's almost intoxicating. Even from a simple glance, it's obvious that she doesn't maintain the same kind of lavish lifestyle.

She'll make for a nice change of pace out of the gate. Starting on the right foot and all that.

I do wish I could get a look at her notebook, see what she's drawing, but I'm not feeling confident enough to press my luck like that. The important thing is that the feeling is there, the sensation of someone creating something from my inspiration. And while it might just be a sketch on the page of a cheap notebook, that doesn't matter. What matters is the person themself. And Penny is shining, for sure. I barely had to give her a push.

Feeling quite satisfied with myself, I go back to my book. It's not like it's just for show. I've never actually read these stories before, so I figure there's no time like the present. I find a more comfortable position in my chair and indulge in some classic literature for a while.

I manage to get through two chapters when I feel something… shift.

It's not easy to describe—like knowing you're off-balance even with your eyes closed. My people, we have an acute connection to the movement of emotion and creative energy, even more so when we're putting out inspiration into the world. But the experience is keenly different when we become the subject of that art.

Penny is drawing *me*.

Some of my more conservative siblings have very strong feelings about it, claiming we were never meant to be depicted. Our only task is to be the whisper, the drive, the impulse. Always the bridesmaid, never the bride. So when it happens, there's something about it that feels just a little bit rebellious, a tad naughty. Which is maybe why I enjoy it so thoroughly.

I know now I've found someone worth putting more time into. And the fact that she's already started drawing me means there must be some level of connection here. So I decide to push things forward just a bit more and properly bait the hook.

Looking up from my book, I finally glance toward Penny and catch her eye as she goes to study me again. I flash a warm smile—something encouraging, inviting even.

But she just gapes back at me with an intense, deer-in-the-headlights panic. As cute as it is, I also feel a bit bad for surprising her. Just as suddenly, she averts her gaze, face going deep red from an intense blush.

I intend to say something, to explain that it's all right, or ease whatever worries she's having in that moment. Unfortunately, I don't get the chance. While I'm busy thinking up the right thing to offer, she starts hastily shoving all of her things into her bag.

"Um! I've got to go. But it was nice meeting you!" She has a terrible stage whisper, and it carries to every corner of the reading room. As if to drive home the implication that she's some kind of spooked wild animal, she awkwardly climbs out of her chair and starts practically scrambling for the doors out the hall.

Perhaps if I weren't so out of practice, I might have been able to convince her to stay. I'd forgotten what it was like to be so green. So I'm forced to watch her leave, bemoaning what a shame it is to let someone with so much potential slip away. But it's never been my style to actively pull artists into my world—perhaps it was a given that my first attempt would be so fumbling. If only I knew what made her so skittish that she would run away like that.

Things with Penny may not have gone as well as I would like. But I'm still working out all the kinks from my lengthy absence. It's bound to happen. The important thing is that I keep at this. So I eventually check out my book and leave the library to poke around the city a bit more. I do pass a few people on the street who have that familiar hole in their heart, so I leave them with a tiny spark as I walk by. It's not much, but by the time they reach the end of their day, they just might turn that energy into something beautiful.

In a nearby station, I find a young woman with honey-blond hair playing a melancholy tune on a weathered violin. I throw some money into her case on the ground and listen to the rest of the song. When it's over, I gently touch her shoulder and smile. "That was wonderful, thank you." Tonight, with any luck, she'll discover the first few notes of her next masterpiece.

After a while, though, I have to admit that my day started at its high point and perhaps I shouldn't push myself anymore. Soon enough, I'll remember how to really sustain it. For now, helping a few souls is more than I've done in ten years.

On my way back to my apartment, I stop off at my favorite coffee shop. Savage Roast is only a short walk away from home, and the atmosphere is quite cozy. They don't try to be hip and cool, nor fashionable and upscale. They have comfortable couches and simple music and plenty of plants to give the place a charming, welcoming feel. I've gone in at least once a week for almost two years now.

As always, the bells on the door ring to announce my entry, and a familiar face is working the register today. Raine is a student at Boston University who somehow always manages to have a bright smile despite juggling all the coursework required for a double-major-double-minor bachelor's degree. She digs her hands into the pockets of her canvas apron and gives an excited little bounce. "Heya, Anthea! What are we up to today? The Gardener?"

Behind her, scrawled across a series of blackboards in Technicolor chalk, is the café menu. Savage Roast makes some wonderful drinks. They also make some very *bizarre* drinks. On a whim, I'd started going down the list in order, trying a new one each time I stop in. "Hello, Raine. I actually had that one the other day. I'm not sure coffee is really meant to have a shot of jasmine in it."

"And yet people keep buying it. So it must be appealing to someone."

"It takes all kinds. So I suppose that brings me to…" I trace my eyes over the list and coo with some genuine enthusiasm. "Ooh, the Green Monster." Green tea and pomegranate. That sounds like exactly what I need right now.

"One monstah for the lady with the lovely name." Once it's paid for, Raine passes a mug and a ticket to her associate making the drinks. "We'll have that ready for you in a couple minutes."

I head into a quiet corner where I can curl up on a couch away from everyone else. While I mess with my phone, I find myself thinking about that Penny woman in the library. It makes sense, of course. Her call was powerful enough to draw me there in the first place. I actually exchanged words with her and gave her a more sustained supply of influence than anyone else today. Our interaction, such as it was, also had the most dramatic ending. One moment, everything is going well enough, and the next, she's rushing out of the place like Cinderella two minutes before midnight.

Already I know that I'm focusing on this singular person more than I should. That's the kind of behavior that led to me getting hurt and burnt out in the first place. So it's only natural I should fall right back into old patterns now. This time around, I need to do things differently. I need something shallow and selfish and easy. Matilde does that better than me, and I did promise I'd let her know how things are going. This is perhaps a bit earlier than I'd intended to do it, but I need some sage advice before I get trapped in my rut all over again.

The other barista comes over and sets down my mug with a more subdued and polite smile than Raine. I'm pretty sure I'd be getting the neutral look if my tip hadn't been so sizable. I nod gratefully before picking up the mug and blowing on it slowly, then take an experimental sip. It's earthy and lightly sweet. I'm fairly certain I've just found my new favorite drink here.

While waiting for it to cool a bit more, I work up the nerve to call Matilde.

"Darling! Already phoning to tell me that you've had an absolutely perfect first day, and to thank me for my excellent suggestion of a temporary break instead of quitting altogether?"

What a brat. "If only. It wasn't terrible, as far as first days go. But I wouldn't call it a rousing success. Still, there was this woman with an incredibly strong pull."

"Oh, Anthea…" There's some very real pity underneath that bless-your-heart tone of voice. "I really hoped you'd manage to go a couple months before this happened. Or at least a few weeks."

"Matilde, you know me. You know what I'm like, how I get. I can't help myself! And her energy was so different from the others. No raging fires or thundering storms. Just…warmth and light. I mean, notes of neuroticism with a hint of desperation, sure. Nobody's perfect. But it really was a good start." While it might seem absurd to speak about all this so plainly in public, there's really no point in worrying or censoring ourselves. Human minds can ignore a great deal when the uncanny grinds up against their grounded reality. They'll either block it out completely, or assume I'm talking about some New Age nonsense.

Like earlier today, Matilde is quiet for a long while. "Sweetie, I'm afraid I'm going to have to put my foot down. It's too early to be choosing a single artist. No more tuning in to this woman's frequency."

"No danger of that. She…started drawing me, and caught me looking at her, then promptly ran for the hills. I'm the last person she'll want to see. And honestly, after that, I did have a pretty good string of random gifts. Some passersby, a busker, that kind of thing."

"But…?"

"But. I can still feel the old me wanting that particular brand of trouble that comes from putting all my eggs in one basket. And I'm trying to keep that from happening. So, please, tell me how you do it. Impart your wisdom unto me, your poor baby sister, who knows nothing of dividing her attention the way you do." I'm laying it on thick, but I need this. I can't do what I did before. Something has to change this time around.

"You've always taken your inspiration far too personally, Anthea. And as a result, you treat the process like a relationship, like making love, or something even more poetic and gag-inducing. Me? I know it's a lark. An engaging bit of amusement.

You're always so *serious*, darling. From the outside looking in, I have to imagine it must be exhausting."

She's right, though I won't say it out loud. It's overwhelming sometimes, being me. And I'm fairly certain being yourself is one of the few things that should come naturally.

"So maybe what we need to do is rethink our terminology, eh? It's not the Work, it's not our Grand Purpose. It's…the Game!" She snaps excitedly, and I can almost picture the enthusiasm on that expressive face. "I rescind my previous point. You should absolutely find this woman again."

"Well, that doesn't sound ominous at all."

"It's simply not viable to waste the time and energy turning you into me, or even teaching you how to do what I do. However, I believe it may be possible for you to 'find the fun,' in your own special way. So, I say, pull this woman to you when you're ready, and accept the fact that you're an ageless being with the capacity to give or take your inspiration on a whim. Enjoy just how much power this gives you over her! Strut a little."

This is…actually not terrible advice, though I'm sore at just how easily my sister can read me. And she's managed to sum up in so many words our different approaches. Matilde has always seen herself as a goddess doling out gifts. And I usually tend to operate more like a guardian angel—taking on a personal, supportive role lifting up a singular artist.

If I'm being honest with myself, there was something attractive about making a pretty woman get all flustered and embarrassed with minimal effort. It would be quite thrilling to do it again on purpose.

"I cannot believe I'm about to say this…Matilde, you may be right. It's worth trying, anyway." Really, what's the worst that could happen? Perhaps I end up getting too attached anyway. There are worse fates. So long as I keep that healthy distance, it shouldn't matter too much. I pick up my mug of tea and take a sip, finding it has cooled to just the right temperature, and let out a contented little sigh. "Okay. Thank you. I'll do my best. Don't let me keep you any longer."

"I already told you once, the world could be beating down my door and I'd still make time for you. Kisses, darling!"

With a plan in place, I feel almost ecstatic for the future, and cradle my mug close. Perhaps a little fun is just what I need.

CHAPTER THREE

Penny

Running away. The Hartwell Twins Special. When things get too tough, we just leave.

I knew full well I was trans by tenth grade, but I put off coming out for years. It was too much, too scary—and so easy to run away.

The moment my brother and I graduated, we got the hell out of Amherst and came here. Why bother dealing with a family that barely tolerated us?

When Theo realized that he just wasn't the right fit for college, he dropped out. No point spending all that money just to have professors teach him things he already knew or didn't believe. Music is more than just theory.

And relationships? Forget about it. I had one serious girlfriend in grad school, and when we broke up over compatibility issues, I didn't bother fighting to make it work. I hit the bricks.

So when I get caught looking this woman over and drawing her, you bet your ass I'm not gonna sit around and have some awkward conversation about it. I'm not going to laugh it off or try and be cool about it. All I have to do is cut my losses and never, ever come to the library ever again. Easy as that.

Knowing this about myself doesn't mean I'm proud of it, or that I've never tried to work on it. But even now, the door is quite the enticing mistress, albeit a shameful one. By the time I'm outside the library, I'm feeling even worse than I did when this day began.

And that's made even more painful by the brief, glimmering moment where I was creating again. My pencil was moving with an enthusiasm I haven't felt in years. I didn't just sketch the reading room. I *captured* it—the beams of light and motes of dust, the sense of awe and wonder I felt the first time I ever saw it. I was making art. In my hubris, I fucked up.

God, it feels so gross to even think about!

This poor woman. All she wanted to do was come out to the library and read a classic children's story. It should have been enough to just share a few words together and let that be it. But in the moment, she looked so picturesque, and I just couldn't help myself. Ideally, she should be carved in marble with features like those. Unfortunately, an artist can only work with the tools they have.

If I'd managed to finish the picture without her noticing, I'd have probably only gone home with a fistful of guilt instead of this millstone around my neck. Or maybe an albatross is the more fitting metaphor here. A good luck charm, until I went and screwed everything up.

Setting down the roll of cheap paper towels on the kitchen counter, I think maybe I'll just veg out on the couch for a while and try to forget my shitty behavior. So it comes as quite the surprise when I feel that twitch in my hand again and my feet carry me to my room instead. In something of a fugue state, I'm back at my computer and working with passionate fervor on my backlog of commissions.

In spite of my mistakes, the actual drive to create hasn't left me. It's an ember compared to how I felt in the library. But it's enough.

The next few hours pass in a blur, and I've already sent one of the pieces off to the client before putting a significant dent in the next. I'm pulled from my tunnel vision by a knock at my bedroom door, followed by Theo's muffled voice from the other side. "Penny, soup's on. Or, uh, spaghetti. Whatever, get your butt out here."

As much as I want to try and finish this other project before taking a break, the prospect of a hot dinner is too good to pass up.

True to his word, Kai has put together some food for the rest of the apartment. It isn't much—store-brand spaghetti, cheap sauce, frozen meatballs, powdered parmesan—but it'll fill our bellies and keep the starving artists from going hungry another day.

The three of us sit together in the living room, eating while watching reruns of crappy MTV dating shows from the midaughts—our default when we don't know what else to watch. When that's done, Theo and I do our due diligence and take care of the dishes. He washes, I dry. He splashes me with sink water, I whip him with my dirty towel. And Kai sits on the counter with a handful of Oreos, egging us on.

"So, how'd your journey into the city go, Penny?" Theo asks conversationally as he tries fruitlessly to fully remove the sauce stains from the warped pot. Like they aren't practically melded with the metal at this point.

"Mostly good. Ended up going to the library downtown."

"Ah, more of a pilgrimage, then."

Kai crunches through his cookie and asks with his mouth half-full, "Wait, pilgrimage? Explain."

I run the towel over the damp bowl with its chipped edges, looking back at him with a smile. "You remember that classical music performance you took me to in college?"

He lets out a weary groan and washes down his "dessert" with a glug of milk. "God, please don't remind me of our ill-advised date."

I'm not sure why he acts so surprised when I bring it up. I do it at least once a year, just to keep him humble. In Kai's defense, it was very sweet. I hadn't been "Penny" all that long, and he stumbled through asking me out in a way that was very charming and did wonders for my dysphoria. "Well, I may not have fallen in love with you that night, but I did fall in love with the library. I go back there every so often when I need an artistic pick-me-up."

"Happy to be of service, I guess."

Theo passes me the pot to dry. "Did you find what you were looking for?"

Whatever look is on my face must speak volumes. I try to busy myself with toweling off the pot so I don't have to see the glance that no doubt passes between them. "It went okay." I'm trying to remain evasive. Truth be told, I want to get back to my room, back to work. I think I can eke out a little more of this energy I've found.

He chuckles and shuts off the water, moving to lean up against the counter next to Kai, unsubtly stealing a cookie from his hand. Theo shoves it in his mouth before he can be stopped. "There's a story there."

"It's nothing, really. I just—" I cut myself off with a sigh and put the pot into the dish rack with slightly too much force, rattling the other items inside, then turn to look at them. "There was this woman."

"You dog!" Kai grins at me eagerly.

"Can you please not accuse me of anything lascivious until I've actually told you what happened?"

"Apologies. I'll save my judgment."

"We just talked for a few minutes. But it was nice. I was almost a regular, human person for a moment. I'm not gonna lie and say I was smooth or anything, but I held my own in polite society despite my weirdness. Not only that, but I was finally able to draw again. I felt good. And there she is with her book and her contented smile, and she looks like freaking Galatea. So…I drew her. Just a sketch. But she saw me doing it, so I probably soured her whole day."

The two of them share another glance, both looking confused by my confession, before shrugging in turn. Theo looks back my way with a sigh. "Penny, you're absolutely overthinking this. Do you know how many random women have inspired songs for me over the years? This is nothing to be embarrassed about."

Kai nods and offers me the last Oreo, a Double Stuf olive branch. I take it and shove it into my mouth, if only because it will stop me from talking for a while—unlike these two inconsiderate jerks, being all nice and supportive. How dare they? "Besides, there's how many people in this town? You're not exactly likely to run into her again."

He makes a pretty good point. But it also feels like it's not that simple. This isn't just about the embarrassment, though that's part of it. Anthea was just trying to enjoy an afternoon reading, and I wrapped her up in my art block crisis without her consent. But I'm not gonna take a dump all over their well-intentioned support. "Thanks, guys. I'm gonna get back to work. Bring home the imitation bacon and all that."

My hand is aching a little and my eyes are strained, but I finally get another piece out the door. Leaning back in my chair, I scrub at my face and sigh. Whatever I found today that gave me this burst of energy, I think it's just about run its course. Reaching down into my bag, I pull out my sketchbook and flip it open. There's already a bunch of other drawings in here, and I flip past them until I find my re-creation of the reading room at the library. My hand hovers for a moment before I bite the bullet and turn to the next page.

Even though the sketch is rushed and unfinished, something about it shines. There's that same stupid guilt I've been feeling all evening, but underneath it is something else entirely, something that's harder to pin down. In spite of my exhaustion and strained hand, I find myself reaching into my desk to pull out a small plastic container. There's still one last precious nub of charcoal in here, and this would be a worthwhile way to use it. Make some adjustments, maybe a few embellishments.

As badly as I want to—or need to, perhaps—the energy is gone, leaving a void in its wake. I'm tired and frustrated and still a bit disappointed with myself. But my head is buzzing with something ineffable. Tired in body, tired in spirit, but mentally charged.

I need a drink.

Heading out of my room and into the kitchen, I find Meagan hunched over a plastic container filled with the last of our dinner. She's still wearing her black uniform T-shirt from the pub, her curly red hair somehow corralled into a ponytail. If I had to guess, she came straight back from her shift to the fridge to scarf down the leftovers. Meagan gives me a small nod of recognition before resuming her noisy slurping.

Our collection of booze is small and inexpensive, but I also don't plan on taking much. I pour out a single shot of vodka from the chunky plastic bottle and knock it back in one fluid motion. Unfortunately, part of the downside of drinking the cheap crap is the sheer severity of it. The burning agony leaves me coughing and sputtering like a high schooler at their first party. "Augh! Fuck…"

"Hell yeah. Partying tonight?" she asks in her thick Bostonian accent.

"Opposite, I think. Moping."

"Yeah, ya look a little…" Meagan gestures to me with her fork, trailing off as she starts really scrutinizing me. "It's weird. Yer kinda glowing. But in a sad way? Or sad in a glowing way?"

"That sounds about right." I tap my fingertip against the shot glass for a second before pouring out a second portion and drinking that too, this time with only a light cough. "You ever done something that felt really good, but also made you really guilty?"

"Hell yeah," she says again. "That's, like, my signature move."

She says it so confidently and without a shred of self-consciousness that I can't help but laugh. "How do you deal with it? The feeling guilty part?"

Meagan spears a meatball with her fork and shoves it into her mouth while she explains—does no one in this fucking apartment know how rude that is? "Oh, that's easy. I learned to get off on it. So now it's just a sweet, sweet recursive loop."

"Come on, I'm being serious."

"So am I. It's important to embrace the cringe. More often than not, that guilt is from something innocuous, not anything ya should actually be worried about."

For a moment, I gnaw on my bottom lip. "Okay, and what if you were to, say, draw a woman without her consent?"

"In that purely hypothetical situation? I mean, I'm no artist or nothin', so I don't know what's 'normal.' But if some stranger drew this mug, I'd consider it a compliment, personally." Chuckling,

Meagan takes the Tupperware container over to the sink and starts washing it out. I think that's the end of the conversation when suddenly she says, "So, what're ya going to do about it?"

That's a very different question from what either Theo or Kai asked, and it catches me off guard. "Do about it? I mean, I doubt I'll ever run into her again. But in a perfect world or whatever... I'd want to apologize."

"Because it'll make ya feel better?"

"Nah, I doubt it would. But I did a gross thing, and she saw me do it, and I think she deserves that much."

She nods and fluidly tosses the plastic container into the dish drainer. "There ya go, then."

"There I go what? I don't understand."

"Yer all hung up on this thing you did. It's good to be repentant," she says while reflexively making the sign of the cross, "but not if yer only reaction is self-flagellation. Don't make it all about yer weird anxiety, because then yer just centering the narrative around *you*. I doubt ya actually ruined her day or made her life worse. And hey, if ya do ever run into her again, apologize and then move the fuck on."

It's so glaringly obvious when she says it like that. I'm trying so hard to be contrite that I'm just overshooting instead and coming out the other side kind of selfish. "Thanks, Meagan. You're pretty good at that."

In a move that's either affectionate, infantilizing, or both, Meagan pats me on the head with a sleepy grin. "Ya pick up a few things bartending. Like how to play therapist to poor, lost souls. You'll be all right, kiddo." She's a few years younger than me, and yet her worldly wisdom makes the term of endearment feel natural.

CHAPTER FOUR

Anthea

My first impulse is to start making some kind of grand plan for how to approach Penny. The next day, I spend an hour jotting down some ideas, only to eventually scrap the entire thing and toss it all in the garbage. For all I know, this is yet another facet of my problem. I want so desperately for everything to go perfectly, even knowing that it's a fruitless endeavor. Sooner or later, something unexpected will come along and throw me for a loop.

If the goal is to change my approach, then I have to get rid of this notion that I can control things so tightly.

Instead, I'm going to focus on a single goal—find Penny again and propose a partnership. Simple as that.

Just like last time, I home in on that same warmth that had drawn me so powerfully. She's farther away this time but just as enticing, like a signal fire. I make my way down into Copley station, noticing the eager bounce in my step, and take Green Line B out west along Commonwealth Avenue. The car is packed, but with each passing stop, it empties out little by little. By the time I'm within walking distance of Penny, all that's left is myself and a few scant passengers.

I step down onto the small platform and glance around. The Allston-Brighton area is quiet, roughly halfway between Boston University and Boston College, and well outside the part of the city I'm familiar with—closer to a suburb than a city street. The only thing I have guiding me now is the knowledge that Penny is close by. So I set off in the direction of her glow.

Two blocks south from the station, I finally reach my unexpected destination—a small gas station with only two pumps out front. There's rust on the awning and grime coating the windows. Yes, it's safe to say that Penny leads a very different life from my last few artists. Dirt and grit be damned, there's something comforting about that.

With a deep breath, I pull open the door, and a beep sounds to announce my entrance.

Penny is hunched over behind the counter and doesn't even bother to look up. She's got her weathered little notebook out and she's idly doodling, only bothering to mutter a perfunctory, "Welcome, let me know if you need anything."

I step up to the register and lightly clear my throat. "Well, hello there, Penny."

Her brow furrows slightly and she blinks a few times before finally glancing up from her sketching. She's shocked to see me, and who can blame her? I have absolutely no reason to be here. It stretches the bounds of mere coincidence.

"Anthea?"

With a bit of concentration, I manage to give her a normal smile, suppressing the thrill I feel. "It would seem someone told me a fib. You're much more than an artist." That's good—keep it light and playful.

"Yeah, but 'register jockey' doesn't have quite the same ring to it," she says with a nervous laugh. Even if she feels as awkward as I do, at least she's playing along with my banter. "So, uh, what are you doing here?"

Even with all the time I had on my trip here to think up an excuse, I wasn't able to come up with anything airtight. So I remain vague. "I was just down this way on an errand and needed to pop in somewhere for a quick drink. A woman's got to stay hydrated, after all." To maintain the ruse, I move over to the nearby coolers and hastily extract a large bottle of water before coming back to the counter to set it down.

The good news is that Penny seems far too stunned by my presence to really question this paper-thin explanation. She scans the bottle, and we take a moment to go through the capitalist song and dance of paying for a basic necessity. As she passes me my receipt, she locks eyes with me and goes a bit serious. "Hey. Um. Maybe you being here is Providence or whatever. I actually wanted to…apologize."

An apology is the last thing I expect. "What for?"

"The library, the other day. You were just trying to find a quiet spot to read, and I drew you without really asking if it was okay or whatever. Maybe it's not even that big a deal to you, or maybe you felt like it was an invasion of your right to go out and not be creeped on. But either way, it was a weird thing to do, and I'm sorry for that."

For a moment, I can only stand there and stare at her. As if I needed any other proof that Penny is a completely different breed. "That's—Thank you, I appreciate it. Truth be told, I didn't actually mind. If anything, it's nice to know I've still got it." That's about as close as I can get to being honest for now.

Penny's shoulders lose some of their tightness and she stands a bit taller. "Thank goodness. I felt really shitty about it."

As much as I want to immediately launch into what I actually wanted to talk with her about, I don't think this is the right place. Even if it's quiet at the moment, a customer might eventually come through. I would rather the two of us had somewhere else to do this. Luckily, I know the perfect place. "Hmm. It would seem that what I took for an innocent interaction has left you a bit rattled. There's a coffee shop downtown that I'm quite fond of, and I'd like to treat you to a drink."

She looks at me in surprise for a moment, no doubt trying to piece together what my angle is. "Seriously?"

"I wouldn't offer if I wasn't serious."

With a bewildered chuckle and a shake of her head, Penny finally relents. "Okay, I guess. I've still got a couple more hours to go here. And, uh, I should probably shower and change." She glances down at her maroon uniform polo self-consciously. "I can meet you there at like…four-ish?"

I check my watch and give a firm nod. "Wonderful." In an unnecessarily dramatic move, I pluck the pencil from her hand and write down the name of the café and the address next to her sketches, then start for the door before turning back to look at her over my shoulder. "Oh, and bring the drawing you did. I'd love to see it."

Just before the door swings shut, I see the bright burn in her cheeks.

Matilde was right. This is fun.

I spend the early afternoon doling out some more inspiration to the city, but I do so sparingly. I'm holding on to some of my spark for when I meet back up with Penny.

Even with a designated time to meet, I still end up getting to the coffee shop early. To calm my nerves, I take a seat at one of the outside tables and pull the borrowed book from my purse. The story gives me something to focus on so I don't get too carried away wondering how this will go. My connection with Penny is undeniable, but that doesn't mean she'll actually be interested in working together. Yes, she agreed to come all the way out here, but that's small in the grand scheme of things, and I am plying her with a free beverage after all.

While it's easier when I'm focusing, even on a subconscious level I can feel Penny drawing closer. My decade spent dulling myself has also made me that much more aware of how powerful my family's abilities are, seeing it all with fresh eyes.

Before I know it, she's coming up the sidewalk toward me. Winter's spell is finally starting to break, and everyone is able to shed their heavy jackets—at least until the usual cold snap around early April inevitably hits. Penny is wearing a well-loved black hoodie with some artwork on the front that probably has some significance, though I can't place it—two rapiers crossed in front of a large, stylized rose.

"Hey! Hope you weren't waiting too long?"

"Not at all. Just a few minutes." It's a white lie, but it was my fault I got here so early anyway. Foolish enthusiasm and all that. I stand and open the door for her, and she enters as her cheeks go slightly pink.

Raine is working the register again today, and it doesn't escape my notice the way she gives Penny the once-over before looking my way with a knowing smile. While she's not quite right in her assumptions…she's not exactly wrong, either. Matilde called me out so easily the other day. There is something romantic about the way that I work. Start with a bit of flirtation and testing the waters, then slowly get closer—more intimate, more open. And always, inevitably, that moment where the line between our partnership and our personal lives blurs so much it becomes nonexistent.

But if I can keep my focus, this time, I won't—Well, I won't end up in a place where I feel like quitting. "Heya, Anthea! Ready for the next drink on the list?"

Considering what I'm planning to do here, I'm not sure I need to burden myself with a new concoction that might turn out as disastrously as the Gardener. So I play it safe for today. "Let's do the Green Monster again. I quite liked that one."

"You got it. And for you, ma'am?"

Penny fidgets and glances over at me for a moment before looking up at the chalkboard with an even more helpless expression. In her defense, it's a mammoth string of rainbow text, and it can be hard to pick something from it on the fly. That's half the reason I even started going down the list in the first place. "Can I just do an iced coffee?"

"Absolutely. Cream and sugar?"

"Please."

I pay for our drinks, and we step aside to wait for them. "Not a fan of complicated orders?"

She flushes and idly messes with one of the strings on her sweatshirt. "That's a nice way of saying I'm basic."

"Even if that were true, it's not like 'basic' is a dirty word. Basic is important. Buttered noodles are basic, and they're delicious."

"Comparing me to buttered noodles. That's high praise. Yeah, I guess looking at it that way, I am kind of a simple woman."

She takes a brief glance over toward the register where Raine is speaking with another customer, then back to me. "It sounds like you come here a lot."

"I do. Honestly, I've been rather…uncomplicated myself lately. Mostly, I just visit my usual haunts. Not much in the way of branching out."

"Yeah, I feel that. Weird, living in a city this big and diverse, you can still find a way to settle into a routine."

"Well," I say with just a hint of suggestive mystery. "I'd say we both still have time to shake things up in our lives."

Once the second barista sets our drinks down, we take them to a quiet table away from the other patrons. Penny sits across from me, looking me over warily before taking a sip of her coffee. "So you really wanna see the sketch I did?"

"Of course. Did you think I might change my mind on that in the last few hours?"

"Sorry, I don't know, it's embarrassing still. Even if you don't mind, you have to admit it's weird."

"How about you let me see it, and I'll decide if it's all that weird."

Bashfully, Penny reaches into her bag and pulls out the spiral sketchbook, flipping to the offending page and passing it over to me. The book doesn't look terribly expensive, but I still treat it with a bit of reverence. It doesn't matter if she bought it for five dollars or fifty. It's one of her tools, filled with her art, and it demands to be respected.

The image on the page is good, even if it is a fairly simple sketch. I can also see the point around my hands where the drawing looks less polished—no doubt this was where I caught her and she rushed out. To a mundane viewer, it might look like a simple sketch of a middle-aged woman reading a book. But I can feel the energy radiating off it, some of the lines practically shimmering with my lingering influence.

Penny's eyes are boring into me, and I imagine she's holding her breath while waiting for my final judgment. As much of a thrill as it is to keep her hanging on the precipice, I don't have the same instincts for playful teasing as Matilde. So I take pity on the poor woman and look up at her with as warm a smile as I can conjure. "You really don't have anything to be ashamed of. This is good. Hardly the work of someone 'creeping' on me."

Somewhere between the smile, the compliment, and the reassurance, I can finally see some of that worry leave Penny's face.

The drawing is about halfway through the sketchbook, and I feel a primal need to see more. I've gotten a good sense of who Penny is as a person. Now I want to get a sense of her as an artist. Whether they're just doodles or serious pieces, it doesn't matter—they're all important in their own way. "Would you mind if I looked at what other treasures you've got hidden in here?" Okay, maybe I have a little bit of a knack for teasing.

She flushes and takes another long sip through the straw in her cup. "Mm. Don't know about 'treasures.' But knock yourself out."

Grinning, I start moving backward through the pages, giving each image the appropriate attention. Prior to drawing me, she did a marvelous re-creation of the reading room, taking the time to play with light and shadow, rendering the various visitors as wandering silhouettes, as if they're haunting the space.

The next few pages feature various characters I don't recognize. They could be from movies or television shows, or original creations, and I wouldn't really have any idea. One of them is a pair of women sharing a passionate embrace, and I can't help but smirk before quickly hiding it by taking a drink from my mug of tea. There's an image of what I imagine is some kind of spaceship, and a sketch of the Faneuil Hall weather vane with its strange grasshopper feature. Sometimes she goes lifelike, sometimes stylized. But always, that skill shines through, with or without my spark. Penny is talented, she simply needs a gentle push to get her moving.

There's something else here, something I don't notice until I've looked at five or six different images—the shading. She uses a lot of smudging, but all of these have been done in pencil. I would expect someone who does this so consistently would have more charcoal drawings, even in a basic notebook. It's a technique I recognize well, and some part of me says that this is destiny, even as another part says that's ridiculous.

I can only delay for so long before I need to take the next step. Penny feels like the right choice for my grand return. I don't think I've ever met anyone who would be so contrite over a simple drawing. Besides, she's got the potential that's downright intoxicating for my kind. So I hand the sketchbook back to her and offer another warm smile. And that's when an idea strikes—something so beautifully brilliant I can't help myself.

"Draw me again."

CHAPTER FIVE

Penny

I almost drop my sketchbook. *Draw me again.* The way she says it, I swear she's daring me. Like we're sloppy-drunk teenagers playing party games. "What?"

"You didn't get to finish the first one, so I think it's only fair you have another chance. What do you say?"

My other hand is already diving into my bag, fishing around for a pencil. It's twitching again, which makes it all the more difficult to actually grab the damned thing. I should probably be questioning this, pushing back, trying to figure out if she's got some ulterior motive. But the opportunity to do this again, and do it right, is too good to pass up. Finally, I manage to pry a pencil free before flipping to the next open page in my sketchbook.

While I'm busy getting ready, Anthea has already shifted her posture. She's turned sideways in her chair, back pressed to the wall. Her back leg is propped up on the second chair, arm lazily draped over her knee. The index finger on her free hand is lightly looped through the handle of her mug where it sits on the table.

She's fucking posing. Like she's done this a dozen times. That, or she's a natural. Either way, there's no time to question it. There's art to be done. I lay out my book and start putting down an initial layer to capture her general shape. The world falls away until it's just me and Anthea, her mug still lightly steaming, my cup sweating. I can feel my tongue pressing out the corner of my mouth but I don't even bother trying to force it back in place. There's something weird and intimate and real here, and it feels wrong to make my face behave.

Sometimes Anthea shifts a bit, but it's always very careful and considered. She seems to know just how much she's able to adjust her body and her posture before it will become a distraction.

I have the basics down in record time—her skeleton, the table between us, the windows beyond. But that's just the beginning. Something about that daring tone of hers tells me that this is some kind of test, and I need to do this properly. So I move on to the actual drawing, capturing everything with lines so confident I feel like I'm possessed by an artist who actually knows what the hell they're doing. I shape out the lines of her face, the curve of her gentle smile, the slight shine in her eyes as they half focus on the opposite wall. Before long, my left hand starts to join the fray, occasionally smudging a line for a bit of strategic shadowing.

It feels magical. It feels miraculous. She's intuitively found this perfect pose, and I'm intuitively crafting this amazing image. Just two women, intuiting together.

When the tunnel vision finally shatters and the world comes back into focus, I realize that I have absolutely no sense of time or place. The smell of roasted beans is enough to remind me I'm in a coffee shop. Gun to my head, I couldn't tell you what it's called. I can see out the windows that the buildings around us are casting long shadows, so it's either early morning or late afternoon.

At least there are things that I am certain of, things that ground me. There is a pencil in my right hand, and smudges all over the fingertips of my left. My sketchbook sits in front of me on the table, dangerously close to the pool of condensation from my no-longer-iced coffee. And across from me is Anthea in her effortlessly cool position, with her sculpted face and her tightly curled hair. And I know that she is waiting on me.

I practically shove the sketchbook toward her, not even bothering to really look and see what I've done. My throat is dry as hell and I hastily take a sip from my cup, not even caring that it's become so watered down.

Anthea carefully adjusts herself until she's seated normally again and picks up the finished image. Her eyes trace over every single inch of it, scanning quadrant by quadrant, occasionally doubling back. Nothing else in that book got nearly this much attention, and I'm terrified it's because I made some major error. But to my surprise, I can see just the lightest touch of blush on her cheek. She parts her lips, breathes in almost imperceptibly, closes them again. Her lips part a second time, and she finally speaks. "Okay."

"Okay?"

"Okay. This is…Wow."

She passes the sketchbook back to me, and for the first time since I dropped out of my fugue state, I actually look at the image I created. And it's…Wow.

The translation from reality to page isn't strict. I emphasized the light coming from the windows behind her, making her look like a sacred icon with a brilliant halo. I've accentuated her hair, made it denser, practically its own organism. The plateau of her high-bridged nose sits almost dead center within the golden ratio. The steam from her mug rises up to bloom across the left half of the page in intricate loops and whirls.

I chance another look at Anthea. She's looking right back at me, her smile growing into a cheeky grin. "I want to make a proposition."

A statement like that can mean a lot of different things, and I'm too addled to really make a proper guess as to which she means. I don't want to misread this situation, so I let her finish before I get carried away and embarrass myself with some sordid misunderstanding.

"I've been thinking about commissioning someone to do a portrait of me. Something professional. Something I can frame and display. I get the impression you're a charcoal kind of gal."

My hand starts eagerly twirling and spinning the pencil. Is this real? Is this actually happening? "Uh, yeah. Yeah, not as much as I'd like, but whenever I can afford it. How'd you know?"

Anthea motions to my left hand, covered in graphite smudges. "Educated guess. Only a certain breed of artist will use a technique like that. And you seemed to be doing it almost instinctively."

She knows her shit. Add to that her skillful, natural posing, and I'm starting to get a sense I'm not the first person she's modeled for. She told me she'd retired, and I think I know what she used to do. Or maybe she just has some very interesting hobbies. Either way, I suddenly feel like I'm way out of my depth. "So, based on a couple of drawings, you're going to let me do something this big?"

"What can I say? I have a good feeling about you, Penny." She cradles her mug close and drinks slowly from it, still eyeing me over the rim. "I've always believed in supporting people with potential. And sometimes that means taking a risk. So how about it?"

The more she talks, the more the gaps are being filled in. Crazy as it might seem, I've somehow managed to cross paths with an eccentric patron who wants to give me a major opportunity on little more than a whim and a good feeling. This should absolutely be a red flag, and the smart thing to do would be to thank her before getting out of here. This stuff doesn't happen, and it damn sure doesn't happen to people like me. I'm destined for a life of scraping by, an existence of *good enough*.

And yet it clearly does happen, because it's happening in front of me, to me. And a commission like this, however improbable, would make for a sorely needed windfall. "Obviously I'm going to need a bit more information." I flip to the back of my sketchbook and start jotting down notes. "So you're looking for a proper portrait. How big are we talking here?"

"I'd like something sizable. Maybe…sixty by thirty?"

Jesus, that'd be the most massive thing I've ever made, by a wide margin. This relative stranger has more faith in me than I have in myself. "And you want it done in charcoal? Don't get me wrong, I love the stuff. But I figure it's worth considering if you want something more than that."

"What do you have in mind?"

"Well, traditionally it'd be paired with something like watercolor or acrylic." I can't quite keep the unenthusiastic tone out of my voice. Either of those would be pretty safe bets but not my preference.

Anthea studies me quietly once again. "I didn't ask about what's traditionally done," she says softly with a light smirk. "I want to know what you have in mind."

Flushing, I thoughtfully tap my pencil against the page. I know the answer immediately, but it's a long shot. "Oh, um. Well, there's this really cool effect you can get mixing charcoal with pastels. But that's less common for a reason—you're sacrificing detail for texture. And with a portrait, normally you want to maintain the fidelity since you're trying to accurately capture the subject." Granted, that's an oversimplification. You certainly could get some seriously lifelike stuff if you work with some charcoal pencils and the right set of tools. But there's something about the grit and dust of basic sticks that calls to me. It's a tactile experience to throw down what is essentially compressed powder onto a surface, and come away with a unique work of art.

Either way, I know that I'm hedging my answer here. Everything is ultimately decided by the commissioner. And I don't want to bully this woman into doing what I want just because I'm passionate about the subject.

Even as I try to temper my expectations, I see her eyes light up. "I wouldn't be opposed to that at all. A portrait doesn't inherently have to be a perfect re-creation. In fact, something dreamlike would be lovely."

"Really?"

"Besides, the more confident you are about the medium, the better it will be. And it's obvious you care about this."

I redirect for a moment, bring us out of the ideal and back into the practical. "We're talking about a large canvas and some pretty expensive materials here, Anthea."

"Money is no object."

Fuck. Theo and I left home to get away from the kind of people who can say those four words with a straight face. And here I am, thinking about accepting a job from one. Still, even as I think that, I also find that there's something about Anthea that feels so totally foreign from the world I grew up in. My parents would have scoffed at the idea of an unconventional portrait, but she looks downright excited at the prospect.

If she's serious about this, then I'd be an idiot to turn down this kind of opportunity. I need the scratch, and the experience alone would be priceless. If she has even the bare minimum of connections, I could actually meet the kind of people who want more than gay fanart for a fistful of dollars.

"Hmm, all right. Do you want to do this in person, or am I just working from a reference?"

"I'd much prefer to do it live, if that's not an issue."

"Yeah, that's no problem for me. We'll have to schedule sessions around my job, though."

"Certainly. I'm in no rush to get this done. Whenever you have a free afternoon or evening."

"Here, give me your contact info," I say, unlocking my phone and opening the address book before passing it off to her. While she does that, I continue to make a few scribbled notes. "I'll have a few more questions for you while I'm hammering out the contract and estimate."

"But of course. Take all the time you need, and don't be afraid to pester me for clarification." She finishes entering the information before swiping out of the application, and her lips spread into a much more natural smile of amusement, a soft giggle bubbling out of her. "Hmm. I'm sensing a pattern here."

Shit. My wallpaper. Some art my friend Marina made for my birthday. Utena and Anthy sharing a kiss in a field of roses. I hastily take my phone back and shove it into my hoodie pocket, blushing furiously. Like I need this woman thinking I have any other reasons for accepting her generous offer. "Right, well, I'll uh…'pester' you soon. For clarification."

We shake hands and go our separate ways. At the nearest station, I lean against the wall and pull the new contact up on my phone. Anthea Corey. *Just what kind of woman are you?*

As soon as I get home, I sit down to start working on the contract. And the first thing I realize is that I have no idea where to start. I've got some really basic stuff for my quick commissions, but that's more of a small breakdown about turnaround time and avenues for requesting adjustments. This is bigger, and really demands proper documentation.

When it becomes obvious I'm too lost to just do this from scratch, I decide to reach out to Devon, a friend from art school. He runs his own gallery out in Portland and he does this kind of thing on the regular. So I figure he's probably got what I need.

"Hey, Penny. What's going on? Wait, shit, I'm not missing the drawing session, am I?"

"Nah, that's not for like another week. I wanted to ask your help with something."

"Sure, anything you need."

"So, I landed this kinda unexpected commission, and it's bigger than I'm used to. I know you do a lot of portrait work. Do you have any kind of boilerplate contract on hand that I can crib from?"

"Oh! Absolutely, I can shoot you my standard form. And hey, congrats."

"Thanks, man. I'll have more information for everyone next week. Just feeling out of my depth, and I figured you'd have a better grasp on how an actual professional would go about this."

He clicks his tongue softly and sighs. "Penny…You *are* an actual professional. Same as any of us."

"Doesn't always feel like it."

"We all get that way from time to time."

"Hah, very funny." That's easy for Mr. Successful Gallery Owner to say. Not all of us had the luck of a family business to use as a springboard into the Pacific Northwest art scene.

"I'm serious. We're always our own worst critics, and we know how to think those thoughts that really hurt."

"Yeah. That's for damn sure."

"So no matter what you might tell yourself, you've earned your stripes. You're an artist." I wasn't really prepared for any kind of revelation during this call. But there's something comforting about it, to think that even a guy as confident and talented as Devon can feel like a fraud. "But I'm glad you're getting a shot to really prove it."

"Here's hoping I don't screw it up."

"You won't."

Well, it's nice to know someone has confidence in me. Maybe by the time I finish this portrait, I'll learn how to have some in myself. "Thanks, dude. Looking forward to hanging out again."

"Likewise. I've got a cool exhibit coming up and I wanna show everyone pictures. You're gonna dig it for sure. Take it sleazy."

With a chuckle, I hang up and turn back to my laptop. While I wait for Devon to send me the goods, I take some time transferring everything I jotted down from my notebook to a text document so I can get it all laid out neatly. It still seems so unreal. Penny Hartwell doing an actual portrait. Things are looking up.

CHAPTER SIX

Anthea

The moment I get back to my apartment, I go straight to my kitchen, crack open a bottle of wine, and pour myself a healthy portion. I drain half the glass in a single motion before bubbling up with slightly delirious giggles. Against all good sense and reason, I have managed to secure myself a new artist.

I've never done it like this before.

There are plenty of ways for muses to connect with their targets, but there are two major approaches. There are those like Matilde that take the active path. They insert themselves into the life of an artist and directly influence them. But I've always preferred the passive route. I would linger around someone with the right energy, and then put out enough inspiration until they couldn't help but notice me. I provided the space for them to make the first move, make the decisions, make their grand masterpiece on their terms.

Anthea is back, and she's doing things differently.

It is, perhaps, a bit early to be feeling quite so victorious. A handshake and a promise to pester further is hardly ironclad. But everything is so spectacularly new that I'm willing to indulge in some foolish optimism. "Honestly. 'Money is no object.' Who even says that anymore? Oh, Matilde would be so proud." For a moment, I think I should phone her, but I decide against it. Despite what she's told me, I don't know if I should be constantly chatting her ear off with the play-by-play of my foray back into the world. I'll let her wait a while for the next update.

What can I say? This confidence thing is rather empowering.

So I'm going to take my wine into the living room, curl up with my book or a movie, and luxuriate in this feeling for a while. Before long, Penny will have that contract worked out and I'll gladly agree to pretty much any demands she might have. That's just formality on my end. I have my Artist, she has her Project. And I am feeling…*Potent.*

* * *

I'm still riding that high from yesterday when something brings me crashing back down to Earth.

After spending the day mostly relaxing, doing a bit of cleaning, and making food, I get an unexpected call. Not recognizing the number, I answer hesitantly while tending to my pot of pasta boiling on my stove. "Hello?"

"Hi, is this Anthea Corey?"

"Speaking."

"Great! I'm calling from the Massachusetts Society for the Arts."

"Hmm, did something go wrong with my last donation? I'm fairly certain all my information is up to date."

The woman on the other end of the line with the pitch-perfect phone voice laughs softly. "No, ma'am, quite the opposite. According to our records, you've been sponsoring us for ten years now, and the amounts have been…quite generous."

"Ah, and was this just a thank-you call, or…?"

"Actually, I wanted to let you know that we'll be holding our annual gala soon, and we'd love to have you there so everyone can put a face with the name. The Boston Museum of Fine Arts is hosting us this year, and the caterers are the same group that did my wedding, so I know their food is to die for!"

My chest starts to go a bit tight. I can already picture it—the museum, absolutely packed with people, all of them wanting to come up and shake my hand and thank me for my generous contributions. They'll probably march a whole troupe of children in front of me so they can show off their talents and tell me that, because of my money, these kids can follow their dreams. People staring and hoping and—

And none of them will ever know why I did it.

Without thinking, I mutter, "I really should have been doing this anonymously." Thankfully, with a little grace, I manage a respectable dismount. "I'm not looking for attention. Simply trying to make the world a bit brighter."

"Oh," she says with an almost performative level of disappointment. I can't help but think she's trying to guilt me. It becomes clearer when she adds, "Well, you'll also be getting a formal invitation in the mail. If you don't plan on attending, RSVP so we know not to bother you in the future. And if you wish to switch to anonymous donations, please let us know and we can figure something out."

Worst of all, the guilt trip is working. I shut my eyes tight and sigh softly. "I'll consider it. Sorry, I just have a very busy month coming up and my schedule is all over the place," I say, lying so blatantly that it's practically an insult.

"Thank you so much, Ms. Corey. And if you can't make it, then at least allow me to say how much I appreciate your dedication to our organization."

I somehow manage to finish the conversation without getting overly flustered, but I hang up the phone perhaps a few seconds too early.

I don't have to go. I have almost no reason to. It's better for everyone if I stay home, because then they don't have to expend the energy dealing with me. Far easier to tell myself that's why.

Because if I dig much deeper, I'll have to face what really scares me—finding out that I've forgotten how to seem like a real human. I can handle going to the coffee shop, or small interactions one-on-one. And walking through the crowds of the city, you might as well be alone for how little you actually participate in anything with the people around you. But a gala means remembering my manners and my social games, keeping my story straight, wearing a series of elaborate masks.

It's far too much. I won't go. Muses aren't meant for hobnobbing. We're meant to be viewed at a distance by our artist—and even that is a scandalous take, according to my more conservative family members.

I'll make sure to include a note with my RSVP, apologize profusely, maybe make my next donation a bit bigger with a request to go anonymous from now on.

Matilde was right—there's no way to turn me into her. She goes where she pleases, does what she wants, and damn anyone who would look down on her. But here I am, terrified at the prospect of attending a simple party. I've spent most of the past decade hiding away in my hole. Where did I get the idea that I could emerge, ready to immediately take on the world?

After dinner, I nestle myself onto my couch to spend another quiet evening. But this time it's less celebratory and more a way to nurse my ridiculous anxiety. I'd been feeling quite proud of how I handled everything with Penny. Sure, it took some work to get there, stepping outside my comfort zone, but I did it. And now here I am, realizing that I've still got a long way to go. One successful negotiation does not a confident muse make.

Did I really think things would be all that different? The last few times I went to any events like this arts society gala, it was on the arm of my artist. All I had to do was be paraded around for a while, shown off like the trophy I so clearly was. They could take the spotlight, waxing poetically about how their inspiration comes from "love, beauty, life itself." And now that I have a chance to go stag and assert my independence, I shrink.

A whole decade trying to prove I could make it on my own, and all it takes is a few days to prove how little progress I'd made. Perhaps if I had spent some of that time doing a self-inventory, actually working on my problems, this wouldn't feel like such a monumental roadblock. But no, I just sat in solitude, licking my wounds. Nothing truly productive.

It feels like I might take the rest of the night to dig nice and deep into a hole of self-deprecation, when my phone starts buzzing against my thigh and I look to see what fresh hell could be bothering me now. Thankfully, it's not a call this time, but a text.

Hey, it's Penny!
Just realized I never messaged you so you could have my contact info too

In spite of my roiling mind, I do feel a smile tug at my lips.

Anyway I'm just thinking more about contract stuff
This is new for me
Still shocked you wanna do this

After moping all evening, I'm starting to think that maybe everything with Penny would be a good way to find my fire. She only knows me as this enigmatic, wealthy woman with an eccentric streak. Maybe if I can learn to develop this persona around her for long enough, I can make it stick more permanently.

You have a good energy.
And I meant what I said. I think you deserve a real shot.
Wait, it's Saturday night and you're working on our contract?
You lead a glamorous life.

Rather than a message, she sends me a series of pictures.

The first is of a wobbly-looking card table that's probably older than Penny, and it's straining despite only holding up a collection of shoddily folded shirts. All of them bear the same logo of the words "Terra Vertebrae" against a stylized line that forms a mountain ridge on one side and a sound wave on the other. In the corner of the shot is a small portable card reader.

The next image reveals what I can only assume to be Terra Vertebrae themselves. There's the blonde at the mic, guitar in hand, midvocalization with a look of raw energy that might be anger or perhaps euphoria. Possibly both. Behind her is the drummer, who's mostly a blur, but I can make out a shock of blue hair somewhere in the mess.

Standing out the most is the bassist. The resemblance is immediately obvious. Taller, lankier, sure. His hair is shorter but just as dark and messy. The chin is more defined and covered in stubble. But in the stance, there's something familiar—sloppy and casual, uncertain, but trying very hard.

The final shot is a selfie, and I'm not at all prepared for what I see. Penny looks quite different than either of the last two times I saw her. That first day at the library, she was rather…worn down. When she showed up at the café, hoodie aside, Penny seemed to have put a bit more attention into her appearance.

Not here. In this image, she's got on black lipstick, with heavy liner and shadow on her eyes, one of them shut tight—I can't quite call it a wink given how aggressive it is. Her pierced tongue is hanging out of her mouth. Her hair is back in a ponytail, and the hand not holding her phone is throwing up the Horns. The studded bracelet on her wrist completes the ensemble perfectly.

Even though it's not how I'm used to seeing her, I know instantly that there's something real and true about this look on her. Maybe it's not her everyday appearance, but she wears it comfortably.

It's attractive in a grungy sort of way, and I can feel my face flush as the room grows warm. She really is so unlike my previous partners, here more so than ever before. And I find myself hoping that I can eventually summon the necessary confidence to take us beyond the bounds of our simple arrangement.

I am not immune to a woman with an edge.

While I'm distracted by the dramatic look, she adds clarification.

My brother's band has a gig at this bar tonight
They needed me to play roadie and run the merch table

Looks like my life is actually even more glamorous than you first thought :P

An artist and a rock star.
Quite the talented family.

Rock, yes. Star, no.

I flip back through the images to get another look at her brother, but I inevitably find myself returning to that picture of Penny. I study it, the playful aggression, the confidence she hadn't really shown before. If she can manage to find it, then so can I.

Can I get a sample?

There's just long enough of a pause that I think maybe I've crossed a line. Which is when I see that Penny has initiated a video call, and I accept.

Obviously, the quality is pretty rough. The chatter and cheering of the bar patrons are messing with the acoustics somewhat, especially with the tiny microphone in Penny's phone. But eventually the lead singer manages to get everyone to quiet down. "Thank you, Crafty Taps! I'm Celeste, that's Cameron, and he's Theo. We've been Terra Vertebrae, and you've been awesome. This last one's called 'Circles and Squares,' and it's dedicated to all the weirdos out there."

There's another cheer from the crowd. "We'll be sticking around after this to enjoy some more tasty beverages if you want to come and chat, pick up a shirt, or pledge your undying allegiance. And hey, seriously, tip big tonight. That's not a fucking joke. I wanna see that glass jar on the bar top overflowing with cash."

I laugh softly and quickly put in some earbuds so the sound isn't doubly crunched trying to play through my phone's equally pathetic speaker.

Penny's brother kicks off the song with a bass solo. Music isn't my specialty, but I know enough to get by. So I can tell that, even if it's a bit rough, the technique is there. It's "slappy." Only when the other two join in does everything come together. The drummer, Cameron, is enthusiastic and primal, but with a shockingly precise sense of rhythm. And Celeste's voice is smoky and sultry, but it grinds in a pleasant way when she gets amped up.

The song itself is a strange mix of peppy and sardonic—played in a major key but with lyrics about growing up being shoved into lockers and trash cans. There's a bounce to it that feels strangely sarcastic. But it's undeniably *good*.

Even though I'm nestled in the corner of my couch, for just a moment I let myself get swept up and pretend I'm there. The stench of stale beer and staler bar snacks, and the music filling the space until your ears start to hurt. Even thinking about being in that crowd of people doesn't fill me with quite so much anxiety, not when I imagine myself there with—

Hell, I'm still doing it. Damn it, Anthea, we're trying to get away from that. Flirt with Penny, not with danger.

I push aside the urge to fantasize and focus on the music instead. Even with these subpar conditions, it's obvious that Terra Vertebrae has a lot of potential. It would seem that it runs in their family. Or, at the very least, these two siblings share it in spades. It would explain why Penny puts so much effort into supporting her brother.

When the song finally comes to an end, Penny flips the camera back around to face herself and grins with pride before ending the call.

Good shit, right?

They show exceptional promise.
And I'm very much looking forward to seeing their inevitable meteoric rise.

Cool, that brings their grand total fans to like five lol

Then I won't rest until it's double that!

Best of luck to you, Sisyphus

I think about leaving it there, but I also realize in the wake of our conversation—now that the thrill of watching Terra Vertebrae play has started to die down—that Penny has left me with a good excuse to see her again. After thinking for a moment on how to phrase it, I finally make my move.

You know, if you're having trouble with the contract…
I'd be happy to go over things with you.
No point in trying to do it alone.
We're partners, after all.

It takes just long enough for Penny to respond that I worry I might be pushing my luck. But then my phone dings again, and I can't help but smile.

If you don't think that will completely bore you, sure
Got a free afternoon coming up
Savage Roast again?

CHAPTER SEVEN

Penny

I make it to Savage Roast with a few minutes to kill, so I'm sitting at a table and idly messing around with my phone while I wait. Hesitating just a moment, I pull up my conversation with Anthea. I've been overthinking her texts pretty much since I sent that selfie.

It was a fun time, but I don't know where in the hell that burst of confidence came from. All I really had to do was take a quick snapshot of the bar and the band. Hell, I didn't have to send any pictures at all. But I was kind of rocking the roadie thing. I looked good, and actually felt it for once. My makeup was on point, and there's something about wearing a studded bracelet that just makes you feel like a badass.

Most days, I'm kinda just this vaguely girl-esque blob. But for one night, it felt like there was something really solid about my presentation. I was Penny Fucking Hartwell, Lugger of Drumsets, Peddler of T-Shirts. I wanted to preen and strut a little bit.

Although I have to wonder, why was Anthea the one I decided to show off to? Perhaps because there's something so unique about our entire situation. I may be new to doing a professional portrait like this, but I'm fairly certain we're operating outside the usual bounds of the artist-model relationship. Nothing about the way we've done things is normal. And she called us "partners." Do any of my professional friends consider the models they work with their partners?

Still, there are benefits to doing things the unorthodox way. I'm grateful for any help I can get on this damned contract, even from Anthea herself. It's not easy to figure out all these fiddly details. There are so many factors I haven't had to deal with before.

It's a blessing to have someone write you a blank check. But if you have even an ounce of integrity, you're left with a lot of extra work. What's the price range for a portrait like this? How much do the materials cost? What am I worth as a person and as an artist? Please, miss, will you give me an advance, please, so I can make sure that we're not late on rent again next month, pretty please?

The bells on the door jangle pleasantly, and I look up to see Anthea entering. As usual, she's nicely dressed in her fancy clothes—crisp black slacks and a cozy cream sweater—dramatically contrasting my own grubby shirt and jeans. I love grit and grime, but sometimes I wish I didn't. Sometimes I wish I could be a little more…normal. Moments like these, where I'm in close proximity to someone so amazing, make it so obvious where I'm lacking.

In spite of all that, she walks right up to my table with a bright smile, as though she were greeting an old friend. "Good to see you. Want something to drink before we get down to business?"

"You don't have to—"

"You're right, I don't. But I want to. I tell you what, I'm going to buy two drinks from the menu that I can confidently say are amazing. That way, if you decide you don't like it, I can drink it myself."

I seriously cannot get a read on this woman. But if she's going to insist on treating me again, I'm not strong enough to stop her. "Sure, couldn't hurt."

"Back in a flash." She walks over to the register with a bounce in her step, taking her time to share a few friendly words with the barista. Jesus, she's cool.

Before long, she's making her way back to the table with two steaming mugs, planting herself in the chair across from me. "So! This contract. What do you need?"

I pull a spiral notebook from my bag and flip to a page already covered with various notes. Hesitantly, I lift the closer mug and blow on it before taking a small sip. Coffee, chocolate…with cinnamon? There's something else in there too, a hint of apple, maybe. Regardless, it's impossibly perfect, and I wish I was half as good at reading people as Anthea seems to be. Because right now she looks like some kind of clairvoyant compared to Human Disaster Penny Hartwell.

I can feel myself in danger of getting hung up over such a stupid, small thing, and I press on to get us back to the task at hand. "I figure we should get down in writing what exactly the work is going to look like. Obviously it's a portrait of you, but just to be safe, a few extra details wouldn't be a bad idea."

"Such as?"

"Well, let's start with the general style. You mentioned that something dreamlike would be nice. Are we talking loose but still realistic? Or do you wanna go more abstract with it?"

Anthea laughs softly. "As long as you don't take the Cubist approach, I think I'll be happy with just about anything. But something vaguely Impressionist would look quite nice." She says the last part with a kind of forced casual tone that intrigues me. It's pretty clear that an Impressionist portrait would be meaningful for her, though I'm not brave enough to push her to say more.

"Yeah, for sure, I can work with that." I jot down a few things. "Hmm, dreamy also makes me think you're probably wearing like…a gown or whatever. I can see you rocking the elegant look."

Her eyebrows lift for just a moment. "Oh? Clothed? And here I thought we'd be doing a nude portrait."

Lord, kill me now.

Just as suddenly, she bursts out in bright laughter. "Sorry, sorry. I agree. So many options, though. It might take me some time to choose."

"Not a problem. We probably don't need to be quite *that* detailed in the contract. I just wanted to pick your brain, see if you had any thoughts so I know what to expect."

"Once I've made my decision, I'll let you know." Anthea props her chin in her hand and hums thoughtfully. "How about my pose? Perhaps something dramatic and emotive."

"Given how long this might take me, I was actually thinking we might take a more casual approach. Sitting in a chair or something, looking pensive. That way, you've got somewhere comfortable to rest while I work."

A look of legitimate surprise crosses her face. "Surely a dynamic pose would make for a more interesting subject."

"It can. But any posing can be made to look more dramatic with the right shading and environmental touches. Besides, if we're talking about the kind of portrait you want to hang on your wall, then something cozy and inviting might be good. Instead of you standing there formally with a serious look on your face." Anthea remains difficult to read, but I at least get the sense that she's wrestling with this. "Sorry, obviously if you want to do something striking, then I'm happy with that too. I just wanted you to know the option was there."

Finally her face softens again, and she smiles at me warmly, her cheeks just a bit pinker than they were a moment ago. "No, I think you're right. It would make for a nice change."

"Okay, cool." I haven't the foggiest idea what's going through her head, and it doesn't feel like it's my place to ask. We're both good with a comfortable pose, so I write down a bit more, then flip to the next page and pass the notebook over to Anthea. "So here's the price breakdown I've worked out so far."

I'm honestly hesitant to show this to her. Even being careful to choose media and tools that are quality without being super expensive, this is a hefty chunk of change. No matter how readily she said "money is no object," there still has to be a breaking point. So I've prepared myself for the possibility that she might talk me down to a lower commission price or less pricey materials.

Her brow furrows slightly, and I feel a lump forming in my throat. I'm already anxious, and what she says next throws me completely off-balance.

"This seems a bit low."

I think for a moment that maybe I've misheard her, or there's a smudge on the page that's screwed up where my decimal is. "One thousand is low?" I spent a long time looking at various websites and articles, desperately trying to figure out how the math works on something like this. A portrait this large really ramps up the price, but artists traditionally charge less for charcoal and pastel compared to something like a classic oil painting. Factoring everything in, I figure a cool thousand is a good starting point, even if I have to negotiate it down a bit. "Felt like a solid ballpark to me. Why, what are you thinking?"

"You could easily bump that up by a factor of ten," she says, almost casually.

"You're shitting me." It slips out before I can stop myself, and I have to fumble for a more graceful follow-up. "Look, I can accept that I'm a good artist, but there's no way I'm good to the tune of ten thousand." What is even happening here? This is a negotiation, that much is clear, but everything is backward. A smarter woman than me would see that I'm being given a golden opportunity and just accept it. And yet this feels so ludicrous that I can't help but try to be the voice of reason. "For someone at my level, this is a totally reasonable price tag."

"Oh? And what level is that?"

Jesus, I don't know how to clarify that, it's just a vibe thing. I went to art school, I make money doing art, but it's all nickel-and-dime commissions to keep me afloat. "Somewhere above amateur but below professional."

She looks me over coolly for a moment, then down at my notebook, then back up at me. "How long have you been making art? In general, I mean, any art at all."

"Since I was able to hold a crayon, I guess." Already I can see where she might be going with this, but it feels ridiculous.

"Mm-hmm, and how long have you been doing commissions?"

I have to actually think about that one, and it takes me a moment to reach back far enough. Mikey Burns found out I was a "drawer" and wanted me to draw him "Cammy, y'know, from *Street Fighter*, with the great tits" for twenty bucks. And I was enough of a smartass that I went as literal as I could. The next day,

I handed him the drawing of the muscular blond fighter with a pair of blue-and-yellow birds on her shoulders.

Sadly, my genius was lost on him, but he paid me anyway.

"Sixteen years or so?"

"A decade and a half of experience, that's quite a lot." This should feel infantilizing, or at the very least patronizing. But Anthea says it with such conviction that I start to fall for it.

So, what the hell, I go for it. "Unless you stop me, I'm putting ten thousand on the contract. Then it's in writing, which means no takesies backsies in lawyer-speak."

Frustratingly, she just lifts her eyebrows and smiles mysteriously at me.

So. I write it down. Ten thousand. In writing. Confirmed. No need to freak out, nothing to see here, that's just enough money to cover my share of rent for an entire year. "Suit yourself. What about the list of the supplies, does that all look...copacetic?"

Anthea nods, then stops herself and points at something on the list about halfway down the page. "Though now that you mention it, I'm curious about the disposable gloves."

First, my asking price is too low, and now she's confused about something so minor. I *cannot* get a bead on this woman. "Uh, yeah, for smudging. So I don't get oil from my fingers all over the canvas."

"Why not brushes?"

"They're fine, I guess. I just...really prefer doing it directly. It's more tactile, and honestly gives me way more control. And anything that requires more precision, I just need a stump or tortillon or whatever. Not a big deal."

"Fair enough. Well, let me know if you need to add anything to the list before we have our first session."

As easy as that, huh? The way this is going, I'm starting to wonder if I can convince Anthea to become my permanent patron. Or at least introduce me to someone else looking for an artist to do their portrait.

Please, miss?

"Right, will do. Um, I think that covers pretty much everything I wanted to talk about. Unless you had anything?"

"What's the rush? Why don't we stay a while, enjoy our coffee, and just chat? I'd like to know a bit more about the woman I'll be working with."

"Seriously? Can't imagine why you'd want to spend any extra time with a coal-dusted gremlin like me." It slips out so easily. I normally only save that kind of self-deprecating stuff for friends or my own internal monologue. This coffee shop suddenly feels blazing hot. I'm positive that kind of talk will absolutely make Anthea uncomfortable and she'll find some excuse to head out.

Instead, she just lets out more of that bright laughter. "Now now, no need to poison the well. You might be coal-dusted, but I bet you're far more than a gremlin."

I bring my mug up to my lips and take a slow sip, though I'm mostly just using it as something I can hide behind for a moment. How dare she be so nice? "Well played. What'd you want to know?"

"Well, I've seen a few of your other sketches and things. But what about your bigger projects? What else are you working on?"

"Eh, I haven't really had anything major to do in a long time. It's mostly just commissions for peanuts. Between that and my glamorous day job, there's not much time for any grand visions."

"That must be frustrating." She looks legitimately sad to hear that, and I feel a sudden need to not make myself sound quite so pathetic.

"Yes and no. I do at least have the luxury of choosing which requests I accept. But it's definitely a lot of fanart for TV shows, movies, anime, that kind of thing. And even when someone commissions a character I really like, they aren't able to shell out for a fully detailed piece. Line art and flat coloring against static backgrounds. Basic stuff. So I'm glad to have something I can sink my teeth into."

That gets her to smile a bit. "Regardless, I'd like to see more of your art. Anything else you feel comfortable sharing with me?"

I fiddle with my phone for a moment, even more hesitant to show her this than I was my list of supplies. There's a definite through line in my art, and she's bound to pick up on it quickly. "I mean, I have my online portfolio. Just a website I built with some cheap software. Um, here." In spite of my nerves, I pull it up with a few quick taps before passing the phone over to her.

Anthea takes her time swiping through everything I've felt comfortable posting, occasionally smiling to herself or even cooing appreciatively. But then she gets to one in particular and holds my phone back out to me with a grin. "Okay, I have to ask. Do you get a lot of requests for this kind of thing? Or are these… pet projects?"

Just like the other day with my wallpaper, it's a blatantly gay image. And this time, I don't even have the excuse that it was a gift from a friend. Just a lovingly rendered picture I made on a whim of Madoka and Homura enjoying a well-earned quiet moment together after a harrowing adventure.

"A little from column A, a little from column B. People on the Internet really like paying money to see their favorite ships played out. But I do occasionally…dabble in my own obsessions."

"Such as?"

"God, I don't know, do you have a couple hours for me to go down the whole list?"

"That's all right. I doubt I'd actually know most of them anyway."

"Bet that's not completely true. I'm sure even you've heard about…I don't know, *Sailor Moon*."

"The name sounds vaguely familiar."

"*Final Fantasy*."

"Is that a book series?"

Maybe Anthea is right. We come from two very different worlds. I know this is a pretty mundane conversation, but it really does perfectly highlight how bizarre it is for the two of us to be not only working together, but spending any time with one another that doesn't include the portrait. "Gotta be something. Uh…Harley Quinn and Poison Ivy from *Batman*."

"Oh! I know *Batman*. Which movie were they in?"

I sigh despondently. "Still waiting for the two of them to get their own movie together." With a chuckle, I shake my head and look at Anthea curiously. "I'm starting to think you need some kind of gay nerd pop culture primer. Or a crash course or something."

"A boot camp, perhaps? Are you volunteering to be my personal drill instructor?"

Does she ever not find some way to twist our conversations into a tease? If I'm not careful, I'm going to be in a constant state of embarrassment around this woman. "I guess I could. No idea where to even start."

"Give it some thought. I'm sure you'll find something approachable I can get into."

"How did a meeting about our contract end with you giving me extra homework?"

"To be fair, once you figure it out, you'll be the one giving me homework." She fiddles idly with her empty mug before suddenly perking up again. "Oh! I know something else I wanted to ask you."

"Hmm? Sure, hit me."

"Your brother's band, do you…have any recordings of them? I was hoping to hear a little more."

That's something of a shock. I mean, I know that Anthea said that she liked what she heard the other night. But part of me honestly kind of assumed that was just a bit of friendly banter. The fact that she's going out of her way to ask about them, to listen to more? I couldn't have predicted this. "Well, they're obviously still pretty small-time. They haven't had a chance to do any professional recordings. So most of what I have was recorded on my phone in the drummer's garage. I don't really know how, uh, pleasant it would actually be to listen to."

"I don't mind. I'm just curious, no pressure."

Anthea really doesn't strike me as someone who would want to actively pump literal garage band rock into her ears. But…she's asking, so I hesitate for a moment before pulling my headphones out of my backpack and plugging them into my phone before passing them off. I figure we should probably start with something approachable, so I pull up the recording of "Stunning Friendships" that Celeste had her engineer friend tape for them, and press play.

It's a kind of jangly song, made more so by the cheap mic used to record the impromptu session. But it's also pretty boppy with the syncopated rhythm and "ooh la la-las" that Theo and Cameron throw in.

When Anthea starts bobbing her head in time, I flash back to a decade ago when I spent that summer religiously watching *Garden State*, desperately wishing I could find my very own Sam. Only now *I'm* Natalie Portman, sitting there grinning as I share something sonic and meaningful with a relative stranger. At least I didn't promise that this song would "change her life." I don't think I could recover from the embarrassment.

When it ends, she pulls the headphones down from her ears and passes them back to me, her smile mirroring my own. "Yes, definitely a fan. Quite different from what I'm used to, but… maybe that's what I need these days."

I assume, at first, that she's just making some kind of excuse for her faint praise. But there's something in the way that she says it that hints at a much deeper meaning. What that meaning might be, I couldn't begin to guess. I'm just happy to know that maybe we can find some common ground. This would be a pretty miserable partnership otherwise.

CHAPTER EIGHT

Anthea

A dress. I need a dress.

Inside my massive walk-in closet, I flick my way through all the various dresses I own, giving each a quick inspection before moving on. Only one in ten even makes me pause, and fewer still actually receive the honor of being pulled down and draped across my bed to be tried on. It takes a full thirty minutes just for me to conclude the initial perusal, but finally I have a stack of potential outfits laid out. Now, it's time for round two.

First up is the classic little black dress. I figure, it's a classic for a reason, you can't really go wrong with something like this. But as I tug it into place and look myself over in the mirror, smoothing it out and checking the fit, I quickly realize that it's not going to work for this portrait. The hem is too high, the straps too thin—I look like I'm getting ready for a night at the bar with the ladies, and it's still the nineties. This is no good.

Something classier. What had Penny said? "Elegant." A flash of scarlet catches my eye, and I smile. This is the one for sure. A floor-length gown with enough extra layers in the skirts to give my artist some opportunities to play with the shadows. I'm certain I'm on the right track until I actually pull the zipper into place and turn to look at myself again. It's striking, that's for sure, but perhaps…too much. No one would lounge around in a getup like this—it's made for parading around a ballroom.

It happens again and again. Every time I try something on, I feel like I've found a winner, until I actually look myself over and the flaws start to scream at me.

This lovely, sky-blue tea dress? Cute, and comfier, but it makes me look like a housewife.

The asymmetrical dress with the long sleeves? The designer went with a shade of brown akin to burlap, and it doesn't play well with my skin tone. In retrospect, I'm not sure I've ever actually worn this one.

My periwinkle Versace dress? It would definitely be fun for Penny to re-create in charcoal and pastel, but the runway fashion completely clashes with the vibe we're going for in this portrait.

Before I know it, there's a kaleidoscopic sea of fabric on my bed, and I'm standing there in my underwear looking over the wreckage with my lips set in a firm pout. "This is no good. I think it might be time for plan B."

Despite living in close vicinity to several highly rated clothiers, I haven't actually spent much time during the last decade buying new outfits. There's not much point when you become a homebody recovering from myriad heartbreaks.

So I end up picking a shop at random based on the positive reviews and make my way over in search of the perfect dress.

Time/Reality has quite the strange name, but if my cursory search is to be believed, I should have better luck here than with my own wardrobe. I'm relieved to step inside and see that it's not quite as sterile and whitewashed as some of the establishments I've been to in the past. The interior is all exposed red brickwork and golden lighting. Something about the atmosphere reminds me a little of my treasured café—down-to-earth without trying too hard. Both walls are lined with a mix of clothing racks and accessory displays. Mannequins in the windows display specially chosen looks, enticing visitors to purchase the latest fashions just in time for the encroaching spring season. Another day, perhaps. For now, I have my singular goal, and I refuse to be distracted from it.

A man at the nearest rack of clothing, carefully rearranging a selection of blouses, looks my way when I enter. He looks to be in his midtwenties, in a crisp white shirt with the sleeves rolled up past his forearms, revealing a plethora of tattoos, and sporting a buzzed mohawk and horn-rimmed glasses. "Hello! Let me know if there's anything I can help you with."

"Perhaps there is, actually. I'm on the hunt for something specific, but I'm afraid I might be overthinking this."

He claps his hands together with legitimate enthusiasm. "Ooh, a challenge. Tell me more."

"I'm having a local artist do a portrait of me. But nothing I own really fits the project."

"What are the vibes?"

"Elegant yet relaxed? Preferably something not too sleek that drapes a bit, so that she has plenty of interesting textures to play with."

"Hmm. Textures…" He studies me for a few moments, steepling his fingers together in front of his mouth, deep in thought. "Standing?"

"Reclining. On a fainting couch."

A few more seconds passes before he suddenly snaps and starts bustling toward the back half of the store, and I hurry to chase after him. "I know just the thing. Where the hell did that beauty go…" Just as suddenly, he stops at a seemingly random rack of dresses and begins swiftly swiping through them, humming atonally. One-third of the way down the line, he apparently finds what he's looking for and dramatically whips it off the rack, holding it up victoriously. "Success!"

Just judging by the dress's beautiful shade of Castleton green, I already know that he's found something worthwhile. I'm excited to try it on and see how it looks. With a light coo, I gently take the hanger from him and glance toward the dressing rooms in the back. "Do you mind if I—?"

"I'm going to have to insist."

Just a few minutes later, I step back out wearing the dress, feeling utterly delighted. The green looks amazing against my skin and will undoubtedly provide just the right pop of color. The design is vaguely reminiscent of a toga—hanging off the left shoulder with a cape sleeve. Its skirts hang down to the middle of my calves, with plenty of gathered fabric to give Penny those shadows she wants. There's even a braided rope that cinches the waist. Despite the modest price tag, I don't think I've felt this good, this *right*, wearing a dress in a long time.

I snap a picture of myself posing in the triple mirrors nearby and send it off to Matilde. "Sir, you are a blessing. How did you get it in a single try like this?"

"No need to call me 'sir,' it's Elijah. And what can I say? I'm good at what I do." He crosses his arms and looks me over with a firm nod. "Very good indeed. Something about you in repose, it just screams 'classical, but with a twist.'"

"She's going to love it," I say excitedly, without thinking, and don't catch myself until I hear Elijah start to chuckle.

"Because of the textures?"

"Yes, exactly. The textures. For the portrait," I mutter, blushing. Goodness, am I that obvious? No denying, I can only hope that Penny finds this look appealing. It will certainly help me play the Game more effectively. If the art she showed me is anything to go by, there might just be room for the two of us to have a bit of fun down the road.

The dress could still use a bit of alteration, so Elijah fetches a small pack of safety pins and begins finding the spots where it needs to be taken in or adjusted.

While he works, I continue to look myself over in the mirror, filled with giddy anticipation. "I don't know how to thank you for your all your help today."

"Leave us a review online, give me a shout-out, and I'll consider us square." He very carefully pins near my hip, his hands steady and sure. "Oh, and don't hesitate to stop in again the next time you're looking for a new outfit. For a portrait, or...y'know, any other reason." He chuckles again and starts working on shortening the skirts slightly.

"Five stars, no question." While he works, I glance idly around the store when I catch the name of the place in the window again. "Okay, I have to ask, what's the story behind 'Time/Reality'?"

"Ah, everyone asks that one. The owner couldn't decide if she wanted to go with 'Stitch in Time' or 'Fabric of Reality,' so she split the difference. To her credit, it's eye-catching." Just like that, he stands up and claps excitedly. "All right. Go ahead and get changed and I'll have our people work their magic. We'll give you a call as soon as this beauty is ready for the canvas."

I'm beaming as I leave, nearly floating on my walk back home. This day has been more successful than I ever could have hoped.

"Anthea!"

I have to pull the phone back from my ear so that my sister doesn't deafen me. "Mm, I appreciate the enthusiasm, dear, but there's no need to injure me to show it."

"I'm sorry, but you just look so stunning."

Matilde would likely call me stunning even if I were wearing a stained sweatshirt and ripped-up jeans. But the fact that she would mean it, no matter what, is touching. "I chose this darling little shop, practically at random, and I'm so happy I did. The man who helped me was a miracle worker. I was worried it might take me several hours to find what I needed."

"And just what, pray tell, *is* the occasion for such a striking look?"

"Well, I followed your advice and went after Penny again. I've commissioned her to do a portrait of me," I say as I feel my lips spread into a wide smile.

There's a bit of breathy laughter on the other end of the call. "Ooh, how naughty. I'm so proud."

"You were right," I say, knowing just how eagerly she'll drink in those words. "This is already such fun, and we've only just started."

"Tell me more about this woman, Anthea. I must know just what sort of creature could capture your attention in such a fresh, new way."

It's a normal choice of words for Matilde. But it is a bit apt for her to refer to Penny as a "creature." At the coffee shop, she'd called herself a "coal-dusted gremlin." While she may have intended for it to be a playful jab against herself, I just found it that much more endearing. "Penny is even more of a change than I initially realized. Talented, with the potential to do amazing things. And yet there's none of that self-aggrandizing pomposity. Some part of her knows what she's got. But I get the impression that something in her life has blocked her from really accepting it."

"Yes, yes, she's a prime candidate, I'm sure. But you know that's not the only thing I'm asking about here, darling."

Oh, hell. I should have known she'd go there eventually. And I find myself fumbling slightly for the right words, because there's something ephemeral about Penny that a simple description wouldn't be able to capture. Slightly on the shorter side, a bit pudgy, with shaggy black hair and a relatively one-note fashion sense. I could share the picture she sent me from the other night, but that would still only reveal a single facet of who Penny is.

"It's the eyes, I think. They're very intense for someone trying so hard to seem mellow. Looking intently at everything around her, analyzing the interplay of light and shadow, the colors, taking it all in so completely." That's still not exactly what Matilde is looking for, but at least it's an honest assessment. Still, I decide to throw out a morsel for my sister to sink her teeth into. "And she blushes so easily."

"There it is. I knew you would get to it eventually."

"It's been a lot of fun teasing her. I'm starting to see the appeal."

"That's my girl. Anyhow, I just wanted to let you know the dress is stunning and that I can't wait to hear more. Have fun with your plaything!"

* * *

The day of our first session has arrived. I wake up well before my alarm goes off, bursting at the seams with energy. Penny won't even be arriving until early afternoon, which leaves me with almost half a day to putter around anxiously.

I decide to get my breakfast down at Savage Roast. Raine isn't around today, so I go through a much less protracted transaction at the register before settling in to enjoy my latte and chocolate chip muffin on one of the couches, idly scrolling through the news on my phone. For just a moment, I consider sending a text to Penny, letting her know how excited I am for today. But I suppress that compulsion. The Game demands I continue to play it light and easy for now.

By the time I get back to my apartment, I find I've only managed to kill an hour or so, which means I've still got almost five hours left. Looking around, I suddenly feel like this place is an absolute disaster, and I want to make sure Penny is comfortable here. So I set to work putting my home in order.

The decor is eclectic, to say the least, and I've tried desperately over the years to find some way to give it all a kind of cohesion. A genuine Japanese screen divider, my framed playbill from the premiere of *Into the Woods*, that Woodstock poster—assorted knick-knacks, bits, and bobs from my life as "Anthea Corey." Though I do have an old Grecian urn from a much earlier life that's no doubt worth more than this entire building.

But I do my best to at least make sure that everything is straightened, dusting as I go. Seeing just how much detritus my duster has accumulated, I become aware of the way I let the last decade go by in a fixed state. I just…existed. It felt good to coast, but was it ultimately *productive*?

Well, it's too late to worry about that now. I'm starting over with a new artist, and the best I can hope for is that Penny is just as fresh and different as she seems to be.

My cleaning spree takes me through the kitchen, and I alternate wiping down every available surface while snacking on whatever food I have available. By the time I look at the clock again, I'm happy to see that I've been at this for nearly two hours now. That's good, but that means I still have a good long while to wait. So, I carry that momentum into the hallway bathroom, since I figure there's a good chance Penny might need to use that at some point.

I spend the last bit of my focused tidying in the spare room I've been using as my personal library. This is where Penny and I will be working, and I've already set up an easel with the canvas, and all her requested tools. And centered on the paisley rug, a fainting couch where I'll be posing. I allow myself a small, excited smile before I set to work dusting the shelves and making the room look as nice as I can.

One last hour to go, and my nerves keep growing.

I take a long, luxurious shower, then get changed into my beautiful dress, lingering in front of the mirror. Yes, this is going to be amazing. I'm sure of it.

Just as I get the final touches of my makeup in place, I hear a knock at the door.

It's time. Here goes nothing.

CHAPTER NINE

Penny

It's not until Anthea sends me her address that I start to experience a new wave of anxiety.

Newbury Street. She lives on freaking Newbury Street. You don't get an apartment in a high-end shopping district like that without some serious coin in your bank account. God, she probably trades stocks. I bet she has fine-china dishes, mahogany bookshelves, and plush leather furniture. She could pay a real, actual artist to do the job, instead of this little charity case. And yet here we are. She signed the contract, she's already sprung for the necessary materials, and we can use her spare room—she has a fucking spare room!—as our studio.

The entrance to her building is just next to a clothing store that I couldn't even afford to set foot inside of, much less buy a bra or pair of jeans. But who knows? Maybe by the time we're done, I actually could.

Oh, who am I kidding? First thing I'm going to do is cover everyone's rent for a month and celebrate with fancy pizza or something.

I push my way through the revolving door and step into a lavish lobby. It's been ages since I've seen decor this swanky, and for just a moment, I'm shot back fifteen years to when our family visited Boston and spent a few nights in an insanely opulent hotel. At least there's not a chandelier hanging from the ceiling or anything.

A woman strolls past me in workout gear from REI, popping AirPods into her ears, on her way out for a jog. She looks better going to exercise than I do on my best days. Being here feels wrong. I'm not meant for a place like this. My jacket and jeans are frayed and dirty. I'm wearing one of my nicer button-ups, but it's still pretty wrinkled from the fifty wash cycles it's been through. I probably smell like drugstore deodorant and anxiety.

There's a giant desk staffed by a woman in a sharp blazer who looks over at me curiously. Her shiny, metal name tag reads "Sierra."

Nervously, I step my way over and clear my throat. "Hi, uh, I'm here to see Anthea Corey." I pull my ID card from my bag and pass it over to her.

Sierra nods and studies it for a moment. "Right, she mentioned she was going to be having a regular visitor. You're an artist?" It's obvious by the way she looks at me that she's having some trouble correlating the way I look with the person she'd conjured in her mind.

"That's what my degree says, anyway."

She passes back my card with a curiously raised eyebrow before swiftly putting back on a more generically friendly face. "Well, the elevators are just down that way. She's up on the third floor, apartment 318." She motions down a side hallway before giving me one last professional smile.

Once the elevator arrives and I've pressed the button for Anthea's floor, I huddle into the corner and nervously tap out a rhythm on my thigh. I'm sure that if I can just make it up to her apartment, I'll probably be able to shake some of this stupid insecurity. I tell myself that it doesn't matter what some random concierge thinks, all that matters is whether I'm any good at my job. And I definitely am. But if I can't reliably put on the persona of a master artist, then I'm never going to get any actual respect except from eccentric, wealthy people like Anthea.

The elevator lets me off on the designated level and I follow the signs—you need signs to find your way around this place!—toward door 318. I give as firm a knock as I can and bounce on the balls of my feet while I wait. From somewhere inside, I hear her call out, "Just a moment."

Eventually the door opens, and I'm bowled over by what I see on the other side.

Obviously, her place is nice. It would have to be in a building like this, almost by necessity. To the left is almost nothing but floor-to-ceiling windows, with a sliding door leading out onto a large balcony that wraps around the corner and connects to what I assume must be the main bedroom. The main area is all open concept, with shiny hardwood and white walls. The kitchen has a brushed-steel fridge and a fucking island. It's not completely sterile, at least. Anthea has decorated the place with plenty of personal touches, like a framed Woodstock poster and some lush plant life.

But most of my attention is captured by Anthea herself. She's wearing a gorgeous, flowing green dress, hair in an elegant updo, with stunning gold jewelry hanging around her neck and decorating her upper chest. Her makeup is seamless and understated, which means it took ages to get right.

My right hand twitches yet again. Like every time I look at her, the only thing I can think about is capturing her likeness. I unconsciously reach over with my left and massage the palm, gently reminding the little guy that we'll be doing exactly that in a moment. He just has to be patient.

"Did you want to come in, or are we doing this in my doorway instead? That seems quite inconvenient." She grins at me, playful and daring. She looks good, and she knows it. Not in an annoyingly cocky way, but because it is an incontrovertible fact—as universally true as "fire is hot." The same way I had to accept that I had some measure of talent, or else I would never actually get anywhere in the art world. Growing up isn't all about accepting your flaws. You also have to have the grace to recognize your strengths.

"Sorry, just—You look great." Again, it's plain as day, there's no point in skirting around that. "Please, lead the way."

To my surprise, there's just a bit more warmth in her cheeks that wasn't there a moment ago. She's blushing. I make her blush. Score one for Penny. "Right to it, then." Anthea steps aside and lets me in before heading through the living room area and into the second room, where she's set up our makeshift studio.

A few pieces of furniture have been pushed aside to open up the space, so the only things of note are my workstation and her modeling area. A large canvas and easel for me, a fainting couch for her against a backdrop of huge wooden bookshelves.

There's also more of those tall windows along one wall offering tons of gorgeous lighting. Natural light is useful for how it can affect an image, but it's also a harsh mistress. Any changes in weather or season can drastically alter the shadows, which are hard enough to get right even when you're working with a carefully controlled environment. So I'll be taking a few pictures for reference, to have something static to refer back to.

Next to my canvas is the other major acquisition. A repurposed end table holds a pair of fancy cases, my tools for this project. Charcoal and pastel. Difficult creatures, but capable of making impressive art in the right hands. And for all my insecurities, I at least know this one thing—I can use them. My hands are the right hands. I step forward and crack open the case of charcoal sticks, then the pastels. They're absolutely gorgeous—deep, chunky blacks and brilliant colors. I can hardly believe my luck. As if I'm not already getting the chance to make something special and earn a proper paycheck, I get to do it with these beauties.

Once I'm done admiring those, I reach over and brush my hand across the surface of the canvas. Heavy cotton with a fine tooth, the good stuff. A sheet of plastic lines the floor beneath my feet to ensure I don't get a bunch of dust and grime all over the fancy floor.

With these amazing materials, I just might be able to do this project justice.

Anthea has been quietly watching me this whole time, studying me as she sometimes does. "Do you want me to leave the room? Give you all some time alone?"

"Uh." I flush and clear my throat, almost violently snapping back to reality and remembering I'm not alone. "No, sorry, I'm good. It's just been…a long while since I've gotten to work with materials this pristine. Grad school was the last time I was even in the *same room* as something from Unison. And this canvas? I honestly wasn't sure you'd be able to get them in such a short time frame and—I'm rambling. Just, um. Go ahead and make yourself comfortable."

With a throaty chuckle, she steps past me and over to the chaise lounge, practically draping herself across it dramatically. "Ah. This will definitely be one of the more comfortable modeling sessions I've done, that's for sure." Anthea wiggles her hips, sighing happily, and looks for all the world like she might start taking a nap.

God, even when she's goofing off, she still looks picture perfect.

Before I end up staring at Sleeping Beauty, I remember the final important tool I'll need to do this properly. "Oh!" I reach down into my bag, and after a few seconds, manage to extract my treasured Bluetooth speaker. It's ancient at this point, purchased years ago from a tiny electronics shop a few blocks from our apartment, but it still works like a charm. "Do you mind if I play some music while we work?"

"Not at all." Anthea cracks an eye open and looks at the chunky little circular device with another teasing smile. "You know, I think I've got something a bit more powerful if you'd prefer to use that instead."

"Nah," I say without missing a beat, voice tinged with a bit of pride. "Listen, I get it. Sound quality is important. But I've been using this thing for almost a decade now. It's small and it makes the music really tinny. But that's part of the magic."

She shrugs and opens her eyes fully, turning her head to watch me curiously. "Far be it from me to interfere with your method," Anthea says before chuckling.

"What's so amusing?"

"Nothing, really. I just think I'm starting to see…I don't know, the shape of your aura, I suppose."

"You didn't fully suss out the shape of my aura before commissioning me? Bold, Ms. Corey."

"I'd seen enough to know it was a good one. Now I'm in the confirmation stage. For example…" she says, looking at my speaker with a cheeky grin. "I'm fairly certain you're about to play something…jazzy."

For just a moment, I contemplate putting on one of the few metal albums I still have from my edgier days. But the mood in here is so good that it's not worth it just for the bit, so I pull up my carefully curated playlist on my phone and set it to shuffle. The room soon fills with opening bars of a wailing jazz song, made slightly warbly through my trusty speaker.

Anthea's grin grows wider. "I knew it."

"I'm a stereotype, what can I say?" I switch over to my phone's camera app. "Now, let's get some reference pictures while the light is still good."

She holds the relaxed pose for a few moments longer before finally relenting. Anthea sits up and, with some careful backward shimmying, gets herself positioned against the curve of the arm, then reaches down to the floor to pick up a hardcover book of plays she'd set aside for a prop. The dust jacket has been removed, so it's just an otherwise nondescript tan cover. Anthea crosses her legs at the knee and finds a good way to hold the book that won't strain her arms too much or look awkward.

Just like in the coffee shop, she finds the pose so easily and so naturally, I can't help but be impressed. While I start snapping pictures, I do my best to casually prod and confirm my suspicions. "So come on, be real with me. You're too good at this. Were you a legit model or something?"

Her eyes flick up from where they're resting on the page, then back down again. Her lips are already carefully crafted into a light smile, but I swear I see them crook just a little more. "I was, once upon a time. Like I said, I retired, when I started to age out of it."

"Blech. 'Age out.' Such bullshit." I scoff, then snap a few more shots and finally move back behind the canvas. From my bag, I pluck a sketching pencil and get to work putting down a basic layout. "As if a woman suddenly loses some ineffable quality at twenty-five or whatever. As if that's not when she finally starts really hitting her stride."

She laughs lightly from the throat to keep herself from actually moving too much. "Ah, I see. So you prefer older women, then?"

The question catches me off guard, and my pencil briefly defies my orders and swings out wide. I rush to grab an eraser to fix the errant line. "Er. I guess? I mean, I like people in my age range or whatever. But yeah, if some silver vixen trained her sights on me, I would absolutely be okay with that."

Anthea laughs again. "Good to know."

What the fuck is that supposed to mean? I'm like…eighty percent certain she's just messing with me. But it's so hard to really pin Anthea down on pretty much anything. And it's not like I've ever been very good at telling the difference between joking, teasing, and flirting. All I know is that my interrogation has ended with me shoving my foot in my mouth. In the interest of not wasting our first session together, I focus on the task at hand.

As I finally fall into the zone, without even thinking about it, I start to quietly sing along with Ella Fitzgerald's far superior tones.

"You have a nice voice."

I gasp, but this time I manage to keep my pencil under control, even as my nerves jump and my face burns. "Um, thank you. I was never super good at music stuff, that was always Theo's department. But I guess we did kinda get a fragment of each other's talents. His sketches are better than he thinks."

"Don't sell yourself short, Penny. I like how you sound."

"You're too kind," I mutter, more earnest about that than the platitude might imply. Anthea has been pretty supportive of me almost since the moment we met. Even when she's teasing me, I get the impression there's some legitimate appreciation underneath. And something about the things she says, and the way she says them, makes me want to believe her.

"On the contrary, I'm just the right amount."

I don't really know what else to say, but that's just as well, because my focus suddenly tightens up again, and my hand starts moving almost of its own volition. We lapse into a surprisingly comfortable silence, coated in a cozy fog of Billie Holiday, Bessie Smith, and Brandi Carlile.

CHAPTER TEN

Anthea

A bright chirp interrupts the music pouring from Penny's speaker. She pauses her work to reach over and silence the alarm on her phone. "Okay, that's time."

I'm grateful for her careful attention to the time, because it means I can finally release my hold. Saved by the bell, so to speak. Ten years without flexing my spark has left me severely out of practice. It was easy enough to do in the library when I was giving Penny only a fraction of it. And even during our test portrait in the café, I took it easy on her—and on myself.

Today, I offered up my influence readily. Perhaps too readily, with no consideration for my own reserves. Rising from the chaise lounge, I lift my hands high over my head and let out a little squeaking yawn as I stretch out my body. "Ah…I really am glad you convinced me to go with a relaxed pose."

She grabs a small rag from the table and wipes some errant graphite from her hand and arm, giving a small shrug. "Hey, I'm just the artist. You're the one who'll be hanging this up in your home. I didn't want to press the point too much, but I figured it would be better for you."

For a moment, I can only stare at her in disbelief, grateful that she's not looking my way. When it finally passes, I lightly click my tongue and shake my head. As if to confirm something for myself, I step quietly around the other side of the canvas to see her progress. Obviously, it's just a sketch layer with a few random arrows to get a general sense of the room, my posture, and the effect of the light and shadow. But as a first step, it's incredibly solid work. I'm really quite eager to see what it looks like when she actually starts laying down some charcoal and pastel. "Hah. 'Just the artist,' she says. Usually it's 'I'm the artist, and what I say goes.'"

"Well then, sounds to me like you used to work with a real pack of assholes." As soon as she says it, Penny freezes up and her face starts to turn bright red.

I have another moment of pure shock, but just as suddenly I'm laughing—practically cackling—as I slap her shoulder. "Penny! God, what I wouldn't give to watch you say that to their faces. You're right, they were…a handful."

Still blushing, she busies herself with putting away her things. "Anyway, this was good. Looking forward to next time."

Of course, I could just let Penny take off for the day. But I want to keep her in my orbit a bit longer. And I am trying to do things differently this time around. So I take the leap. "We should celebrate our successful first day."

The look of surprise and the lingering heat in her cheeks is intoxicating, and I think I could get used to this. "Really?" The poor thing always seems so shocked that I'd want to spend time with her.

"I offered, didn't I?"

For a moment, Penny stares down into her bag as though she's found something especially fascinating inside. I worry she might balk and make a run for it. But finally she gives a quick nod. "Um, okay. Sure. What'd you have in mind?"

"Nothing complicated. Let me go change, and then we can crack open a few beers and see where the evening takes us." That might be a tad more suggestive than I intend, but I'm still finding my new rhythm.

"Far be it from me to turn down free beer."

As I move past her and through the door, I look back over my shoulder and grin. "You should know by now, nothing in this world is truly free. You're earning that beer by putting up with me."

Back in my bedroom, I take a moment alone to recenter. As good as I feel right now, my energy is also running incredibly low. I wanted to make our first session a productive one, to hook Penny in properly. But now there's a kind of soreness in my limbs, a tightness in my chest, and I'm getting a bit drowsy. At least this will be a nice chance to recuperate while getting to know my artist a bit better. So I'd say it all balances out.

I wipe away my makeup and decide just how dressed-down I want to be. Given the kind of casual outfits I've seen Penny in thus far, I ultimately decide to lean in to it and throw on some jeans and a T-shirt. I've shown off enough for one day, no harm in letting the woman see me looking more natural.

Well, I suppose "natural" is a complicated concept for my kind, so perhaps "unadorned" would work better.

As I step into the kitchen, I can see Penny wandering around the living room, looking at my treasure trove of random odds and ends. She traces her finger down the list of names on the concert poster, muttering them to herself.

"Sorry for the wait." I smile to myself and pop the caps on two bottles of beer before heading over to rest on the couch, passing one off to her as she joins me.

"No apology necessary. I was all caught up in looking at everything in here."

"I know it's a bit eclectic. I've been meaning to find a way to get some proper order out of all this chaos." I told myself I would do that back when I first started my little constitutional and then promptly never did it. How the time flies.

"I dunno, I kinda dig it. It's got character."

"Noted." I take a slow pull from my bottle while eyeing her curiously. "So, I have to ask, how did you end up doing the whole…starving artist thing?"

"Truth be told, it was at least a little bit out of spite." That's not at all what I expect to hear, and I'm sure the surprise looks pretty plain on my face because she chuckles softly before taking a drink. "I mean, that sounds worse than it is. Me and Theo come from a really conventional, successful family. Strong stock, deep roots in New England, big obsession with wealth and status."

"And you didn't buy in to all that?"

"The two of us weren't really allowed to get away with being proper slackers, but we got pretty good at finding ways of maintaining the bare minimum of expectations. Turning in papers written at the last minute and netting a solid B-plus. Pulling just enough weight in group projects. That kinda thing."

"You must be pretty close with Theo to still be so tight knit all these years later."

"Well, I guess it's just one of those twin things. We always had each other. And we needed that companionship to stay sane."

That would explain the exceptionally strong resemblance. "I'm glad you had him, then. Is it true what they say about twins? The ineffable link, where you can almost tell what they're thinking or feeling at any given moment? I can't remember if that only applies to identical twins, or if you get it from a fraternal bond too."

Her blush swiftly returns, and Penny idly picks at the face of Sam Adams on her bottle. "Uh, we actually...*are*...identical."

Oh. "Sorry, I didn't—I wasn't trying to make you—Well, I feel a bit silly now. But thank you for clarifying." Excellent work, Anthea.

"No, it's totally fine. Hell, I appreciate the little shot of gender euphoria, if anything. I transitioned back in college, so I've had plenty of time for the hormones to do their thing."

There's a part of me, the old me, that wants to tell her that I actually spent some time as a man, how I mostly did it to get social capital I wouldn't have had otherwise, and how it never felt right for me. But I can't think of an easy way to say so without opening an entire can of worms. Besides, I'm trying to avoid revealing too much if I want to keep that healthy distance. So I press on. "Anyway. Old-fashioned family."

"Right. So we've got a dad with a cushy office job, mom's a professor at Amherst College, our older sister has a big law firm, and our younger sister is a freaking biology wiz working on her doctorate. And then there's the two of us, a pair of black sheep. We were only able to get away with it because Theo used to play a mean cello and got first chair in the school band, and I earned a few awards at state-level art competitions."

"I see. You were allowed to follow your passions as long as it meant accolades and a future."

"Bingo. It was stressful as hell—eighteen years of constant anxiety about not measuring up. Coming here for college felt like a chance to finally find ourselves, to see who we were away from them. And it's absolutely fantastic, I'm totally thriving. I thought maybe I'd slack off my first year, but I realize that once I'm free from those monumental expectations that I actually do like school. But Theo, it's just not for him. He confessed to me that he was thinking about dropping out. He'd been moping for weeks and finally worked up to it. And uh…" Penny's face falls slightly. "I told him that he needed to be honest with Mom and Dad about it. Wasn't sure he'd find the courage, but when we came home for Thanksgiving, he actually did it. Only thing, he did it in the middle of the meal, plates still half-full. Our parents go fully apeshit, with our older sister, Annie, getting a few jabs in herself. Our younger sister, Liz, is totally silent and completely passive. I couldn't let all that stuff stand, especially since I was the one who had encouraged Theo to be honest in the first place. So I jumped to his defense, confirmed just how much we'd both been affected by all the lectures and judgment and impossible expectations. Worst of all, Dad seemed completely unconvinced, asking our sisters if they felt the same way. Obviously Annie took their side, and Liz was too busy staring down at the floor to be of any help."

She sighs heavily before taking a long sip of beer. "It was ugly, and things got personal, *fast*. They brought up how much of his potential he always wasted, he fired back with how uptight and shitty they were. They called him a failure, he told them they had iron rods up their asses. And that's all pretty bad, but Mom just *has* to have the last word, every time. Only…she took it way too far."

This already sounds bad enough, I can't even imagine what could make it worse.

"There's no good way to prepare yourself for your mother telling your twin brother, 'You were a mistake I wish I had never made.' And the kinda wild part is that I didn't even care that I was catching strays. I was just furious about how they were treating him. I dragged Theo upstairs so we could pack our bags and get the hell out of there, stopping just long enough to let them know that they'd hear from us again when they were ready to apologize."

There's a tightness in my chest that I don't expect, a flash of recognition that we are kindred spirits, in our own disparate ways. But obviously I'm not about to get into that. "I'm so sorry. That sounds awful."

"It's fine, we've had more than a decade to recover. Since then, it's been me and him scraping by and doing our best. Thank god for scholarships and assistance programs. He was always able to crash with me when he didn't have anywhere else to couch-surf."

"I take it none of them have ever reached out?"

"Dad stays silent. Mom likes to dangle little carrots in front of us from time to time. 'Shape up and you can come home. Enjoy the finer things again. No more generic-brand food and shitty mattresses.' But that's not an apology, so we don't go for it. No matter how nice that sounds, they've clearly made their choice." In spite of this heavy topic, her lips do quirk into a slight smile as she continues. "Liz, to her credit, likes to send us covert little messages from time to time just to see how we're doing. Unfortunately, she also has some very heady ideas about getting all of us to reunite someday, and I don't think her efforts have yielded a lotta fruit. Still, she's coming into her own, figuring herself out just like we did. The messages get a little more frequent, the conversations a little longer. She's a good kid, and I think maybe she'll understand eventually and make her own tough choice."

"It's good you've got someone else in your corner. And I'm glad I can provide a lucky break for you."

"Hey, if this works out, feel free to become my full-time patron. Or pass me off to any other rich friends you have," she says with a light chuckle.

"Ah, I'm sorry, Penny. I'm afraid I don't have much of a social circle to vault you into." The urge to say more keeps gnawing at me, and I'm doing my best to push it back down. This whole deal I've made with Penny was supposed to be a way for me to get to know her better, and to find a little companionship, maybe a bit of fun. She's not my therapist, and I don't want to reveal so much of myself that we get dangerously close to one another. It wouldn't end well for either of us, and I legitimately like Penny enough that I refuse to do that to her. "I burned some bridges while extricating myself from that lifestyle. It's…complicated."

Rather than take the hint, Penny takes my evasiveness as a chance to press a bit more. "How'd you get into modeling in the first place? Were you pushed into it by family or something? Y'know, like a stage mom kinda situation or whatever."

"Something like that." I keep my focus on the bottle in my hand. Because if I look up at that searching face, I'll be in danger of saying more. "It's still a bit raw, even after all this time."

Finally, she relents and looks idly around the room. "Enough soul-bearing, then. I say we get started on that crash course. Let's watch something." She says it almost petulantly, and I'm grateful for that. Penny knows she's doing me a favor, and pivoting in such a childish way eases the tension in the room significantly.

It's enough to actually make me laugh softly. "Okay, sure. What'd you have in mind?"

She motions to the massive television hanging on my wall. "You got Netflix on that thing, or is it just for show?"

The teasing is a lovely surprise. For the most part it's been mostly one-sided, which has been fun. But to think that Penny might finally be feeling brave enough to fire back is encouraging.

Matilde's voice pipes up in the back of my mind, like she's the angel on my shoulder. Or perhaps devil would be more apt. *It's not the Work, it's not our Grand Purpose. It's…the Game!*

There's something thrilling here that I'm excited to indulge in.

"I do, though it tends to go woefully underutilized. Are you looking to change that?"

"Yeah, after thinking it over, I'm pretty sure our best bet is *The Haunting of Bly Manor*."

The name sounds somewhat familiar, and it takes a moment for me to connect the dots. "Does that have anything to do with *The Turn of the Screw*?"

"Yes! Okay, perfect, you know the book it was based on." Without a shred of self-consciousness, she gives herself a high five. "Excellent work, Penny. Thank you, Penny. Let's do this."

Giggling at her antics, I pass Penny the remote before rising from the couch, taking our two empty bottles to toss in the recycling. "Refill?"

"Please."

Toward the end of the third episode, I notice that Penny starts to fade a little. That's not so surprising. Even with the relaxed atmosphere, I did give her a pretty sustained dose of my spark. That can sometimes create a sort of high, which means there's bound to be an inevitable crash. I'm sure with enough time and practice, I can keep that from happening so much.

I rouse her gently, and she gets ready to head out.

The two of us stand at the door of my apartment, me on the threshold, Penny in the hallway. We go through a slightly drawn-out farewell, all awkward half waves and pleasant smiles. But it feels a bit stilted, and as much as I'm trying to keep this woman out of arm's reach, I don't want her to think that today wasn't a success. It absolutely was. I can tell that she's the right artist for the job, and I have legitimately enjoyed our time together. But there's a very careful dance that I have to perform to keep us both safe.

So I need to offer her something supportive, at the very least. "Thank you for a wonderful first session, Penny. I'm looking forward to the next one."

"Likewise." I can hear the enthusiasm in her voice, see it in her posture. Thank goodness she's not deterred. If anything, perhaps she's been energized. I certainly hope so.

"And thank you for spending your evening with me."

"Hey, I'm not gonna complain about beer and Netflix." Her cheeks go a tad pink, and she adjusts her stance slightly. "I mean, obviously you're good company too. Seriously, I'm happy to spend time with you."

And now it's my turn to blush slightly. It's a relief to know my brief caginess wasn't too much of an issue. "Well. Just let me know when you're free and we can pick back up."

"Will do." She takes half a step forward, then stops herself and offers another quick wave instead. "Until then," she says hastily before heading down the hallway.

Once I shut the door, I lean up against it and release a low sigh. The Game is afoot, and I am still figuring out how to play.

STEP TWO: SHADE

CHAPTER ELEVEN

Penny

"Click the link, coward. Do it. Open it. Reveal your fate."

"I'm doing it! You gotta give me a second."

This is the usual patter of our regular get-togethers. Unlike me, my friends from art school have left Boston and are spread out all over the country, so we have to find companionship wherever we can get it. Usually, that means voice chat and dumb art games.

I click the link that Marina sent me, and it pulls up a random character generator. Everyone is watching on my shared screen. "Come on, big money," I mutter to myself.

After a second, the next page loads with my randomized prompt—a shy, boisterous gargoyle.

Devon's laughter pipes straight into my ears through my headphones. "No such luck, Penny. I have no idea how you're going to pull that off."

"You gotta give me a little more credit than that, man. Besides, the challenge is half the point." I switch over to my art program and start putting down a few lines, getting a feel for the shape of the gargoyle. That part is easy enough. I used to draw nasty little guys all over my notebooks in middle and high school.

I feel myself break into a smile. This is good. We haven't been able to do this for a while. What used to be a weekly event when we were in our early twenties turned into a monthly gathering during our late twenties. These days, we're lucky if we can do it every two months.

"Okay, while Penny performs her sacred duty, how's everyone been doing?"

My hand switches to automatic as everyone goes over their latest news and achievements. Spouses, houses, and kids, oh my. Ricky just signed with a major comic label. Marina moved into a new place with her husband. Devon's second kid is learning to walk. And Penny? Why, the other day, she was able to eat a meal made with real chicken instead of the precooked stuff. Moving on up in the world.

Marina swings the spotlight around to me. "How about you, gargoyle girl? New England still treating you okay?"

While I try to figure out what sort of face a shy grotesque would make, I chuckle softly. "Mostly the same. Trying my best." As soon as I say it, I know that's the wrong answer. This has been happening pretty consistently during our last few digital meetups. Everyone always comes in hot with super amazing stories about what they're getting up to. And then I have to be a Debbie Downer.

Thankfully, Devon comes to my rescue. "She's being modest. From what I hear, someone just landed a pretty sweet commission."

The tension disperses, and I hear Ricky—Mister I Can't Say Who But They Make Movies Now—coo excitedly for me like we're at all in the same league. "How sweet?"

"Ten thousand for a full, in-person portrait. She even footed the bill for all the materials—canvas, charcoal, and pastel. The really fancy stuff."

He whistles softly. "Damn, not even paint? Weird choice."

Marina hums curiously. "Did she let you choose the medium? I know those were always your favorites."

"Yeah. She, like, *read* me just because I did some smudging on a pencil sketch. And when I recommended doing pastels, she didn't even bat an eye or push back." I start drawing a baseball cap on my little gargoyle—backward, of course. After some thought, I add a pair of aviators as well. Shades, to look cool while hiding his anxiety. "I'm a little nervous. As much as I love them, they're not easy materials, and a canvas this big leaves a lot of room for me to make a mistake."

"You found a strange one, Penny," she says with a light chuckle. "I'm picturing some eighteenth-century heiress who owns an entire Back Bay brownstone with servants and shit. Honestly, who even gets a portrait like that these days? But hey, whatever, the point is that I'm proud of you. I've got to see it when it's finished."

"Yeah, yeah, if she's cool with it, I'll be sure to throw a picture of it up on my portfolio or something." I put a few finishing touches on my drawing, adding in some texture to his craggy skin, then slump back in my chair with a sigh. "There. Shy gargoyle with boisterous clothing. How'd I do?"

My funky little guy is enough of a distraction that conversation finally turns away from the embarrassing topic.

With my drawing done, the spotlight swings over to Ricky, who starts sharing his screen and pulls up the randomizer for his own prompt. But as he gets to work making a "lewd, criminal librarian," I find myself still thinking more about Anthea. I'd been so eager to have something I could report that I'd kinda turned her into just a model and a source of money.

But she's a lot more than that, and I feel strangely guilty for not really conveying that properly. Like it's a dishonor to who she is. I make a promise to myself then and there that I won't become yet another member of that "pack of assholes." And, more importantly, to use this portrait as a way to really show some of her good qualities. She's given me free rein to get creative with the image.

Of course, that would be a lot easier if I had a better sense of the woman. She's let me see a few things about her now—bits and pieces of her past, flashes of her personality beyond being mysterious and charming. But there's an evasiveness that makes it difficult to properly understand her. And if I can't figure out at least a little bit of who the real Anthea is, then I worry the portrait might suffer for it. But hopefully if we keep doing this Queer Pop Culture Boot Camp thing, more and more of her true self will shine through.

Tonight is another rare occurrence where all four of us are actually in the apartment at the same time, so we're gearing up to watch a movie together in the living room. Kai has been insisting that we watch *Knives Out* for almost a year now, and we've finally caved. Meagan acquired one of those massive bags of bulk popcorn, and I'm putting together sandwiches for the crew.

Kai clutches four cans of soda in his arms, pausing as he passes by me. "So hey, how did your thing go?"

"My thing?"

"Yeah, your thing. You looked stressed as hell."

I had completely forgotten. In my haze to get to Anthea's place the other day, I rushed past Kai. When he asked me what was going on, I quickly muttered something about needing to be somewhere. I kept it vague, and even now I feel kinda weird about just coming out and saying what it was.

I move over to the sink and start washing the sandwich-meat slime from my hands. "Just a new commission. An in-person thing." I keep my tone even and casual as we move into the living room.

Theo perks up a little, taking the soda can as Kai offers it to him. "No shit?"

"No shit," I confirm before passing him a plate as well. "In spite of the absolutely impossible odds, I actually ran into that nice lady from the library the other day. Anthea. It turns out you guys were right. She wasn't even upset that I was drawing her."

"Told you. Chicks dig it when you immortalize them."

I roll my eyes as we continue divvying up our spoils. "Yes, lady killer, I concede. My agonizing was all for naught. Still, it felt good to apologize, regardless." Glancing over, I share a quick smile with Meagan. As humbling as it is to be surrounded by three I-told-you-sos, there is something comforting about how nicely everything has worked out. So it's hard to be all that frustrated. Taking my spot on the floor, I cross my legs and take a bite of the chewy sandwich.

Kai settles in on the couch behind me. "Well, come on. What happened?"

"Yeah," Meagan says while crunching on a piece of popcorn. "Deets."

Over our humble little meal, I run through "deets." Anthea showing up at the gas station, getting coffee, commissioning me. For some reason, I gloss over our test portrait there in the café. There was something almost…intimate about that moment that feels weirdly private. And I'm not entirely sure I can talk about it without getting flustered.

Well, I'm not completely getting through this without some embarrassment, because Meagan interrupts me when I mention Anthea's apartment.

"So it's just the two'a ya, alone, in her home?" Her voice slides into a low, suggestive register, practically purring. "This as tawdry as it sounds?"

It most definitely isn't. Let's be real—Anthea is attractive, mysterious, and witty. She's so high above me, as the song goes. Like Aphrodite. Anyone else would be lucky to find themselves in this kind of scenario. I just so happen to be of a certain disposition where something like that doesn't even enter my head, nor is it what I'm looking for.

Kai comes to my rescue, thankfully. "Nah, that's not Penny's style." He was there for the fallout from the Juniper Situation during my first year of grad school. "Still, she makes a good point. Do you think she's got any ulterior motives?" He's got a hint of legitimate concern behind the question.

On the one hand, beer and Netflix are hardly "tawdry," even by my own chaste standards. But there have been hints of something flirtatious in Anthea's demeanor that I still haven't been able to parse out. I don't want to go asserting anything based on my less-than-reliable vibe detectors. So I just shrug. "Nah, I just get the feeling she's a little lonely. I seriously doubt it's anything beyond that."

"Ten fucking thousand dollars, Penny. Jesus," Theo mutters softly, then takes a sip of his soda. "Jesus," he repeats but doesn't say anything else. There's something heavy in his tone that I can't quite parse.

Regardless, it's an accurate summary of my own disbelief, and I hastily motion to the television. "Okay, no more spotlighting me. Can we please just start the movie already?"

I'm pulled out of the cinematic experience when my phone suddenly starts buzzing. Some small, stupid part of me hopes that maybe it's Anthea. But it's actually someone far more unexpected. A film this good, there aren't many things that could warrant an acceptable interruption, especially when it seems like the big parlor scene is coming up. But this is very much an extenuating circumstance. I tap Theo on the shoulder. "Pause it, pause it."

"What's up?" he says while doing as I requested.

"A call from the Forbidden Zone."

Normally, Liz will just send the occasional text. It's rare for her to actually call either of us. I answer and put it on speaker. "Hey there, kiddo."

"Penny! Theo! Guess what!"

We share a quick look, neither of us able to conjure up a reason for her to sound this enthusiastic. But it must be pretty big.

Without anything constructive to offer, Theo snickers softly while regressing into the older brother shtick. "Chicken butt?"

"What are you, five? No, the NSBS conference is next week— Sorry, the National Society for Biological Studies conference. Anyway, someone in my department had to drop out last minute and gave their spot to me. It's being held in Boston."

"And…you want to see us?" I don't mean for that to come out so incredulous. Liz has always done her best to actually be cool— even if she tries a little too hard to maintain neutrality. So I course correct. "Aren't you gonna be too busy doing science nerd stuff to make time for us?"

"Oh, gee, let's see. What would be more interesting to do with my limited free time in the big city? Hang out with a bunch of Harvard tight-asses, or shoot the shit with my own siblings? It's a really tough call."

We're both still a bit bewildered, but eventually Theo remembers that she's waiting on an actual response. "Sure, I guess we can swing something. Dunno if it's gonna be terribly impressive or fancy. Grab some beers, that kind of thing."

"Literally anything. It's been too long, and the rest of the family just makes it so difficult."

"Yeah, you can say that again. Send us your, I don't know, itinerary or whatever and we'll figure out what we can do."

I chime in. "Just gotta check my work schedule. But I'm sure we can find a couple of hours to hang."

"Yes! You guys rock. Looking forward to it."

Once I hang up, I share a long look with Theo. I can see it on his face too. It would be really nice to see Liz again. But there's just no shaking that deep-seated paranoia. "You think…?"

"I dunno. Shit. She's a good kid, but…Yeah, I dunno."

Our roommates share a look of their own, and eventually Meagan clears her throat. "You two seriously need to sort yer shit out. She's going outta her way to chill, and yer too busy wondering if she's gonna spring some kinda trap."

"Yeah, well, you don't know our parents," Theo mutters darkly. "Fuck it, let's just put the movie back on. I wanna know where this is going."

CHAPTER TWELVE

Anthea

Even though I told Penny I understood that we would have to adjust our sessions around her work schedule, I still find myself growing impatient. I'm eager for the next time I can see her.

If what Penny and I did in the library felt merely naughty, then pushing her to draw me at Savage Roast was downright lewd. But that first day working on the portrait? There was something... *intimate* about it.

Granted, that was the entire point. The two of us, alone in my apartment, all of her attention on me, studying me intently.

Matilde was onto something, comparing my style of inspiration to something romantic. It doesn't happen to many of our siblings, but some of us do have a proclivity for letting our connection to our artists move beyond simple inspiration. The difference is that Matilde is content to keep things purely physical while maintaining a healthy emotional distance. That was a skill I never mastered.

I intend to learn it this time around. So no matter how much I might feel like some kind of excitable puppy, I will keep myself distracted.

I will clean my apartment.
I will read my book.
I will make regular visits to my favorite coffeehouse.
I won't think about how nice it is to be doing my job again.
I won't worry about all of Matilde's I-told-you-sos.
And I most certainly won't fantasize about the little thrill I feel every time I catch Penny looking my way.

* * *

Well, five out of six isn't so bad. Honestly, it's rather shameful the way I light up when my phone tells me that I've gotten a text from Penny.

You available to do a session tomorrow night?

I reach out, intending to type a reply, but swiftly stop myself. Play the Game, Anthea. Take it easy. With some concentration, I'm able to hold off for a solid ten minutes before finally messaging her back.

I think I can pencil you in.

Pencil? No no
Charcoal and pastel remember?
We're starting those next time.

Ah, that's right. The good stuff.
I bet you're quite excited.

That's it. Tease her.

Is it that obvious? I mean, yeah
Super stoked you were willing to buy the good shit

A dozen different responses all flit through my mind, various things I'm tempted to say. Something flirty like "only the best for my artist." Or perhaps even insinuate there are plenty of ways she can show me her appreciation. But none of them seem quite right. Again, Matilde is the undisputed master of these sorts of things. And I can't simply mimic her style or I'll inevitably push my luck. So I continue to keep it subtle and coy.

I know you'll use them well.

lol no pressure

I'm serious. You're going to do great.

In response, she sends me back an emoji of a little melting smiley face, and I spend the next several minutes trying and failing to not overthink that.

* * *

As soon as Penny gets to my apartment, we set about getting ready for our second session, and it already feels a bit like a routine is developing. The two of us head back into the spare room, and Penny prepares all of her materials while I work on finding my pose. Of course, my job is a bit easier than hers, so I'm mostly lying there while she bustles around—adjusting the curtains to tweak the lighting, getting her supplies in order, and starting up the soundtrack for our session. Today's playlist is a bit more upbeat, and it's going to take some mental effort to stop myself from bobbing my head in time.

"All right. Let's get messy." Penny begins unbuttoning her shirt before casually draping it on top of her backpack, then pulls her short hair back into a small ponytail.

It's the smallest of things, and it should be meaningless. And yet, for just a moment, I find myself completely *beset*. It's not that she reveals a wealth of impressive muscles rippling beneath her plain black tank top. Nor is she showing off a lithe figure with ample cleavage and "creamy" skin—whatever that means.

She's chubby, and her upper arms are utterly plastered with freckles and a few pockmarks. There's a scar on her elbow, likely from some fall as a child. And as she goes to tie her hair back, I can see that she hasn't shaved under her arms in some time.

Her body tells a story, like any does. And that is what leaves me so briefly unmoored. I've had moments where I've found Penny intermittently attractive, adorable, and precious. But for a split second, I feel something much more than that, a compulsion to draw her in close and kiss every single freckle on her shoulders.

Oh hell, what is wrong with me?

"Hmm? Everything okay?"

Oh *hell*, I've been staring, and I don't know for how long.

It takes more concentration than I care to admit to find my composure. But finally I manage it and adjust my posture a bit more, putting a teasing smile on my mask. "Sorry, I just didn't realize you were going to be stripping down today."

Finally some of that familiar fluster is back, and I feel victorious again. Though I'm ashamed by the fact that she could throw me off-balance without even trying. I can't let that happen a second time.

"Wh—I'm not 'stripping down'! Charcoal and pastels are messy, and if they get on my halfway decent clothes, there's no cleaning them." She begins sliding a disposable glove on her left hand while muttering softly to herself. "Honestly…"

I suppress the urge to giggle at her expense, figuring that's probably more than enough mutual embarrassment, and I get things moving along again.

There is no easy or concrete way to explain how a muse does what they do, and it differs from one to the next.

For Matilde, she provides her tune for a kind of dance, one where she always leads.

My spark, on the other hand… Well, it depends. In brief moments, when I inspire a passerby, it's little more than igniting one candle with another. Mostly functional, briefly satisfying. But when working on a larger project, spending time long term with an artist, it feels more like making a bonfire from scratch.

Of course, you first have to find a clearing and ensure you have a proper source of wood. The artist, the materials, the project. You have to get it all properly ordered—and for the love of all that is good, ensure there is a ring of safety around the site so you don't cause a forest fire.

Once the preliminary details are dealt with, you have to get the thing lit. In my first few millennia, I was working with the metaphysical equivalent of two sticks. But with enough time and experience, I have become very, very good at starting fires.

Still, it takes effort and care to ensure the kindling catches. I glance over and see Penny standing nervously in front of the two plastic cases of materials. It's obvious from a single look that she's dealing with a pretty major combination of indecision and performance anxiety. After all, she had mentioned that pastels could be "finicky."

So I glance her way, hold her gaze for a moment, and offer Penny a warm, encouraging smile. "Hey. It's all right. You've got this."

Strike.

There's one last moment of hesitation, and finally she smiles back.

Catch.

Penny plucks an earthy-brown chunk of pastel and turns her attention to the canvas. There's a delightful scratching sound from the other side, out of view, and I finally turn my attention to posing. While I can't actively read the collection of plays in my hands in case it ruins the image, I am at least able to occasionally scan a page, then turn when Penny reaches for a new stick of charcoal or color. I should be able to finish up *Saint Joan* today.

The thing about making a fire is that it's not a simple one-step process. Once you get it to catch, you still have to keep it going. More wood, more kindling, more oxygen. The upkeep can be tiring at times. As much as it is fulfilling to be a muse, to live up to our purpose, that does not mean that it always comes easily.

So when I feel that Penny is flagging, I send her a burst of energy. When she can't decide how exactly to smudge that particular shadow, I provide the sudden *eureka*. And when her arm grows tired, my influence can urge her to press on.

But ultimately, Penny is still human, and I'm still out of practice. Sooner or later, you run out of wood or kindling, or you just plain have to pack up camp and head home. Her alarm goes off, interrupting the poppy music, and it seems we're both grateful for it. This was a good session but another tiring one, and I slump down in my seat a little while she stretches and lets out an impressive groan.

"Safe to say we're calling it there for now?" I say, letting my eyes drift shut for just a moment.

"Mm-hmm. Been a long time since I've done something like this. These old bones are still getting used to it again."

Chuckling, I finally push myself to stand back up and once again move to the other side of the canvas to get a look at her progress. Already it's coming along beautifully, though to the untrained eye it might look like little more than a mass of blobs and gradations. But I can see the shape of something great. "Penny, you're thirty, not sixty. You've got a while before you can call your bones 'old.'"

She joins me in looking over the canvas, laughing softly as well. "Yeah, yeah. Youth is wasted on the young or whatever." Reaching up, she thoughtlessly brushes the back of her hand across her forehead to wipe a bit of sweat away, leaving a long smudge of black dust in its wake.

I can't help myself. I break out in bright laughter.

Penny looks at me, confused, until her brain catches up to what she's done. "Did I just, uh…?"

"Yes," I get out once my mirth has subsided enough that I can actually speak.

"Do you mind if I…?"

"Next door over, across from the kitchen."

"Mm. Thanks." She scrambles out past me and over toward the bathroom, face burning bright red, shoulders hunched up high as though she can hide behind them. Her footsteps are rapid and uneven, as if she's scrambling to hide away. It's precious.

While Penny tends to that, I head into my room to get changed. By the time I've finished, she's already cleaned up the rest of her workspace as well and put the temporary studio back in order. With that done, she slips back into her shirt and buttons it up. After a beat, she self-consciously looks my way. "So, uh. You can tell me if I'm being presumptuous here, but…I was thinking maybe we could watch some more *Bly Manor*?"

"That sounds lovely. Shall I order us some pizza while we're at it?"

Her face brightens up a bit at the mention of food, but the excitement quickly subsides, replaced with something approaching guilt. "I feel a little bad about mooching like this."

I start to point out that this would be a drop in the bucket but stop myself. Given how long she's apparently been living paycheck to paycheck, I think the last thing that Penny wants to hear is that I can indulge in delivery basically any time I please without a second thought. So I adjust my answer slightly, as if I have a tiny Matilde on my shoulder, reminding me how important the Game is. "Tell you what. We can take this out of your pay."

"Okay, well let's not go that far!"

I give her a flippant look before making my way over to the couch and planting myself down on it. "Your fault for not putting a line item in the contract for food. A lesson for next time."

"Anthea, don't you dare."

When I can't help it any longer, I finally let the persona drop and begin giggling again. "Honestly, it's my pleasure. Now get over here. I'm dying to know what the deal is with that unsettling ghost, the one with the shiny glasses."

I'm crying, and I don't even care.

What was supposed to be a session of watching maybe another three episodes has ended with me and Penny absolutely devouring the rest of the show in a single sitting.

This would be more embarrassing if it weren't for the fact that Penny is tearing up herself.

"I thought you'd seen this already," I say with a soft sniffle.

Penny laughs and wipes at the corner of her eye with a sniffle of her own. "It's really fucking sad. Can you blame me?"

I agree, of course.

But it's more than just this unexpected love story. It's the pain of a long life, the people we leave behind—both good and bad—and the stories that we tell. It's the beauty in the face of something so dark, and the darkness in the face of something so beautiful. All these things I don't expect to find so relatable in a simple show, and that I can't possibly explain to Penny without severely disrupting her entire existence. So I need to keep the rest of that hidden and out of sight. "Of course not. I'm fairly certain I could watch this again and again, and I would cry every time."

"Yeah, in retrospect, maybe this wasn't the best thing to start with. I would say next time we should move on to *Hill House* or something, but we probably need a breather first. *She-Ra*, maybe?" She pauses, wiping at her eye again before giggling softly. "Wait, no, that one gets super heavy too."

There's a little hitch in my chest when she says "next time," but I quickly push that down too. No need to get too excited. "That's not the worst thing, Penny. It's a bit like going through something traumatic together. It builds camaraderie." It really has been nice, spending time with Penny doing something so casual as bingeing a show together.

Next time.

I'm really looking forward to it.

CHAPTER THIRTEEN

Penny

Cameron lives in an actual house out in Newton, complete with a garage where the band can rehearse. While it's hardly the ideal location, they've managed to turn it into a halfway decent space—cheap soundproof padding on the walls, a battered drum shield, and third-hand amps get the job done. And it does give Terra Vertebrae some very literal garage band credentials.

I'm settled into the corner on a well-loved papasan chair, making a planning sketch for a new piece. My commissions are closed until I complete Anthea's portrait, but I still have one or two that I need to finish up. I've got a reference image on my phone, screenshots from the *Sailor Moon* episode where Ami and Makoto dance together, trying to figure out how to make the posing a bit more dynamic.

The band is working out the kinks on Celeste's magnum opus, "Shuttle Crash." It's one she's been developing since she was in high school, and it shows. There's a lot of love in it, from the raw lyrics to the less-than-traditional chord progression. Most of their other songs are good, but this one is single-worthy, if they ever make it big. I just hope they don't end up one-hit wonders.

But something is different today. I don't have the best ear for music, and even I can tell. It's not until their third time through the song that I realize that it's Theo. He's off-beat with his bass, and his singing lacks its usual edge.

Cameron waits for Celeste to croon the final line, then looks over at my brother with an eyebrow quirked. "You need to take a break? We got real loose on that last one."

Theo takes his hands off the bass and starts shaking them out, then lightly cracks his knuckles. After a second, he gives an embarrassed chuckle and shakes his head. "Nah, man, just have trouble running that one over and over again." He glances over at Celeste. "That riff you wrote me is sick, but it's a fucking nightmare on my fingers."

Sighing, she runs her fingers through her long blond hair. "Sorry, I know this one's a lot to ask from both of you."

"It'll be worth it," Theo says, continuing to stretch out his hands self-consciously. "Why don't we jump over to 'Fool' for a while? I get to do a bunch of sustained notes, and you can drop into that lower register for a bit." I've seen them run "Shuttle Crash" ten times in a row before. I don't know why he's pushing to pivot like this. But hell, I'm probably just blowing this out of proportion. And I want to make some progress on this commission, so I shrug it off.

Celeste seems to take his request in stride too. "We can do 'Fool' in our sleep. It doesn't need much practice. Oh! But what about 'Humming Silence'? I wanted to try speeding up on the bridge."

Cameron twirls a drumstick and nods excitedly. "Yes! That one's been dragging. I love it. Let's try."

With an accord summarily reached, they shift focus, and Cameron counts them all in. Alas, poor "Shuttle Crash," it sounds like you still need a lot more work. But someday they're going to figure that one out, and it's going to absolutely kill. I'm really excited to see it.

Once practice wraps, the four of us head to a local pizza joint. It's one of those perfectly mediocre places with New York-style pies that also inexplicably serves fried chicken. The food is greasy and it's served with paper plates, and the shakers of parmesan and red pepper are always nearly empty. But damn, is it delicious.

Celeste plucks a piece of pepperoni from her pizza and pops it into her mouth, humming thoughtfully. "I'm just saying we should probably save that one for a full-length album when we actually have space for some experimental stuff."

Cameron is quick on the defensive. "Okay, but if we never play it for a live audience, then we have no idea how it'll go over. We have to try it at least once." It's not like he's the Ringo of the band or anything, and "Get Help White Coats" only barely falls under the umbrella of "experimental." But Celeste makes a good point—it's a downer of a song that he wrote about his experience committing himself to an institution a few years ago.

While they go back and forth, I idly sketch out a drawing of someone in a straitjacket on the back of my paper place mat. It takes me a moment to realize that everyone's looking my way, only catching on when I hear Celeste say my name. "Penny?"

"Huh?"

"You're probably the most objective one at the table right now. What do you think?"

I erase a few lines while I think it over. "With the right crowd, that one *could* bring down the house. You've gotten a few gigs in like…coffeehouses and stuff. Pair it with 'Underwater Flood,' maybe one or two other navel-gazers, and I think you'd have a set in your arsenal for low-key venues."

Celeste blinks a few times before giving a small shrug. "Hmm. I've almost got 'Grieve the Purge' figured out. That wouldn't be a bad trio."

"That's what I'm talking about," Cameron says victoriously, thumping out a jaunty rhythm on the cheap table. "Penny, we need your guidance more often. Wanna be our manager?"

Scoffing, I shake my head and outline a grease stain on the mat before using it as the beginning of a tentacled monster. "That's very sweet, but I'm a little wrapped up in a big project at the moment. Also, y'know, I don't know the first thing about managing a band. That seems like a major flaw in the plan. But I appreciate the vote of confidence."

"Damn, that's right. Theo mentioned something about that."

"The Hartwell twins are moving up in the world," Celeste coos. "Our band is making a name for itself, and now Penny's getting contracted for this big portrait. I'm proud of you two."

Theo gives a soft grunt and shoves a piece of crust in his mouth. "Still got a long way to go before either of us are setting the world ablaze." Even through the chewy dough, I can tell there's something a little weird in his tone. There's been something off about him all day. I thought it was just the one song, but now I'm not so sure.

Still, no point in worrying about it too much. God knows we've all had our off days. "I'd settle for just keeping the heat on until we get some proper warm weather."

Cameron chuckles softly at our banter. "C'mon, man. We finally made it into B-Cubed! Before you know it, we'll be huge."

My pencil stops moving. They're gonna play in the Boston Battle of the Bands? Then why is Theo being so mopey?

There's some surprising tension in his face. "First prize in the battle is peanuts compared to her big, fancy painting. Five hundred bucks and studio time. Yippee."

Celeste cuts in. "Studio time means an album. Which means more people can hear us. Which means more groundswell. That's not nothing."

"It's not a painting. Whatever." I'm too distracted by my surprise to process Theo's dismissive tone. "You guys got in? Why didn't you tell me?"

"Found out while you were at work. That's the other reason Celeste is springing for this gourmet meal."

"And here I thought this was to thank me for my tireless service to the band."

"Not everything is about you, Penny."

Whoa. What the fuck was that? My brow furrows and I stare at my brother for a moment. "Huh?"

"Sorry. That was supposed to be a joke, but I guess it landed all janky."

I'm positive now that he's deflecting, but neither of us have the kind of confrontational personality to actually hash this out. So we're all just sitting around in a haze of awkward tension.

Eventually, Celeste slices through it with another casual shrug. "We've got some time before the battle. I'll check in with a few places around town, see if I can find us a low-key gig where we can try out this whole introspective, navel-gazing thing." Slowly she manages to guide conversation back toward potential set lists and future gigs.

While they all get distracted working out some logistics, I get a text on my phone.

Freedom!
The conference is over for today, and I need a freaking drink.
Where are we meeting?

I hold my phone out and show the texts to Theo, who nods and rises from the table. "All right, we've got plans to meet up with our sister. I'll let you handle all the boring stuff, fearless leader." He gently pats Celeste on the head. "I have complete faith in you."

"Yeah, yeah. Leave it to me. Have fun."

He and I share a look of uncertainty. We're not entirely sure how tonight will go. Liz is cool, but it's hard to ever feel totally at ease when it comes to family stuff. But god, would it be nice to have another sibling we can really trust.

Neither of us really have the energy to spend a lot of time or money hitting the town proper tonight. There are places you can go in the city that are free, but more often than not it's all bullshit tourist stuff. So in the end we agree to just hang out at the pub where Meagan works, The Púca. It's got cheap booze and cheaper food, and it's out of the way enough to be quiet even on the weekend.

Theo and I are here a bit early, which leaves the two of us sitting around in an awkward silence while anxiously nursing our beers. Whatever happened earlier, it hasn't dissipated yet, and I have no clue how to broach the subject.

Thankfully, Liz walks in, dressed up in a pressed white button-up and dark wool slacks for her science nerd convention, dark Hartwell hair in a professional bun, sporting a pair of black cat-eye glasses I could never pull off. Both of us perk up instantly, grateful for anything to distract from all the weirdness. As soon as she plants herself in the sturdy wooden chair, she slumps down to rest her head on the cool tabletop—not even seeming to mind the slight stickiness from years of drinks sloshing onto it. "I'm bushed. No more big words for me today. Promise me we'll keep it monosyllabic tonight."

"Ironic," I say softly. "Monosyllabic, I mean. Big word that means small word."

"Shush." After a beat, she finally lifts her head back up and looks between us, breaking out in a wide smile. "It really is good to see you both."

Theo pushes a laminated menu over to her with a smirk. "Here. The whiskey sours are to die for."

Meagan is working tonight, and she makes her way over with a cheerful smile. "Dear god, they're multiplying. Not sure what to do with a third Hartwell around."

He rolls his eyes and gestures. "Liz, this is our roommate Meagan. Meagan, this is our baby sister. So please make sure Mac doesn't spit in her drink."

"No Loogie Special, ya got it," Meagan says with a wink.

Liz goes with Theo's recommendation for a whiskey sour, plus a burger and an order of pretzel bites to split. Once Meagan heads back behind the bar, our sister looks between us eagerly. "So. How have you guys been? I wanna know everything."

I share a slightly strained look with Theo before giving a small shrug. "Not too much to tell, kiddo. Still mostly just slinging gas and busking."

"She's being modest," Theo says, and I can still hear that tension in his voice. "Penny netted a big commission. And hey, the band isn't doing so bad either."

"That's awesome. Are you still with Terra Vertebrae?" It's not quite clear if Liz just hasn't noticed the awkwardness, or if she's ignoring it in the traditional Hartwell style.

"Yup. Think I've finally found a group that fits. So that's pretty cool. And what about you? School treating you okay?"

"Mm-hmm, I've managed to only have two meltdowns this last semester, which is a new record for me."

We take some time running down everything we've missed. I still find myself skirting around some of the stuff with Anthea. It's such a big deal, and for some reason, that embarrasses me.

Once Liz's food and drink arrive, and we've finally pushed past the awkward catching-up phase, things take a nice turn. We swap cute cat videos and dumb memes we've found. Liz gets caught up in a rant about how much she loathes evolutionary psychology. Theo makes us shut up so we can listen to a song playing over the speakers, demanding that Meagan crank it up, and she tells him to fuck off.

It's good. It's nice. It feels like maybe things are looking up again. Like always, we just have to smooth over stuff, make it all okay.

"Oh god, the eggs!" Liz cackles with delight. "Annie hid them so well, even *she* couldn't remember where all of them were."

Theo shudders dramatically. "The house smelled like sulfur and death for weeks."

I wipe a tear from the corner of my eye and finally manage to get my laughter under control. "We finally found the last one and it was—"

"Inside the TV stand, yes! And it was so rancid," Liz says, breaking out in more giggling. When it finally passes and dies down, she sits up a bit, her face going serious with concentration. "So, uh, listen…Mom—"

In tandem, Theo and I slump in our chairs, somewhere between disappointment and anger. "Shit," I mutter under my breath.

"Fucking *Christ*," he adds. "I knew it. I *fucking* knew it."

This was all going so well. Why does she have to do this every time? All these years later, all this progress we've made getting free, and she keeps trying to drag us back into that world. The worst part is that Liz is the one person in this family we hoped we could trust. But she makes it so damn hard.

"Will you please let me say what I have to say before you go on the defensive?"

"You're free to say whatever you want. But that doesn't mean I have to listen." Theo stands up, almost violently, nearly knocking over his chair in the process. "I'm out." He doesn't give Liz a chance before making a beeline for the door.

She looks at me desperately.

I know I should follow Theo outside, but I'm not sure that would be much better. This is bound to put him in a hell of a mood, and he's still upset with me for whatever stupid reason. So I eventually relent and give a defeated shrug. "This had better be good."

"Mom's sick, Penny."

"Okay?"

"No, I mean she's *sick*. The big one. Like, oncology isn't my best subject, but I know enough to be worried."

A long, low sigh winds its way out of me, and I slump even more into my chair. Shit. We couldn't have seen this one coming. Mom was always so health conscious. Honestly, I always figured that she would outlive me. "*Okay?* What does she want, then? Neither of us are likely to have the cure for cancer shoved up our—Whatever. This doesn't magically change anything, Liz."

"Just…y'know, come home for a weekend. That's all."

Hell no. It's been too long, with too much history that never got addressed. Even if we got some kind of deathbed apology, it would be too little too late. Here's a better idea, how about we just let it happen, and wait until she's fully dead and buried? And then she'll be gone and out of our lives and we can finally, actually, really move on.

As soon as I let myself think that, there's a kind of relief, and also a heavy sense of guilt, and it's all getting so complicated in my head and I just want to escape this conversation. "You have to know already that the answer is no. This doesn't change anything, and it damn sure doesn't suddenly fix it. She—" I have to pause for a second and get my head straight. God, the door is enticing. "If that woman truly wanted to reconnect, the time to do that was a decade ago."

I look at Liz—really look at her. She seems so small and scared in that moment, just like she did during that fated Thanksgiving feast. As awful as Mom can be, Liz is legitimately upset about what's happening. And I realize it's a little bit like looking at an alternate version of myself. Wound up tight, always afraid, stressed as hell. If I had decided that a soft bed and a warm meal were worth more than my art, I'd be right there with her.

"What does she have on you? How are her claws in so deep?"

"She doesn't 'have' anything. I just…" Her voice dips down to almost a whisper. "Student loans are a bitch, y'know?"

"I'm fully aware. I have those too."

"Sure, but you just got a bachelor's, and art school was, what, two years? I'm gonna have almost a decade under my belt before it's all said and done."

Jesus, *just* a bachelor's. And why is she acting like "art school" isn't literally a master's degree? Maybe Liz really isn't as different as we hoped. "Wow. Just lay it all out, why don't you."

"Mom and Dad and Annie aren't *actually* that bad. I mean, they always respected your name and pronouns after you came out, no matter how distant you were."

"Yeah, such a high bar to clear. They don't get special brownie points for not being bigots." I sigh and get up from the table too before suddenly realizing that Theo took off before covering his part of the tab. "Fuck. Asshole ran out on the check."

"I'll take care of it. I feel like I owe you that much after all this."

She does, I agree, but I catch myself before saying it out loud. "Thanks. Sorry our big reunion kinda went down like this. Um, enjoy the rest of your conference thing." When I can't bear it anymore, I leg it too.

Theo's already gone by the time I get outside. Which is just as well. I'm not sure I can handle trying to be normal around him after this.

I don't want to go home. Kai is in crunch mode on his latest project, and Meagan won't be there for hours. So it'll just be the two of us, stewing. But I don't really have anywhere else to go, no one else in this city that I spend time with. And I'm not in the mood to huddle alone in my room and pretend things are okay.

It occurs to me that there is one other person in Boston that I could spend time with. It's a long shot, especially with no warning. But putting in some time on the portrait might actually make for a nice distraction.

Hey, can we do a session tonight?
I know this is last minute
I could use the diversion

That's totally fine, I have nothing going on.

Thank Christ
Be there soonish

I hop on the nearest train and make my way toward Copley. Settling into a seat, I feel my phone go off again and I check to make sure Anthea isn't changing her mind. Instead, it's a text from Meagan.

ur sister cant tip for shit.

I don't know why, but that's the thing that breaks me in that moment. Theo, Liz, money, Mom, cancer, Anthea, art. I'm arguably in a better position than I was just a few weeks ago, but back then I felt like I had some kind of control over it. Now, I've got absolutely no clue what's coming next, and it terrifies me. The last thing I want is to be one of those weirdos on the train having an emotional meltdown, and I have to clamp a hand over my mouth to stifle the erupting sob.

Cancer. Jesus.

CHAPTER FOURTEEN

Anthea

I'm happier than I'm willing to admit when I get a message from Penny. It's another quiet night in my quiet apartment, with only Mr. L. Frank Baum to keep me company. Ever since that day at the library, I've been making the occasional excursion back to borrow the next in the series and continue my way through the rest of the Oz books. And while the story of Dorothy's exploits is delightful, it doesn't compare to having another person around.

There's a slight desperation in Penny's tone that makes me nervous, though. It sounds like she needs a place to unwind—something to distract her for a while—and I'm happy to oblige. According to some myths, it is a muse's job to provide a kind of forgetfulness to shield a mortal from their worries. So it's only fair that I live up to that ancient belief, even if just for one evening.

Next time. I can get back to the Game next time.

I think about getting changed while I wait for her to come over. But those messages leave me concerned. And distant though it may be, even from here I can see there's a flicker in Penny's warmth that is…troubling. If she's bringing some kind of fractured energy with her, then it might not be the wisest idea to immediately go rushing into work. Practically speaking, the work might be poorer for it. And it's ten times harder to do my job if my artist isn't in the right headspace, which will just lead me to overextend myself. Then we're both suffering and nothing productive comes from it.

So I read a bit more, and when I sense that warmth drawing closer, I preemptively fill up my kettle and put it on the stove.

Even the knock at my door is slightly frantic, and I move quickly to answer. I find Penny pacing in the hallway, turning to look at me eagerly when she hears the latch. "Hey." Her eyes are a bit red, eyelids puffy, and she doesn't quite manage to hide the quick sniffle.

"Hello. Is everything all right?"

She sighs softly and enters as I step aside, closing up behind her. "It's nothing. Family drama."

"From what you've told me, you all are barely on speaking terms."

"Exactly. Therein lies the problem."

Before I can ask for any further details, the kettle in the kitchen starts whistling loudly. "Make yourself at home. I was just about to have some tea," I say while bustling over to attend to the shrieking. A small white lie, but a reasonable one. "Would you like some?"

"Um, yeah, I guess that could be good." She perches herself nervously on the edge of the couch, looking around awkwardly.

"How does chamomile sound?"

"Probably better than something with caffeine," she mutters with an awkward laugh.

I carefully load up my infuser teapot with some loose tea, then pour in the hot water. As an afterthought, I put together a small platter with all the necessary accoutrements—mugs, honey, and some small cookies. When I return with the tray and set it on the coffee table, she looks at it, then up at me while rapidly tapping her fingers against her knee. She's at least put her backpack on the floor, but she still hasn't settled into the couch. "You really didn't have to go to all this trouble. I was just hoping to distract myself for a while."

I take my usual spot on the other side of the couch and give a firm shake of my head. "You're scattered right now, Penny. And I hope you'll forgive me for saying this, but I don't think we should be bringing that kind of energy into the studio, or putting it onto the canvas."

It quickly becomes obvious why she hasn't let herself get properly comfortable as she shoots up to her feet, glancing toward the door before scrubbing at her face for a moment. "Shit, sorry, I know, you're right. I'm just not good with this stuff."

Just as she's about to grab up her bag and leave, I reach out and take her firmly by the wrist. "It's all right. Stay. Have some tea. It will do you good."

She stares at me silently for a moment but eventually relents with another soft sigh and a quick nod. My touch lingers against her wrist for just a moment too long before I hastily let go, and she sinks back down onto the couch.

Penny considers the teapot, then huffs impatiently. "So, are we having some or not?"

"It needs a little time to steep."

"Me or the tea?"

A bit of laughter bubbles out of me, and after a beat she joins in, finally dissipating some of that built-up tension. "Both, I guess. If you need a distraction, we can watch something, or I can loan you a book. You could work on drawing something else. But I would prefer it if we save the portrait for when we're in the right headspace."

Penny hesitates for a moment before finally pushing off her shoes and curling up into a more comfortable position with her legs crossed. She fishes her sketchbook from her backpack and flips to an image of two female characters dancing.

There's a primal urge within me to give her a little push, something truly base and simple. I offer up a small flicker of my influence and watch her pencil start to fly.

So we sit together on the couch, her sketching, me reading. When the tea is ready, I pour us each a mug, and we spend a bit of time in a surprisingly comfortable silence enjoying an impromptu teatime.

It's nearly half an hour later when Penny's pencil finally stills and she looks bashfully in my direction. "Um. Thank you for all this. I know I kinda just imposed on you—"

"Penny. It's all right. Honestly, I'm grateful for the company." And I really do mean that. I'm glad to see her again, regardless of the circumstances. "We might be partners or associates or what have you. But I hope by now you realize that doesn't mean we can't also be friendly with one another. If you need a place to escape to for a while, my door is open."

She gives another soft sniffle, and I worry briefly that I've overstepped. But then she smiles and laughs gently. "That's fucked-up. You're seriously too kind."

Once again, I join her in laughing softly. What a strange reaction. "Seems like maybe you deserve a little kindness. A chance for something good."

With a sigh, she tucks her pencil inside the spiral of the sketchbook. "I dunno, it seems like maybe this blessing is blowing up in my face."

"What do you mean? What happened?"

"It's just been…a whole thing. I was hanging out with Theo and the band, and he'd been acting weird all evening. At dinner, they mentioned they'd finally gotten into B-Cubed—"

"Into what?"

"Oh, uh, Boston Battle of the Bands. That's huge for them. A chance to grow their audience, maybe even record an album if they win. But he was all…distracted, and kinda grumpy and defensive. Said getting into the battle wasn't a big deal compared to—" Just as quickly as she opened up, Penny cuts herself off and stares back down at her lap.

Ah. Oh dear.

"I mean, he wasn't completely explicit about it. That's just the impression I got. But…me and him, we've never really talked things through like responsible adults before. Whenever something comes up, we tend to just kind of paint over it and move on with our lives."

Penny made it quite clear how close she is with Theo. If there's static between the two of them, then it's only natural that she'd be reeling. That also makes this far thornier than I'd really prepared myself for.

"And it sucks, but it's whatever. After that, we went to get drinks with our sister Liz."

I nod slowly. "This is the one that doesn't make you want to tear your hair out?"

"Normally," Penny mutters. "It's been ages since we've actually been in the same room together. I'd been hoping this was a chance for something good to happen—connect with her in a way we never really did before. But then she had to go and fucking ruin it. Doing her whole ambassador shtick. 'Come home. Dear old mumsy is sick with The Malignancy.' As if cancer just… undoes all the stuff they've put on us."

I've caught glimpses here and there of the effect that Penny's family had on her and Theo. But this brings it sharply into focus. It takes a lot of hate and resentment to say good riddance to someone in that kind of situation. I've had plenty of time to watch the way that humans treat one another, and it never ceases to amaze me. They have such a short time on this Earth, and they choose to spend it being petty and judgmental and cruel, often to the ones they're supposed to care the most for.

Penny cradles her empty mug and stares down into it. "I probably sound like a terrible human being right now."

"It's not my place to say." Hesitantly, I reach out and place a hand on her shoulder, hoping that I'm not being too forward with this. "But you don't strike me as the sort of person who would normally be flippant about a diagnosis like that without good reason."

She does her best to give me a smile, though it's clearly strained. "That's fucked-up," Penny says again. "But thank you. And uh… thanks for stopping me from going straight to the canvas tonight. I think you were right, bringing all my shit in there would've been disastrous. I'm free tomorrow night, maybe we can try again?"

"I'd like that."

Penny eventually packs up her things and leaves. She promises to sleep on all of this unexpected stress and to see how she feels tomorrow. With any luck, we can get back to our project and resume our rhythm together. Though I can't completely shake what she told me, especially about her brother. I thought I was doing something nice, supporting my new artist in a way that went beyond inspiring her. But that generosity is having unintended consequences. In some convoluted way, am I partially to blame for the divide forming between Penny and her brother?

After taking a moment to collect myself and clean up from our strange teatime, I decide I should call up Matilde. Whether it's just because I need to decompress with her, or because I've got family on the mind, it feels necessary.

"Darling! I was hoping I might hear from you soon. I've been eager for an update on the situation with this Penelope woman."

There's something in her boundless enthusiasm that buffets me slightly. "Hmm, good, though a bit complicated, I suppose."

"Ooh. Complicated in a fun way?"

I move into my bedroom and switch to speakerphone so that I can get changed. After this, I'll be quite ready to slide into bed and get some rest myself. "Complicated in a complicated way."

"I've got some time, do you wish to talk about it?" On the other end of the call, I can hear some other voices and muffled music that swiftly dies out, replaced by the background noise of Los Angeles.

"It sounds like you're already fairly busy tonight. I don't want to pull you away from whatever you're doing."

"Just a little shindig to celebrate an album release. Nothing I haven't done a hundred times. I would much rather receive an update from my wonderful sister."

Stepping my way into some lounge pants, I settle onto the chair at my vanity and smirk. Matilde truly is a sweetheart. And while she might speak flippantly at times, I immediately recognize that genuine tone in her prodding that I just can't seem to resist. So I tell her about our sessions thus far, and the strange turn that things took tonight.

When I've finished, Matilde gives a thoughtful hum. The gears in her head are turning. "Well, the good news is that Penelope is clearly enough of a change from your usual fare, so even if you are repeating certain past behaviors, it's less likely that she'll act the same way those *malakas* did." She lapses into a few more swears in various languages, some of which haven't been spoken with such fervor in centuries. "Anyway, I imagine it won't be the same. But it's possible that this might still be a difficult situation in its own, unique way."

"I suppose it's unavoidable. Getting close to someone always invites one form of trouble or another."

"Yes, I am a bit concerned you're setting a different sort of precedent with her. How long before she assumes this is a two-way street and starts to really prod back?"

"Would that be so bad? I know it's not the most pleasant experience in the world, but I honestly believe that Penny might be able to handle it. After all, it's different for each one. There's every chance in the world that she might be able to correlate the new reality with minimal stress."

Matilde clicks her tongue softly, then goes quiet for a moment. "It just sounds like you could stand to be a bit more selfish with this Game of yours. The more you start to care about this human—"

I really hoped that Matilde had gotten over this ridiculous conspiracy theory of hers. She's had such a long time to accept that our siblings aren't disappearing just because they get a bit distracted. After all, I went ten years without inspiring anything, and I'm still around. I don't want to get caught up arguing this with her yet again, so I hurry to assuage her fears. "We'll be picking back up in no time. The portrait is still happening. Besides, Penny is harmless—a puppy compared to them."

"So long as you stick to petting and don't end up adopting her."

I roll my eyes and sigh, even as I feel myself smiling. Why must we always torture metaphors like this? "I promise. It was a single night, letting her vent a bit. The Game isn't over yet." Yes, I did tell Penny that she was free to come over any time she needed somewhere to hide. But that's hardly the same as opening myself up to her.

"I'm glad to hear it, love. I just want the best for you."

"Enjoy your 'shindig,' Matilde."

"You already know I won't," she says with a bright laugh before hanging up.

As I climb under the covers and turn off my bedside lamp, I let everything roll around in my mind. Perhaps Matilde is right. It's too soon to just lay everything out for Penny. The risk is too great. There's nothing wrong with letting her open up, but it's just too dangerous to show my hand. Best to stay aloof and mysterious.

Unfortunately, the more time I spend with her, the harder it gets to stay uninvolved. How long can I realistically hope to maintain this?

CHAPTER FIFTEEN

Penny

I'm not going to lie and say that a night's sleep has suddenly fixed everything. But it has at least put the bare minimum of distance between me and everything yesterday. And spending some time with Anthea did help. What I had initially thought was just a sweet commission is swiftly turning into something bordering on friendship. I'm still not sure how to process that.

That being said, I'm thinking I should probably stop dumping everything in this poor woman's lap—no matter how much she says it's okay. I'll give it a few weeks before I go and unleash more heavy Hartwell lore on Anthea again. For now, I just want to focus on finishing this portrait. Once we're out of contract territory, then it might feel more natural to enjoy a girls' night where we can braid each other's hair and talk about boys. Or girls. Or... whatever.

Granted, that might be tough with how little she talks about herself. Can you really say we're getting to know one another when I'm the one doing all the revealing? But who could possibly blame me for wanting to know her better? She's like this weird little puzzle box.

As always, Anthea is already prepared by the time I get to her apartment. I've gotten used to the sight of her in that beautiful green dress, but that doesn't mean I don't still find myself a little intimidated by her beauty and poise. The only defense I have is to toggle Artist Mode and focus on the details—the effects of light and shadow on color, the dynamic lines of her outfit, the particular shine on her accessories. I just have to stay analytical to stay sane.

There's a kind of easy silence as we both get into position. She takes her spot on the chaise lounge, I get my music playing and all of my tools opened and prepped. There's less need to talk now—which is good, because it seems like half our conversations involve Anthea flirting with me. Which would be difficult enough, but it's made all the more complicated because I have no clue if it means anything. Some people seem almost flirtatious by nature. Whether she's one of them, I still don't know.

I mean, it can't *actually* mean anything, right? This woman could have her pick of anyone in the Greater Boston area. So I have to assume it's just her natural state. Far easier than trying to contend with the idea of someone like her showing even a modicum of interest in someone like me. Not like we'd get very far anyway.

Ugh, that's a whole other can of worms I'm not prepared to open right now.

So I set myself an alarm and turn my attention to the canvas. This, at least, I'm confident about. The more time I put into this portrait, the more I feel like I actually know what I'm doing. And it helps that there's something magical here. I don't know if it's Anthea, or this cozy room, or working with such amazing materials. But whenever the time comes to work on the portrait, for these few blissful hours I'm no longer Penny the Gremlin. I'm Penny the Artist.

The canvas is a wash of brilliant colors right now, but it's lacking in a sense of cohesion. Anyone taking a quick glance would mostly just see this big green blob against a sea of browns, reds, and yellows. In my mind's eye, though, I can see the finished product. It's like jazz, seeing what's not there and knowing how to fill in the gaps in a way that makes sense.

So I grab one of the sticks of charcoal and get to work.

The magic is definitely still here. The instant I leave my first streak of dark coal, tracing out the lines of Anthea's dress, I know that today is going to be a good one. Like always, my left hand follows behind to start smudging, creating the shadows in the folds and curves. My mind is focused and my hands are steady.

I've also noticed that I don't rush while I'm here. When you're doing commissions for a flat rate—especially on the cheap—the goal is to get them knocked out as swiftly as you can to maximize your dollars per hour. And yet, despite this being another job, I don't treat it the same. While some of my movements are precise and targeted, I often find myself lingering, really taking the time to enjoy this.

I'm feeling truly fulfilled in a way I haven't since grad school.

A spot on the portrait sticks out to me, suddenly crying out for a bit of texture. Leaning over, I carefully dip the pinky of my left hand into a small cup of water, then draw it across the skirts of Anthea's dress, moving carefully to avoid any errant drips that might ruin all my hard work. But it accents things perfectly, and really shows the way the lights in the room bounce off the bright colors of her outfit.

I'm so deep into my concentration, I don't even think twice about saying aloud, "Holy shit, I am *good*."

My model giggles softly and subtly flips the page in her book. "Yes, you are."

All of my momentum grinds to a halt, my hands freezing. The room feels significantly warmer. "That—Sorry, I wasn't fishing for compliments. Just vibing. Ignore me."

"And I wasn't giving empty praise. You're a talented artist, and I'm afraid ignoring you is out of the question."

It's not flirtation, but it's almost as bad—legitimate support— and I'm flustered enough that I have to make up some excuse about needing a quick bio-break. But even as I try to hide away in the kitchen and drain a glass of water, I find that I'm already itching to get back to the canvas and pick up where I left off. The moment I have the worn-down nub of forest-green pastel in my hand, I go right back into the zone like nothing happened.

Yeah, there's definitely something magical here.

After pouring out a little too much of my heart last time, I expect that Anthea will maybe want a bit of a break from me. But instead, she just casually asks what we're going to be doing today.

"Oh, uh, no clue." I realize it might be better to be productive with all this nervous energy I've built up over the last twenty-four hours. Up to now, we've mostly just been chilling and watching stuff, but I find I don't feel like lazing around and streaming something. "Kinda wanna go out and do something."

"Perhaps we could walk part of the Freedom Trail? Take in some of the historic sites."

I look at Anthea in surprise. She's lived here how long, and she wants to do a bunch of touristy stuff? "Eh, I dunno about that. But now I'm thinking it might be nice to wander the Common for a bit."

"Oh, that sounds wonderful. Boston Common it is, then."

Spring has officially sprung, and even the walk to get to Boston Common is a pleasant experience. The park is full of people outside enjoying the last few hours of sunshine just like us. Families everywhere are having picturesque little picnics, and couples are idling around the pond in swan boats. It's all very… Seurat's *Sunday*… Just with fewer parasols and fancy outfits.

As we wander, we pass by a girl in a sundress and sweater playing a yearning melody on her violin. She's really fucking good—her bowing is confident, the sustained notes vibrating in a way that just feels so beautifully melancholy but with a small glimmer of hope. She looks completely lost in the moment. When I glance back toward Anthea, she's got this expression that borders on proud. "You know her?"

"Oh, nothing like that. I saw her at a station nearby, a few weeks back. Put some money in the case, told her how much I enjoyed the performance."

"Ah, it's all coming together now. So, that's just what you do, then? Support artists you randomly run into?"

She laughs bashfully, shrugging her shoulders a few times. "I guess I do."

There it is again. It becomes clearer the more it happens, this lack of reciprocity. And I know it's sort of fucked-up to just expect that she'll open up to me in return. But part of me also feels like maybe it's kind of fucked-up to stay so cagey.

For all Anthea knows about me, I still know very little about her. "Being able to support folks on a whim. Must be some damn good residuals from your old life."

"Less than you'd think," she says softly. It sounds wistful, until I look at her again and see a bit of suppressed pain in her face. "Lots of careful saving and investing. That kind of thing."

Anthea takes a seat on a bench a little distance away from the violinist, facing out across the large pond, watching the swan boats float past. I settle in next to her and recline with a low sigh.

"Do you mind if I ask—how are things at home with Theo?"

"Pretty much what you'd expect. We each stay in our own corners of the apartment. Any time we have to walk past each other, we avoid eye contact and don't say anything. Literally the only reason we've called a truce is because I had to at least tell him about Mom. We did shots together in her dishonor, but then we went right back to ignoring each other. It's…not great. I'd really like for things to go back to the way they were."

Anthea gives a low chuckle and lets her head dip back, gazing up at the sky that's already starting to stain a bit pink as the day comes to an end. "Siblings." One word, but full of meaning. And I realize that she's actually letting something slip here.

"You have any?"

"Oh, hundreds," she says through a bit more laughter. Just as suddenly, she seems to catch herself and sits upright again. "Or, well, it feels like it. A big, extended family. So I always include… you know, cousins and things in the headcount." She starts self-consciously smoothing out some of the hair draped across her shoulder.

I'm not even sure why I care so much about this, but I do. "Tell me about them."

Anthea purses her lips in thought for a moment before giving a soft sigh. "Not all that much to tell."

"Hey, come on, you can't keep doing that."

With a surprisingly nervous energy, her eyes flick over toward me, then back out at the horizon. "Doing what?"

"You're so evasive." That comes out way more accusatory than I intend, so I course correct by leaning over and bumping my shoulder into hers, trying to seem playful. "You can't tell me you have a family to rival the Brady Bunch and then leave it at that."

She laughs, but it's forced. "I'm really only close to one sister. And I wouldn't even know where to begin explaining her."

"Okay, forget about them, then, we can keep the spotlight on you. I just—I wanna know stuff about you, Anthea. I swear, sometimes it seems like you've got something almost…magical going on, ya know? You're pretty mysterious."

"I promise you there's really not that much to tell. I was just a model, Penny. Practically from the moment I was born. I never went to school for it. I was never in anything big or exciting. I've worked with a lot of artists, and yes, most of them were pricks. And so now, I've got no passions or deep inner life. I'm still…just a model. Nothing more, nothing less."

Great work. You wanted this woman to open up, well that's what she's doing. And it looks like she's got a whole lot more pain than you do, Hartwell. The best thing you can do? Get out now. Get the hell out and give her some space.

I push down that voice as quickly as it rises up, with no clue where it sprang from. The Hartwell Twins Special isn't usually so…chatty. It's an impulse, not a tiny devil on my shoulder. And there's no way I can walk away from this. Besides, it would be pretty shitty of me to just get up and walk off without any warning.

So I focus on studying Anthea, and for just a moment, she looks old. Really old. Not physically or anything, not like a human gets old. An old mountain. An old statue. A kind of invisible quality in the eyes and the set of the mouth that says *I have seen so much, and I am not sure how much more I want to see.* I can't help but wonder how true that might be. She doesn't look forty right now. She doesn't even look fifty. Anthea could tell me that she's a hundred and fifty, and it would make a kind of sense. "I mean, that's clearly not true. You've got a bunch of stuff going on in there. I don't know what any of it is, but it's pretty obvious just by looking at you."

The shoulder devil is back, getting louder now, and my legs are twitching so anxiously they feel sore. *Just go. It's not worth it. You aren't friends and she doesn't owe you anything. And this is so clearly gonna blow up in about five seconds unless you leave. Right now.*

Anthea finally looks my way again, leveling me with a steady gaze and a furrowed brow. She's mad, though whether she's mad *at me* is unclear. "Attractiveness bias. You're ascribing depth where there is none because of my looks. It happens all the time. I'm as boring as they come."

"But—"

"Penny. Drop it. Please." Okay, now she's definitely mad at me.

Yup. Time to book it.

I get up from the bench and start taking a few backward steps away from Anthea, even reflexively putting my hands up like I'm trying to prove I'm not carrying any weapons. "Okay. Uh. I need to jet. So. I'm just gonna—Yeah."

For just a moment, I think maybe she'll call out to me, ask me to stay, explain literally anything about what the hell just happened here. But she doesn't. Anthea just sits there and stares intently at the horizon. And my legs are still twitching enough that I can't wait around anymore.

Fine. Whatever. I hoof it away as fast as my out-of-shape legs can manage, shocked to find a few tears stinging the corners of my eyes. But I blink them away and hastily wipe at my face. Stupid. Get a grip.

I don't even ride that momentum very far. The feeling subsides as soon as I get down into the Boylston T stop.

I seriously stepped in it back there. I don't know exactly what was going through her head, but it was pretty damn clear that Anthea was upset. In retrospect, I can't even say if she was mad or hurt or scared. But it was something bad—that much is certain. And I have no doubt that all I've managed to do is put some kind of wedge between us.

I'm positive now this will mark the beginning of the end of our partnership. My reach exceeded my grasp, and Anthea will realize I'm not worth it and break our contract. And yeah, there's a clause in there about a fee for cancellation, a chunk of change that will at least ensure I can cover rent next month. But that's small comfort in the face of the way I hurt Anthea—way more of a breach than that first time I drew her.

Excellent work, Penny.

You already pushed away the rest of the family, now Theo hates you, and Liz probably doesn't want much to do with you either. How long before Kai and Meagan start to realize that you're garbage too? Any other bridges we wanna burn while we're at it?

Truly, *this* is your masterpiece.

CHAPTER SIXTEEN

Anthea

I wait until Penny is out of sight, then immediately rush for the nearest trash bin and huddle over it, dry-heaving noisily. I hardly even care that a couple is walking past me, casting nervous glances in my direction. I'm too distracted by my stomach cramps and tight chest.

That was close. That was far too close. I was mere minutes away from caving and putting everything out there. But I can't do that to myself, or to Penny. I won't. Even if she hates me, it's better than the alternative. This is all for the best.

Once I no longer feel as though my body is throwing a coup, I stumble back from the bin and head for a nearby corner store to get myself a bottle of water and some painkillers.

As I make the walk back to my apartment, I can't help but berate myself more and more with every step.

Stupid. Clumsy. Foolhardy. Puerile. And downright embarrassing. Matilde was absolutely right. Penny wants to get to know me, and I'm not nearly as good at deflecting as I thought. So I overreacted and shut her out, forcefully.

While I only caught glimmers of it, I can safely say that brushing up against the reality of what I am was not an easy thing for Penny to go through. Her poking and prodding only revealed the bare minimum, but she didn't react well. As soon as she became even vaguely aware that something was wrong, she took off. I can't believe I was so naïve to think that this time might be special or different. Of course she left. The one time I find somebody decent, I chase her away.

Calming down right now isn't an option. I'm buzzing with nervous energy and worry. And while I know I should just distract myself with a bit of meaningless television or reading, I instead find my feet taking me straight to my bedroom. Deep in my walk-in closet, hiding up in the distant corner of the high shelves, is a box of mementos. They should have been dumped in the trash the moment I started my constitutional, but for some stupid reason I held on to them.

Sitting cross-legged on my bed, I cautiously open the lid like Pandora, as though I'm in danger of releasing all manner of terrible spirits upon the Earth. But really, the only cursed one here is me.

Sitting on top of it all is a Polaroid, taken when the photographic medium tried—and failed—to experience a brief resurgence. It was taken at a lavish party in a Manhattan loft. I'm dolled up and drunk, hanging on the arm of a handsome man trying too hard with his waxed mustache and hipster glasses. Dmitri—the one that finally broke me.

You'd think that an ancient being should be immune to insincere charm and smart enough to not fall for a series of well-placed but ultimately shallow promises. This is not the case—or at least it hasn't been for me. Millennia spent living in a corporeal form on this planet, yet always so perpetually naïve.

That man had me wrapped around his finger with layer upon layer of bullshit. He was possessive, obsessive, and utterly self-absorbed. That only got worse after I revealed my true nature to him. Dmitri was certain that my presence in his life was a sign from above that he was destined to become one of the greats. I was both the source of his genius, and his reward for it.

Over time, the mask slipped more and more, until I finally realized just what kind of man I'd ended up with. When I felt strong enough, I would try to talk him down, or even verbally parry some of his harsher turns. Dmitri knew before I did that I was ready to leave. He assured me that I would never find someone like him again, that I would end up alone and unfulfilled. Even after so many times doing the same song and dance with so many artists, some part of me believed him. He promised that if I ever went back to him, I would have to beg and plead on bended knee to eke out even the smallest fraction of his "good graces."

Ten years later and it's still too much to think about. I move on.

Beneath that is another Polaroid, this one taken at an estate outside San Francisco, when the technology was fresh and new. The framing is identical in a way that hurts. The only difference, aside from the fashion, is that I'm hanging on the arm of a woman named Betty. It's strange how Dmitri was so different from her, yet ultimately the same. She put me on a pedestal, treating me like some kind of goddess. But the effect was still painfully dehumanizing. It wasn't deification so much as objectification. I was her prized possession.

I continue extracting trinkets and reminders. The gold tennis bracelet from Ramon, whose praise was always backhanded. The scarf from Agatha, who strangled me with her need for affirmation. And a lock of hair from the sculptor who lied constantly, and who only ever went by an obvious pseudonym—Jackie.

Back in those days, I didn't even have the strength to free myself. Each partnership followed a similar pattern—I was useful and fun, until I wasn't anymore. Sometimes they might bid me a fond farewell before sending me off into the world. Others took a more unceremonious approach and dropped me when something shiny and new caught their attention.

Some learned what I was, others never bothered. But the through line remained the same. I was drained of all my energies until nothing was left but a sad, lonely spirit—in some cases, quite literally. There is no heartbreak quite so poignant as the one that causes you to unmake your physical form.

After running to Matilde, I'd lick my wounds for a while until I felt ready to try again. On and on for centuries. There was nothing particularly special or different about Dmitri, not really. He was simply the straw that broke the camel's back.

As painful as this is, I find the thing that really hurts is how it all just makes me think of Penny. She was meant to be different. And she certainly is. But I did nothing to prepare myself for how to navigate that. Which inexplicably puts me right back where I always end up. As I pack the box back up and return it to its shameful hiding place, a voice in my head tells me this is just my lot in life, all I'm ever meant to be. A voice that sounds an awful lot like Dmitri.

* * *

I spend a few days mostly moping around my apartment. I binge-read the rest of the *Wizard of Oz* series, even though it just leaves me thinking about that first day at the library. Occasionally I open up Netflix and scroll through it, but every time something sticks out to me, I just find myself thinking that I'd rather have Penny here to watch it with me. With each meal I cook, all I can think is that it would be so much nicer to share it with her. All in all, it's quite a low moment for me.

But finally I break, if only because otherwise my spiral will start getting exponentially worse.

I'm craving a mug of something that isn't the same black coffee I've been mainlining. So I make the short trip down to Savage Roast. After all, I still have more drinks to try. Any port in a storm, as they say. Sometimes all it takes is something small to motivate you. When all else fails, there's no shame in using something silly to convince you to be proactive.

On the way out, I also stop by my mailbox to see how much has piled up while I sat hidden away in my hole.

Waiting inside is an envelope from the Massachusetts Society for the Arts. My name and address are handwritten in neat lettering, and something about that eats at me. Someone went to the trouble of personally addressing this to me instead of just slapping on a printed sticker. Surely they wouldn't have gone to the trouble if this was just some perfunctory invitation.

Deep-seated social graces prompt me to open it, even if the only thing I want to do is toss it in the trash. The card inside is embossed and gilded, and the lettering is all fanciful cursive. Location, date, time, and an option for a plus-one. There's also a personalized message, mentioning again that they want to highlight my generous giving.

It stares at me, begging me to RSVP as I step outside into the bright sunlight. Given my mood, I wish the weather were more miserable. I want to throw this damned thing away, but that same guilt prompts me to shove it down into my purse. For now, I need to focus on getting coffee, holding on to that goal to keep me in motion.

It's a relief to hear those familiar bells jingle as I enter Savage Roast, and to see that Raine is working the register again today. Hers is a friendly face that I haven't managed to purge from my shrinking social circle. Or, well, parasocial, at any rate.

While I've done my best to not look so haggard, there must still be some kind of cloud hanging over me. The moment I approach, Raine frowns sympathetically while giving me a concerned examination, forgoing her usual greeting. "Hey, you doing all right?"

I give a half-hearted shrug and a half-hearted smile. "I've been better."

"Y'know, I'm clocking out in like ten minutes. If you want, I can chill with you for a bit and you can vent."

"Raine, I'm fairly certain you have plenty better things to do with your time than that."

"Need all the practice I can get if I want to be a successful therapist someday."

"So should I be expecting a bill in the mail?" I crack a small smile. Something about Raine's combination of practicality and kindness wins me over. "If you're sure."

Today's drink is the Castle—a frothy latte with a shot of caramel, sprinkled with cinnamon. Once I've paid and left my usual tip, I once again hunt down a secluded spot where I can wait until this bright-eyed college student can join me and listen to all my woes. This, too, feels like a bit of a low point for me. But at least that means there's nowhere to go but up. Or, at least, I truly hope that's the case. Sipping at my coffee, I find a pleasant little tingle on my tongue from the cinnamon and a lingering, smooth sweetness from the caramel. It's a little thing, a tiny pleasantry, but it reaffirms that just maybe the world is okay. I might be lonely and sad, but never forget that coffee exists.

Before long, Raine comes over to the couch, sans apron, and settles in next to me. Her posture is easy and her smile is warm. "All right, hit me with it. What's got the usually chipper Anthea down in the dumps?"

"Do you remember the woman I was in here with the other week?"

"I knew it!" Her cry of victory is so enthusiastic that I jump a little in my seat and she has to suppress a giggling fit before continuing, "I'm sorry, I'm sorry, you two were just so obvious. All awkward, getting your drinks together. And then you posed so she could draw you, which feels like something I should put on my bucket list now. How long have you been together?"

All the implications wrapped up in her words aren't necessarily shocking in and of themselves. But to hear it all put together so concisely does make me that much more aware of what my work looks like from the outside. "Er, that's not actually—Our relationship—It's really more of a partnership. She's an artist, and I'm sponsoring her. She's doing a portrait of me." I know I'm not doing myself any favors stumbling my way through what undoubtedly sounds like one big excuse.

Raine raises an eyebrow curiously but doesn't press the point any further. "Hmm, okay. So, what happened?"

"We had an argument a few days ago, if you can even call it that. A tiff, maybe. To your credit, I think it's true that she does want to get to know me better, for this to be something other than a partnership. And I...can't do that. I closed myself off."

Why in the world is it so easy for me to say all this to Raine? And yet when it's Penny asking to get to know me, I shut her out. The answer to that is fairly obvious, and I'm choosing to not think about it.

"Too scary?"

"No, not that. I…have a lot of baggage. Heavy baggage. And it's not fair for me to put that on her."

"And does she know that?"

"What?"

"This big, heavy steamer trunk of history you're lugging around. Does she at least know that it exists?"

If anything, I did what I could to convince Penny of the opposite. I stressed—unsuccessfully, granted—that there was very little to me. I hoped that if she saw me as shallow, she might stop digging. But I couldn't pull it off. One more thing Matilde is far better at. Smart as a whip, but she plays the ditsy blonde trope well. "No. I've been trying to downplay it all. And that only made her more determined. Hence, this pseudo-argument."

"Okay. If you're still interested in my opinion, then I think you're being a little bit too absolutist here. There is a middle ground where you can start from. You don't have to reveal a single piece of information about who you are, what you've done, how you feel, none of it. But it might be worth at least laying out in plain terms just how big and heavy that baggage is."

I quietly sip from my mug, deep in thought, wishing desperately that she wasn't making so much sense. "It's easier said than done."

"Well, yeah. That's life in a nutshell. But at least you've got some idea of what you could do. Alternately, you could just pack it in and call it a day. Maybe it's just not worth the trouble. That's up to you to decide."

"Hmm. Well. The good news is that I think you're going to make an excellent therapist. The bad news is that I don't think you've made my life any easier."

Raine grins and stands up from the couch. "Hey, therapy isn't about making life easier, it's about confronting stuff. So I'd call this a success. Now, I need to get home. I'm staring down the twin barrels of two separate research papers. But I'm sure you'll do what you need to do."

* * *

Penny isn't answering her phone, and it's making me more than a little nervous. It would be fair enough, after the way I treated her the other day. I don't think I'd be too happy with me either.

Just about the time I'm going for my third attempt, I stop and force myself to take a deep breath. I'm panicking, and it's making me assume the worst. There are plenty of reasons why she wouldn't pick up. And if I keep ringing her when it's a bad time, then she really will get annoyed with me and not want to talk anymore.

Once I get my breathing under control, a text pops up on the screen.

???
Everything okay?

Yes, sorry.
I want to talk.
Not as in "we need to talk."
Just regular talk.

At work right now
Later though?
…should we meet on neutral ground or…?

As much as I want to tell her we'll do it at the café or maybe the Common, it's much safer to do this at my place. Even Penny's apartment comes with too many potential issues. I just have to hope she won't mind.

You're free to say no of course
But I would prefer my apartment.

That works just fine for me
We'd be in serious trouble if I refused to set foot in your home
I can be there at like five?

Until then.

I set my phone down with a low sigh of relief. Maybe this bridge isn't burned after all.

CHAPTER SEVENTEEN

Penny

I reach out to knock on Anthea's door but pull back at the last second as the uncertainty and anxiety strikes for the tenth time tonight. I had to fight it just to leave the apartment, and again while waiting for the T when all I wanted was to just go home and avoid all of this. Even with the assurance that this wasn't A Talk, it still feels like I'm walking into something big and important. And considering my track record with tackling big and important stuff, it's taking a lot of effort to push down that voice in my head screaming *run, run, run*.

It takes mere moments for the door to swing open, and there she is on the other side, looking as troubled as I feel. So at least we're still on relatively even footing here. For all that it's worth.

"Um. Hey."

"Hello, Penny."

"I, uh, wasn't sure I'd be hearing from you again." There's not much point in couching it in subtlety. That whole thing at the park was pretty obviously my fault. I pushed way too hard.

Which is maybe why the next words out of her mouth are so utterly confounding. "I meant to do it sooner, but I was nervous. I…want to apologize."

"Sorry. I think maybe I misheard that. Don't you mean you want *me* to apologize?"

She gives me a wry smile, somewhere between amused and pitying, which is better than angry—but not by much. "No point in doing this heart-to-heart out here. Please, come in."

The two of us take up our usual spots on the couch.

Anthea is perched on the edge of the cushion, back straight, with her hands lightly tapping against her knees. "The truth is that I *want* to tell you things about myself. Maybe everything. But I need you to understand that it's not a pleasant experience."

"Is this an organized crime kinda thing? Like you're gonna tell me you used to be some mob boss's trophy wife and now you're in witness protection?"

Her eyes go wide in shock, and suddenly she's letting loose with high, bright laughter. Anthea finally slumps back in her seat, clutching at her belly. "Haha, no! No, nothing like that…" It takes a moment for her to stop laughing, but eventually she continues. At least she's smiling now, even as she grows serious again, still idly rubbing her stomach as she looks at me warily. "But…it's complicated. Difficult, even."

Well, at least I didn't offend her with that wild shot in the dark. But I had to know, and it's good to hear her laugh again. Still, I can't imagine what could possibly be so bad. I'm starting to wonder if maybe she's winding me up so that when the big reveal drops, it'll seem small by comparison. "I meant what I said the other day. I want to know stuff about you. So hit me with it."

After nodding a few times, mostly to herself, Anthea gets back up from the couch and goes into the kitchen. Following a bit of rooting around, she comes back and sets a few items on the coffee table before sitting down—two bottles of water, painkillers, some Pepto-Bismol, and a small plastic waste bin. Like she's preparing for the world's most depressing magic trick. "We'll start slow. And listen, this is going to be strange, unsettling. Some part of you will likely try to reject this entire process. If it becomes too much, tell me to stop, and I will. But it's also important that you understand—we're only going to do this once. Should it backfire, then I believe the best thing to do is for us to part ways. You'll still get your commission pay, and I won't think any less of you."

If this is some kind of elaborate trick, she's really playing it up. But between my desire to understand her and my sheer curiosity, I'm in too deep now. I've run away enough times in my life. Just this once, I want to stick around. "It's fine. I'm fine. Just say what you need to say."

Anthea opens the Pepto and takes a shot of it like it's tequila. Then she inhales a deep breath in through her nose and releases it slowly through her mouth. She turns fully to face me and carefully tucks her legs up under her, finding the comfiest position she can.

I do the same, awkwardly rotating my body and crossing my legs.

"That day at the library, we didn't just happen to run into each other. I was drawn there by you. That's also how I was able to find you at the gas station. You put out this kind of warmth that's so hard to ignore, because of your talent and your potential."

A little shiver goes up and down my spine, and I feel my arms break out in a wave of goose bumps. A war breaks out in my mind. Part of me thinks, rightly, that this is a ridiculous thing to say, that it's clearly some kind of New Age nonsense about chakras or the Law of Attraction or whatever. But a smaller, quieter part of me perks up and tells me this is perhaps the Most True Thing that has ever been said.

All of that eventually gets subsumed by something much more pressing—I need to run. Right now. I need to get the fuck out of here. Because this is the bonkers moment when Anthea lets her freak flag fly, and she shows me just what kind of whacked-out beliefs she has. My legs literally ache with the desire to get up from the couch and get moving, the muscles spasming painfully. But if I do that, then I'll never know what is going on here. And that smaller, quieter part of me is surprisingly stubborn about seeing this through. A whisper demanding to be heard over a yell.

"Okay, cool, so you hit me with some kind of weird hypnotic suggestion or whatever. Great party trick. Can you cut the theatrics and just talk to me normally?"

"No theatrics." Anthea's words come out shaky. She's pressing one hand to her chest, the other to her belly. Her face is greener than it was a moment ago. "Your body is trying to protect you, keep you from hearing this. And my body is punishing me for speaking the truth."

I'm getting scared now, because either Anthea is much more eccentric than I realized, or something supernatural is happening here.

No, that small voice cuts in and corrects me. *This is very much natural. This is primal and real.*

"That's insane," I mutter.

Surprisingly, Anthea laughs softly and nods. "Yes, it is. It's the price for knowledge." She massages her stomach gently while focusing on making her breaths even. "I'm really sorry, Penny. I wanted you to see that I'm serious when I say this isn't much fun, that it's going to be difficult. Just remember what I said. We've really only got one chance to do this."

I should absolutely not stick around. Whatever's going on here, it's above my pay grade. But whether it's stubbornness or something deeper than that, I'm getting too invested. My desire to know who Anthea really is wins out against my instincts. No Hartwell Twins Special today. "You're not looking so hot. Is it going to get worse for you?"

She looks at me with a smile that seems as ancient as the Earth itself, fighting through whatever pain she's feeling. "Oh, Penny. You should know things can always get worse. But…they can also get better. What do you say?" Reaching out, she takes my hands and looks at me intently.

This has gone way past a partnership, or even a friendship. She's inviting me to struggle together in the hopes of something new, and yet very old. It's stupid and impossible—and maybe still a prank, but probably not. And the answer comes to me easier than I expect. "Keep going."

She beams, practically lighting up the room. "I'm being quite literal, about the warmth and the potential. I…I should just come out and say it. I'm not human. But I suppose these days I'm close enough for the lines to be quite blurry."

"Are you going to tell me you're an angel or something?"

I laugh. She doesn't.

"Maybe it would be easier to show you." She gently squeezes my hands again and looks me firmly in the eyes. "I'm going to do what I do best and inspire you with a little story."

I don't really understand exactly what that means, or how it's supposed to make this any easier. But she's so confident that I feel like Anthea could weave a story capable of making it all make sense. "Uh. Okay?"

"I'm…old, Penny. My family, we've been around since the first human told the first story. When your ancestors broke open fruits and used the juices as paint, we gave their arms a nudge. With every new note sung and step danced, we were there cheering you on."

Suddenly, I'm hit with a feeling that is so familiar, yet so hard to place. And while I'm distracted trying to figure out where I know it from, I almost miss the fact that the world is melting away around me. One moment, I'm seated on the couch in Anthea's living room, holding her hands and looking at her beaming face, and the next I'm sitting in a chilly cave with my hands held out to warm themselves near a blazing fire. "What the fuck?"

I thought this was crazy before, but we've officially entered a whole new tier of insanity. The impulse rises up in me again, stronger still, to bolt. But two things are keeping me from doing that. The first is that I'm not entirely certain if I'll be running out into an early spring evening in Boston, Massachusetts, or out into the storm raging beyond the mouth of this cave. The second, and the one that really keeps me grounded, is the phantom sensation of Anthea's hands squeezing my own, as if she were the heat from the fire.

"Remember, this is just a story. Though it is an important one, in my humble opinion. Because this is the story of the night I was born, on a stormy night in a solitary cave, ages ago."

Right, she's just showing me something. I'm not actually there, of course. That would be ridiculous. This is just a vision. A hallucination. No biggie. She just has magic powers or whatever. I can definitely handle that. Probably.

My head is really starting to hurt, and I figure it's probably best if I just ride this out. Because if I tap out now, Anthea said we wouldn't get another chance. And against all sense, I feel a deep need to see this through, to know her.

The woman who is and is not me takes one of the spare kindling sticks and idly pokes it into the fire until it inevitably catches and begins to char. She pulls it out and watches the way the flames flicker and dance before blowing them out. Almost as an afterthought, she idly drags the blackened tip against the nearby stones of the cave wall and watches in wonder as it leaves a chunky black mark in its wake.

In her ear, in my ear, a familiar voice whispers, "Yes."

Something indefinable is ignited in that moment. I watch as this kindred soul starts to use her newfound tool to sketch the face of the woman she loves, who lies sleeping in a nearby bundle of furs.

That voice—it wasn't just encouragement. It was enthusiasm and inspiration and joy and delight and drive and a million other things, injected directly into the brain and the limbs. "The night you were born…"

Then, just like that, the scene dissolves, and I'm back in Anthea's apartment where everything is totally normal again.

Only it's not really "normal." Everything is new and different, too. I get it now. This is so much bigger than I could have imagined.

The two of us sit there in silence for a while, gripping one another's hands with white-knuckle intensity, panting and chuckling. Anthea's looking at me with something bright and shining behind her eyes. "Ahh. There it is. Thank goodness. We can finally talk."

But just as suddenly, she makes a kind of gurgling noise from deep within her core. "Oh, this is the worst part." She releases my hands and lurches over, grabbing hastily for the wastebasket that I'd completely forgotten about. And she proceeds to vomit for a solid three minutes.

CHAPTER EIGHTEEN

Anthea

It takes several embarrassing minutes for the two of us to undo some of the damage we sustained. I have to brush my teeth and rinse with mouthwash multiple times. Penny takes a healthy dose of Tylenol and chases it with half her water bottle to fight off the lingering ache in her legs.

With the contents of my stomach removed, I find myself ravenously hungry and order delivery—a feast of greasy goodness—without a trace of shame. After all, what do I have to be embarrassed about at this point? We're past it now. After hanging up, I take my own large glug of water, wincing briefly as it mingles with the mint of the mouthwash.

My defenses are down, I still feel a bit weak, and I'm wrestling with some complicated emotions at the moment. After all I did to hype myself up, I just couldn't follow through on Matilde's advice or her big plan. I got attached to yet another human and let them in close, knowing full well that this is exactly how I got hurt last time. Penny at least seems like she's not the type to do what the others did, but that's not completely guaranteed. And there are plenty of different ways to hurt someone. That's the risk with seeking companionship.

So when I casually lean my way over until I'm resting with my head in her cushy lap, it feels both supremely right and utterly foolish. Although the light blush in her cheeks and the look of surprise on her face does give me a little charge of satisfaction. There's still something to be said for how fun it is to tease her.

"So…" she finally says, hesitantly dipping her toe into the murky water. "Magic?"

Giggling softly, I shake my head. "Not quite. Perhaps it will be easier if I start from the beginning, now that we're not going to be interrupted by any nasty side effects."

"Please do."

"There's no real universally agreed-upon term for what we are, but 'muse' works well enough for shorthand."

Penny's doing her best to remain calm, but I can sense the waves of confusion and anxiety still rolling off her. "Right. Totally. Of course. So when you say 'we,' and that whole thing about having a big family…?"

"Quite literally hundreds. That wasn't a lie. I got a bit sloppy."

"But isn't the whole thing that there were only nine of you?"

"No, they were just the first to get noticed. We used to be a good deal more…cavalier. But then you all started deifying us, worshipping us, and that didn't sit right—especially with the more conservative muses in our family. So we tried to be more conscientious about revealing ourselves."

Almost absentmindedly, Penny starts raking her fingers through my hair. The sensation is enough that I nearly melt into a puddle right there in her lap, but somehow I hold it together. "Is it always like that? All painful and draining? I feel like that would've come up somewhere in the myths if that were the case."

"It didn't used to be." My eyes slide shut, in part so I don't end up staring at Penny's face and getting distracted any further during this little history lesson. "Back then, humans were more open to fantastical concepts, and they could slot the idea of our existence into their world view easily. But the further we got into modernity, the more treacherous it was to be open. The

Enlightenment was seen as a boon by those who wanted to stay hidden, but not all of us agreed."

For just a moment, I get distracted by a deep sense of melancholy. Those were difficult times, watching humanity forget about us. After all the help we'd given them, the incredible inventions and developments we'd inspired, only to be left behind. Driven into the shadows, forced to learn how to wear masks and lie about ourselves. It was a painful transition. "The world became… smaller, unremarkable. Yet there we were, threatening the very concept of the mundane. To accept it, the mind has to quickly catch up to some pretty big conceptual changes. And revealing the truth comes with its own hefty cost, as you saw firsthand."

"Well, at least now I get why you were so cagey with everything." Her hand stops moving, much to my dismay, but her fingers remain tangled in my hair. "Um, sorry for that, by the way. Pushing you to talk. Running out on you. All that."

"No apology necessary. Honestly, that's…not the only reason I was being so evasive. I've been hurt in the past." I open my eyes but cast my gaze at the ceiling.

"The, uh, pack of assholes you worked with?"

"Precisely. That part was also quite true. I have to admit, you didn't make it easy to hide things. That aura of warmth I mentioned? It's comforting, and it's strong."

Her hand eventually resumes stroking my hair. "And that whole retirement thing?"

"Also true, unfortunately. I had a rather nasty habit of latching on to a particular breed of artist. It got so bad I attempted to quit. But my sister convinced me that I should take a break instead, and after a great deal of negotiation, we settled on a decade. For ten years, no artists, no art. Just a chance for me to figure myself out and reset."

"Wow. So, I'm your rebound…"

That makes it sound so terrible. And it doesn't feel accurate. My eyes flick over to look up at her face, and I smile softly. "You're…my fresh start." That's about all I can manage before resuming my intense inspection of the stucco overhead.

That seems to satisfy her, judging by the light burn in her cheeks. "Well played. I'll take it." She's also staring off at a spot on the wall, some absolutely fascinating bit of shadow, I'm sure. After a moment, she softly clears her throat. "I've asked this before, but I think in light of recent revelations, it bears repeating. Why me? Was it just because I'm a safe bet?"

"Not exactly, and not intentionally. It's just that you were… different. You stood out so brilliantly that day. You still do. But it's more than that, too. I mean, that apology was what really sealed it for me. All the others, they were the types to get so caught up in their art that they never showed consideration for the people around them—me included. And the idea that you would feel so penitent over something so small, that intrigued me."

"Guess I owe my roommate a thank-you at some point for that. She was the one who talked me through some of it. Just… didn't expect that I would ever actually get the chance to say it, especially not so soon." She smiles bashfully. "As long as we're feeding my ego here—it's not *only* that, right? Like, do you think the portrait is actually going okay, or is it all just an excuse?"

I'm torn between two facts. On the one hand, Penny's search for positive reinforcement and her insecurities can be quite precious at times. On the other hand, this poor woman could stand to benefit from the occasional bout of self-aggrandizing. "You're good, Penny. And if anyone knows what talent looks like, it's a muse. It's obvious you worked to reach the level you have. The technical knowledge comes to you easily, and you seem to understand the interplay of light and shadow so naturally. And the way you use colors—Yes. You're absolutely skilled. If I were to inspire a child, they wouldn't suddenly start painting like the masters. So please don't get carried away worrying that this is some kind of charity case. I'm legitimately eager to see what you can do." Reaching up, I poke her gently on the nose, and her face scrunches up in protest. "A little confidence would look very good on you, Miss Hartwell."

She clears her throat and shifts a bit, though not too much to rattle me around. "Cool. I think that's enough about me for the foreseeable future. I still wanna know more about you. That stuff you showed me, it's almost like you were a ghost or something?"

"Hmm, 'spirit' would probably be more accurate, though even that implies something fully sapient. We really do start out as just whispers, mere feelings. It takes effort and willpower to take on physical form. But I'm glad that we can, even if not all of my siblings agree. It's so much more interesting. After all, there are a great many things bodies can do that are impossible when you're stuck as an incorporeal mass of creative energy." For once, I don't even mean that in an entirely teasing way. Having a body means having senses, locomotion, thoughts and ideas, all kinds of wonderful possibilities.

But as I lie here and look up at her face, I know that I mean more than that. Things that I haven't done in over a decade now. Things that, as hard as I try to deny it, I find myself wanting from Penny too. But I know that's dangerous territory to go wandering into blindly. I'm trying to do things differently here, and even if I didn't have the strength to keep from getting close to her, the least I can do is not immediately draw the poor woman into something deeper with me. Matilde can do casual flings, but I've never understood them. It's just not in my nature.

Penny's lap is extremely warm and inviting, I'll say that much.

Whether it's just to continue satisfying her curiosity, or in an effort to pivot this discussion away from my teasing, Penny gently clears her throat and gets us back onto the topic at hand. "So this cave woman was the first charcoal artist or whatever. Is that a thing for you, like a specialty?"

"Yes, just like our famous siblings, we all have a medium or style that we're most commonly drawn to—whatever moment of inspiration and creation brought us into being. It's not strictly exclusive. I've worked with poets and musicians before. But there is a kind of primal draw to earthy materials, and charcoal in particular. Paints, pottery, sculpting—they'll get me close. Still, I was born from the embers, so to speak, and that always feels the most like home."

"And that's part of why you found me so easily?"

"There's a shine to any human in need of inspiration, but it's easier to home in on someone that meets our specialty. We share something in common, and that made you attractive." It takes a moment for my mind to catch up with what I've just said, and I flush, looking away from Penny. "Magnetically, I mean. Which is not to say you aren't also *physically* attractive! I'm—I'm sorry, perhaps I'm not explaining this quite right."

She shifts slightly, making me all the more aware of the fact that I'm lying with my head in this woman's lap and being, perhaps, a bit too honest with her. While there's no point in keeping secrets from her, I know that I should keep my affections flirtatious at most.

Thankfully, we're freed from the awkward moment by a knock at the door. Saved by the delivery man, bringing Chinese food from a local family-run establishment that makes scallion pancakes to die for. I get up from Penny's lap and make my way over, signing my receipt with a flourish and making sure to include a good tip. It's literally the least I can do.

After a bit of rearranging on the couch, I lay out our bounty on the coffee table, and soon we're gorging ourselves on much-needed calories. The conversation goes on hiatus while we eat, until Penny perks up with a sudden thought. "Oh, right, that was something else I wanted to ask about. Your sister, the one that convinced you to take a break instead of quitting."

"Matilde."

"Jesus, do all of you choose such cool names? Really makes me regret picking something so normal."

"I happen to think Penny is a wonderful name." With my energy returning to me, I'm making another proper attempt at the Game—at least what parts of it I can salvage. No doubt about it, I'm becoming quite fond of teasing this woman, and she doesn't do herself any favors by reacting so adorably, blushing at the slightest compliment. "I've known a great many Penelopes in my time. You know, there actually *was* a queen of Ithaca who was quite the skilled weaver. My brother Isaac was her muse. Lovely woman. So don't worry, it's a marvelous name with strong roots."

Right on cue, Penny blushes and stammers for a moment before steering back on topic. "Mm. So, Matilde. Are you two especially close?"

"We are. I suppose in some small way, she has something in common with your brother. Matilde is very good at what we do, but she has certain eccentricities that our other siblings were never much interested in indulging. She is…bombastic, and she spreads her influence out to dozens of people at once. It works for her, but I think some of the others see her as a cause for concern." There's more to it than that, but I'm not sure Penny is quite ready to hear about some of the confusing intricacies of our kind, nor the bizarre conspiracy theories that Matilde subscribes to. "And yet I have always found her such a joy to be around. So while everyone else drew away from her, I gave her more attention. I took the time to really listen to her pain and fears, helping her to find somewhere more productive to direct her energy. We've been thick as thieves ever since."

Unfortunately, mention of Penny's brother causes her face to fall a bit. "Yeah, family can be…tough."

Sitting up a bit, I give as comforting a smile as I can manage. "How are things going with Theo?"

She shakes her head and quickly slurps up a long string of lo mein noodles. "Confrontation is not our strong suit. For all that we've tried to break from our family, we never really got over that whole 'stiff upper lip' thing. It's not in our blood to talk through things. Hatchets don't get buried, they just kinda sit there until the elements cover them over naturally. In a week or two it'll all pass, and everything will be mostly copacetic again."

"I hope so." It hardly sounds ideal, but I'm not exactly in a position to give advice when it comes to families. Still, it seems only fair that I try to offer her something worthwhile. So I take a moment to think over our last conversation about their unfortunate tensions when something pops into my mind. "You mentioned that Terra Vertebrae got into a local battle of the bands?"

That gets her to perk up and nod enthusiastically. "Yeah! I'm so proud of them, they absolutely deserve it."

"You should make sure he knows that, then. Even if you feel it all goes without saying, sometimes it can be surprisingly meaningful to say those things anyway."

"I'll have to remember that. Thank you."

Perhaps for want of a bit of mundanity, our conversation slowly winds its way back to more ordinary matters and planning our next session. There's a shared energy and excitement that fills me with a wonderful warmth I haven't enjoyed for ages. It took some stumbling to get here, but I've found exactly what I needed to start properly recovering from everything that happened to me over the last few decades.

I'm a very lucky muse.

CHAPTER NINETEEN

Penny

I had assumed that once our food arrived, I wouldn't need to worry about Anthea being so close to me again. It was nice, don't get me wrong. It's clear that Anthea is simply happy to have someone she can be vulnerable around, and the physical proximity is just a by-product of that. We can talk openly, and that encourages a kind of special intimacy.

I'm really hoping it's nothing more than that.

But even so, when she ends up putting her head in my lap for the second time tonight, I can't help but feel a little shiver run up and down my spine excitedly. Her head nestles so perfectly in my crossed legs, and it leaves her staring up at me with this look on her face that I'm a bit scared to decode. So I blame it on the lingering high from her big reveal and ignore everything else.

"Are you doing okay? I know it's a great deal to process."

"Still a bit overwhelmed, honestly. My brain is kinda starting to settle, but it's slow going."

"That sounds about right. Take your time, as much as you need."

Even though I'm still buzzing with energy from tonight's revelation, I surprise myself with a rather impressive yawn. "Alas, finding out that the world is more magical than you realized can take it out of you. I should really get back to the apartment before the trains stop for the night."

"Not magic. No more than what you do with charcoal." Anthea stays right where she is in my lap and looks up at me with a small pout. "You can always just spend the night here. As you can see, the couch is quite comfortable."

I pray she doesn't say something about her bed being big enough for two people. "That's really nice of you, but I'm still a homebody at heart. I have trouble sleeping anywhere but my own bed." It's a thin excuse, and maybe she knows that, but a tiny seed of panic threatens to sprout in my belly at the idea of staying the night here. Especially when there's all this energy between us that feels…complicated.

Finally, she pushes herself up to a seated position and frees me with a small smile. I know that Anthea is lonely, and that she probably craves company after ten years alone without anywhere to direct her "spark." But I need some room to breathe.

The two of us share another one of our protracted farewells, but somehow I finally manage to pry myself away from Anthea's apartment. As nervous as I am about the change in our dynamic, it's also got a draw to it that feels inescapable. I'll be back here before too long, so I can't avoid it forever. For now, a girl needs her rest. Especially after that particularly harrowing experience.

The train I catch is packed, and I have to stand in the press of the crowd and hold firmly onto the dangling handle to keep myself from bumping into someone. And yet, I also feel strangely isolated.

A muse.

Anthea is a freaking muse.

I can't get the thought out of my head. I want to shout it to this car full of strangers. I want to grab them individually by the cheeks and look them dead in the eyes and tell them, "Magic is real and anything is possible."

Somehow, though, I keep a lid on that impulse. It's not exactly easy, but with enough concentration, it's doable.

By the time I get home, I'm bursting at the seams with excitable energy. My heart is racing and I'm mounting the stairwell with an enthusiasm I haven't felt in years. I barely get winded, which is practically a miracle in its own right. For all I know, there's an obnoxious halo of light around my head right now. I start to open the door before remembering I need to unlock it first and laugh softly at myself as I struggle to get the key in properly with my hands lightly shaking.

And who should be there in the living room, watching MTV reality show reruns, than the one person that would be able to put a damper on that? Whatever I'm projecting out into the world, Theo notices it and gives me a quizzical look. "I guess somebody had a good night with her fancy lady in that fancy apartment."

Normally, this would be the part where I'd just shrug this off and go back to my room. But fighting so hard to finally know Anthea, going through what we did together, and the advice she gave me? My feet remain planted firmly in place, and I realize I can't just walk this one off. So I take in a deep breath through my nose, head into the living room, pop a squat next to Theo on the couch, and look at him levelly. "Dude, is everything okay?"

He's avoiding looking my way, still staring at the television. "Yeah, why?"

"Because I've been getting weird vibes from you lately. And that really sucks. So if I'm imagining things, then that's on me. But if I'm not, I don't want some kind of void to form between us."

For a moment, it looks as though he's just going to keep watching *Next* and ignoring me. But finally, with a weary sigh, he turns the television off. "I dunno. Worried, I guess."

"Worried about what?" That's not even some kind of leading question. I can at least tell that he's developed this one-sided beef over the portrait. But beyond that, I'm clueless.

It looks like it's a struggle for him each time he has to open his mouth. Like he's writing whatever he's going to say in his head, then erasing it, and trying again. "You know how your job at the gas station sucks? Like it's kinda just soul-crushing and shitty, same as pretty much anything where you're earning minimum wage?"

"Uh, yeah, I'm fully aware."

"When you first got it, I was honestly kinda jealous. Look, I know it's always been you and me. But, fuck, I don't know. You managed to finish college *and* get a goddamn master's degree on top of it. At least you're contributing something to society beyond just making art. I'm coasting by, as always. I've been part of like four different bands, never able to hold down a simple job. And *just* when Terra Vertebrae gets this huge break, you randomly land a commission that's, like, ten times cooler."

"I swear to god, you better not accuse me of emasculating you with my big, throbbing bank account."

He looks my way with a hangdog expression and a half-hearted shrug.

Unable to believe what I'm hearing, I revert to a childish display of familial affection and punch him in the shoulder. "Jesus, there's your problem! We cut out the rest of the family to get away from that shit. It's not a contest, Theo. It's you and me and art, and that's it. Everything else is details. If I get rich and famous, you're coming along with me. And I would hope the same is true for you and the band. Terra Vertebrae is battling! And I'm gonna be there, decked out in merch, cheering you on until my throat is raw and bloody. Not because I feel sorry for my poor, unlucky brother, but because art is the only thing that really matters. Supporting each other is how we survive, emotionally or whatever."

"That's all well and good, to get poetic about art and beauty and whatever. But when Callahan was beating down our door for rent, it didn't matter if we were holding on to a pair of priceless masterpieces. We need a place to live, we need food. To get those things, we need money. And getting money…" He trails off, as though he expects me to follow his line of thinking, but I'm totally lost here.

"What, it's hard and time-consuming and it sucks and it kills all our creativity? Yeah."

Theo purses his lips and stares off into space, deep in thought for a moment. "Getting money *changes* you. Annie used to be our kinda cool, smarty-pants big sister who liked to teach us about stuff when Mom and Dad were too busy. The whole reason she became a lawyer is because she used to care about doing the right thing and standing up to bullshit. But somewhere between Harvard and joining her first firm, she lost that spark. She turned into them."

I want to debate that. I want to point out that he's putting way too much of the onus on money. Maybe Theo has let himself forget that even when she was a teenager, Annie could be kind of a bitch. But he's not completely wrong either, especially as I think back to what Liz said. It was the student loans hanging over her head that made her feel duty-bound to our parents' bullshit.

It's becoming clearer now, what's really going on here. My first impulse is to give him another affectionate punch, but instead I just rest my hand lightly against his shoulder. "Okay, then. Let's table the idealistic talk about art and make a new sibling agreement. We watch out for each other, and we actually talk about our shit. Even after all this time, we're still unlearning eighteen years of bad habits. And I swear to you that if this portrait job really does launch me into a world of fame and fortune, I'm not going to abandon you."

"And I swear that if Terra Vertebrae really does make it big, I'll totally put a thank-you somewhere in the liner notes of our first album," he says while chuckling softly. Finally, Theo is smiling at me again. Really smiling. He leans forward and bumps his forehead against mine, like an affectionate cat. "Who the hell are you, and what have you done with Penny?"

"Guess some stuff lately has kinda shaken things up for me a bit."

He stays leaned up against me for a moment longer before pulling away. "Okay, then. All sarcastic comments aside, I guess things must be going okay with uhh…Shit, what's her name, again?"

"Anthea," I mutter softly. "And yeah, they kinda are."

"*Anthea*," he repeats, significantly, with just a hint of a terrible English accent. "Sorry, hard to shut it off all at once." After a beat, he smiles. "What's she like, anyway? All the time you've been spending over there, she must be pretty all right."

That impulse I felt on the train is threatening to rise back up, the urge to say, "Actually, since you asked, Anthea is also a muse and she's got magic creativity powers, so there's that." Thankfully, I manage to come up with a more reasonable answer instead. "Honestly, she's pretty down-to-earth, all things considered. Smart too. And she used to be an actual, factual model, so it's been a breath of fresh air to work with someone so professional." I'm underselling it like crazy. Anthea is warm, witty, supportive... But if I go gushing too much, it's bound to get annoying.

"Is she hot?"

"Wow. Your priorities, my dude. Incredible."

"That's not an answer to my question," he points out with a cheeky grin.

"Ugh, she was a model, so yes. Obviously. But that's beside the point."

"You're doing a portrait of her, so I'd say it's absolutely the point."

I need to pivot away from this particular line of questioning. "She's also a fan of the band. Says she likes what I've shown her so far."

Theo laughs and sinks back into the couch. "Shit, you should've just led with that. Think she might be interested in cheering us on at the battle? We'll need all the support we can get."

With a yawn, I remember that I desperately need to get some rest, and I push to my feet. "I'll pass along the invitation. Dunno if it's necessarily her scene, but she might be interested."

"Dope." It seems like maybe that's going to be the end of the conversation, finally, when Theo looks at me a little more intently with a disarmingly sincere smile. "Hey, thanks. For, like, calling me out. I was being super uncool, and the passive-aggressive bullshit just made it worse."

Honestly, I still don't know how I finally managed to do it, and for a moment I can only shrug. "It's not easy, all this stuff. But I'm glad we're dealing with it, even if it sucks." Okay, yep, that's more than enough responsibility for one night. I head back to my room and leave Theo to his reruns of *Next* and *Parental Control*.

It's crazy to realize just how much progress I've made in a single day. Things are looking up.

* * *

Now that we've managed to lay everything out, I find myself infinitely more excited to get back to work on this portrait with Anthea. But I still have my stupid mundane job, which means three days in a row of suffering through running the register at a rinky-dink gas station only to slump home and pass out from exhaustion.

By the time we actually get in another session on my next day off, I'm practically vibrating with excitement.

Part of me worries that being aware of Anthea's power will lead to some kind of diminishing returns, or that it will somehow change the dynamic of our time together. And while it's true that I do notice when it kicks in now, my awareness only makes it all feel more natural. It's like I know that she's there for me, that she's got my back.

It all makes so much sense now—the focus, the confidence in each stroke or smudge, and the sense that I'm actually living up to my potential.

More than that, it feels like there's something reciprocal going on here. Like every time I notice my attention drift, she pulls me back. And when my arms start to get a little tired, I sort of…reach out and feel her there giving me a push. It all happens without a word, the space filled by The Hush Sound pumping out of my precious speaker.

My alarm goes off, the tunnel vision clears, and I'm filled with pride as I really look at what I've done on the canvas. Maybe I'm starting to understand what Anthea means when she tells me I need to be more confident, because I hear myself say, "Hell yeah, this is going great," without a trace of irony. The background is still mostly untouched, but my rendition of Anthea has been getting more and more refined with each session. It feels like I've finally managed to capture some of that ineffable energy she has. The grace, the poise, but also the slight hint of melancholy and loneliness—though I hadn't been able to put a name to those until she told me her story. It makes a lot more sense now.

I glance around the side of the canvas to see Anthea stretching out slowly. "Think I'm ready to call it for today."

"You know, I actually wouldn't mind going a little longer."

I click my tongue and shake my head. "Uh-uh. No way. You told me yourself that using your…spark thing can take it out of you." After hearing more about what her other artists have put her through, I refuse to do the same.

She stands up from the fainting couch and takes a few steps closer. "I'm serious. My reserves are plenty deep."

"All the more reason to not push it. We've got all the time in the world."

Rubbing her arm self-consciously, Anthea steps around to join me in looking over the portrait. Her entire posture is weird—kind of hunched and awkward—and there's something in her energy that feels off. She tries to just study the canvas, but her eyes keep flicking over toward me. After a few beats, her attention is entirely on me, and it's intense. Even her breathing is uneven and weird. She looks like she's about to have some kind of panic attack. Anthea parts her lips, then closes them again.

"Hey, everything okay?"

She catches herself and puts on a forced smile, then catches herself a second time and shakes her head slowly. "Damn it, we went through all that nonsense about me not opening up, and I'm still doing it."

I take Anthea by the arm and walk with her over to the fainting couch, urging her to sit down with me. "All right, walk me through it, then." After a second, I realize my hand is still lingering against her skin, and I pull it away bashfully.

Anthea releases a shaky laugh. "Normally, my inspiration has this kind of…addictive quality to it. I'm so used to my artists slowly getting obsessive or manic, demanding more of my time and spark. And the fact that you don't seem to feel that way, it makes me worry that—" She sighs softly and starts rubbing her arm again while staring off into space. "I feel like I've done something wrong. Like you won't need me anymore. Why aren't you demanding 'just one more hour,' then two, then four?"

Jesus, they really did a number on her, didn't they? I don't have a solid answer for her, but I figure I have to try. "Trust me, I'm not going anywhere. And look, just because I'm not acting the way they did, that doesn't mean I don't notice what you're doing for me. It's fucking incredible. So, maybe your spark just…works differently for me. Their loss is my gain."

Anthea finally cracks a smile, even chuckling softly, breaking some of the tension and hopefully easing that anxiety of hers. She puts her hand on my shoulder. "No doubt about it, you're very different. In the best way possible." Just like I did moments before, her hand lingers for just a moment while she looks at me, and then finally she pulls away, giving me a smile full of warmth. "I know you think you're just doing what comes naturally, but I'd like to show you my thanks regardless. How about I cook something for the two of us?"

"Um, sure, that sounds nice."

"Wonderful. Let me get changed and then I can see what I've got in the fridge."

Once she disappears into her bedroom, I take a moment to catch my breath. I'm glad that Anthea feels like she can talk to me now. But holy shit, there's even more going on there than I realized. And this new dynamic we share, it's going to take some getting used to.

CHAPTER TWENTY

Anthea

The moment my bedroom door closes, I lean against it and take a minute to let out a few more shaky breaths and collect myself.

The same thoughtfulness that first surprised me so much about this woman is returning with a vengeance. I'm fascinated by Penny, almost as if she were some kind of oddity. I'm in awe of both her potential and her talent. But there is no denying my growing attraction to her on top of all that. It's a great deal to process, and it's taking me longer than I hoped to settle down.

Once that wave of complicated feelings finally subsides, I hurry to get changed into some jeans and a T-shirt, eager to get cooking. Penny continues to be a blessing for me, and I can only hope this will help show her just how much I appreciate it.

I find Penny leaning up against the counter in the kitchen, idly messing with her phone. When I walk out, she looks my way, and I swear I see a glimmer in her eyes as she smiles at me. But I chalk that up to wishful thinking and push it back down. Probably better to just worry about making food. That will give me something to concentrate on.

Poking around my fridge and inside my cabinets, I start plotting out a few possibilities for dinner. Pasta is usually a safe bet, or I could maybe go for something a little more inventive like some curry. But then I hit on the perfect idea and look over at her with a smile. "How do fish tacos sound?"

"Fantastic. Haven't had those in ages."

With a plan in place, I start grabbing out everything we're going to need, laying it out across the counter.

After watching me quietly for a moment, Penny pipes up. "I know you offered to do the cooking to thank me or whatever, but do you want help with anything?"

Of course, the whole point was to do this myself, but I also know that working together would be just as rewarding. And she did offer. So I pull out a cutting board and motion to my knife block. "If you want to take chopping duty, that would certainly make things go a bit quicker."

"I think I can manage that. I don't have a ton of culinary expertise, but that's fairly straightforward."

"Really?"

Penny takes the head of red cabbage from the pile of ingredients before removing a bread knife from the block, as if to unintentionally prove her point.

With a light chuckle, I carefully put it back before pulling out a more appropriate blade.

She blushes and gets to work hacking up the vegetables. "I mean, Mom and Dad were both too busy most of the time to do much cooking, so we just ate out a lot. College and grad school was a lot of desperation meals. Even now, I mostly stick to a handful of reliable staples. Not like our kitchen is big enough to do anything complicated unless we really go out of our way to use what little space we have efficiently. So I never learned to make anything impressive. Honestly, watching someone cook is pretty awesome to me." Just like in the studio, Penny sets some music playing while we work in tandem to put our meal together. "You know, this raises another interesting question. Do you actually need to eat?"

I hum thoughtfully while mixing up the various sauces for our tacos. "Any muse who takes a physical form does so by expending a certain amount of willpower. So I suppose if one were to take enough time and energy, they could perhaps make a body that truly requires rest and sleep. But generally we get close enough by becoming an approximation of human. I don't really get hungry or tired in the classical sense. I experience similar sensations because that's just how being alive works and so that's how we must work to maintain the facade. It's all very…*conceptual*. After a while, you get so used to it that you hardly even think about it. Regardless, there really is nothing better than an excellent meal and a night's rest."

"Damn, wish I had a magic body that didn't require so much upkeep."

"Not magic."

Penny laughs mischievously. "Oh! I almost forgot to mention. Theo wanted me to extend you an official invite to the battle. He was pretty jazzed when I told him that you liked Terra Vertebrae."

"I would be delighted to attend. And I'm glad things have been patched up, given how important he is to you. And it will be a nice chance to meet everyone. If…that's something you're okay with?"

"Of course."

I spoon a bit of the sauce for the fish and go to taste it, but an idea strikes me. So instead, I turn toward Penny, holding out the spoon, my other hand cupped underneath to catch any drips, and offer it to her instead. I get that blush I'm hoping for, and she eagerly takes a small taste. Her face instantly lights up, and she lets out this noise that's close enough to a moan for my mind to momentarily short-circuit.

Now I'm the one blushing.

We stay like that for just a moment, and then she quietly mutters, "It's good."

With some embarrassed laughter, each of us returns to what we were working on. "I should hope so. I'm slightly modifying a recipe I got from a dear friend in Guadalajara years ago."

"Are we talking decades or centuries here?"

I just give her a mysterious smile as I get the fish into the pan, sizzling delightfully, before warming the tortillas one by one in a second pan.

Any curiosity about the sauce's origin is quickly forgotten as the smell of the cooking fish fills the room. "*God*, it really smells amazing," Penny says, her voice full of awe. It's a tone I don't think I've actually heard from her all that often. Perhaps it's true what they say about the way to a woman's heart.

Our meal tastes incredible, and I can't stop myself from thinking it's all the more superior because we made it together.

I'm just tucking into my second taco when my phone vibrates against the table. I check to see who's calling me, and my face falls.

"What's up?"

For just a moment, old instincts kick in again and I start to tell Penny that it's nothing to worry about. But that was what led to us having our nonargument in the first place. And she's earned the right to know about my silly little nonissue. So I put my phone away and let the nice lady leave me a message. "The Massachusetts Society for the Arts is waiting on me to RSVP for their upcoming gala."

She looks me over curiously for a moment, head tilting slightly. "And you don't wanna go."

"Sort of. I suppose it's complicated."

"Easy enough. Tell them 'thanks but no thanks.' You don't owe them your presence or whatever. Fuck those people."

I should probably be getting used to her attitude toward these things by now, but I can't help but clutch my pearls just a little regardless. "Wow, tell me how you really feel."

Just as suddenly, she's chuckling with a small shrug. "I submitted a few things to the art society when I was a kid and I still had all that pressure to do big things."

"They rejected you?"

"Worse, they selected me."

Now it's my turn to flash a confused look. "I'm not sure I follow."

"All I really wanted to do back then was just mess around and make fun art. But that wasn't good enough, I had to Be Somebody, Do Something. And I guess the arts society was kind of the culmination of that whole struggle. Proof that I could make something that fancy people would approve of. I spent a couple of weeks fighting every single one of my instincts and did this technically competent—but otherwise totally lifeless—bit of fluff, and everyone ate it up. Which I think was also when I decided that, as soon as I could, I was going to forge my own path. No more cranking out meaningless bullshit to appease some judgmental asshole." She chuckles again, though it comes out a bit hollow. "Which was a great plan until I had scholarships to maintain and bills to pay. Idealistic postmodernism is all well and good, but there's a reason that so many groundbreaking artists were either destitute or lucky."

I nod along slowly, picking up a stray chunk of fish and popping it into my mouth. "I've certainly seen the compromise play out before plenty of times, and it's never pleasant."

"Anyway, I guess there's something about my experiences with the MSA that feels significant to me. Not quite a trauma, but… close."

"I'm suddenly feeling like kind of a monster for donating to them."

"Eh, you're not. The arts society isn't actually the problem. And they do provide great opportunities for kids who wouldn't get them otherwise. Honestly, even when I was younger, I mostly felt gross for taking a spot that probably should have gone to someone who needed it." Penny glances over at me curiously. "How about you? What's your not-trauma with them?"

"When I took my…constitutional, I wanted to at least do something that was passively akin to my actual work. And I had all these extra funds sitting around that were basically going to waste. So I figured I might as well put it somewhere meaningful. And maybe it was also my penance for choosing to neglect my 'Grand Purpose.' Or for always doting on artists who honestly didn't need the leg up in the first place."

"And what about this gala specifically?"

"They want to thank me for my contributions, to spotlight me, however briefly. And that was never the intention. I donated out of guilt, not the goodness of my heart. Besides, there's a pretty deeply ingrained part of my people's culture that you're not supposed to be front and center. We're meant to do our job from the sidelines, let the art and the artist speak for themselves. Besides, ten years is plenty of time to forget how to function in polite society. And the last few times I went to events like this, I was always there as the mysterious arm candy to whoever I was working with. Going alone would feel…foreign."

"Hmm, I suppose there's another option here, then."

"Oh?"

"Bring your own arm candy. That way, you've got someone there to lean on. Not to mention an excuse to duck out if you get overwhelmed."

"Would you like to go with me?" The question leaves my lips before I actually take the time to think it over, and I regret it immediately. Penny just told me that she's got her own complicated feelings about the arts society, and I get the impression she's not much for elaborate gatherings. There's no way that she'd actually agree to that. We'll laugh this off and move on with our lives.

That's not what happens, though. After a bit of stammering, Penny manages to respond, "I mean, I'm more like a melty bar of chocolate than arm candy. But considering everything you've done for me, I think I could probably slog my way through it to pay you back."

We sit there quietly together for a moment, each of us nervously looking at the other, simultaneously realizing just what it is we're both tentatively agreeing to.

"Okay," I say softly, and it comes out a bit shaky.

"Okay?"

"Okay. Then I guess I'll give them a call back. And…we have a few things to figure out."

The spell finally breaks a bit, and she gives me another quizzical look. "Like what?"

"Can you tell me with a straight face you have something to wear that's black-tie appropriate?"

"Touché."

* * *

A dress. We need a dress. And I know just the man for the job.

Elijah's face lights up when he sees me walk into Time/Reality, and he breaks out in a massive grin the moment he spots Penny trailing just behind me. I let just enough slip the last time I was in here that he knew I wasn't buying that dress just for the sake of the portrait.

"Hello again. I was wondering when I might see you come back through here."

"Well, I find myself with another sartorial conundrum, and I had such good luck last time, I thought it was worth stopping by." I gesture to Elijah while glancing over at Penny. "He helped me find that incredible green dress."

"This is the artist, then?" He steps forward and offers her a hand.

She takes it and shakes, nodding slowly. "Penny, yes. And, thank you, I suppose. It's a great accent to the work."

"So what's today's 'conundrum' then?" Elijah asks, turning my way.

I shake his hand as well. "A gala at the Museum of Fine Arts. Penny is in need of a dress. Something with a bit of a unique flair to it."

Just as he did with me, he takes a moment to really study Penny, pressing his hands together against his lips with a thoughtful hum. "But not so unique that she becomes the center of attention, I take it?"

She flushes at being scrutinized and read so easily, rubbing her neck and glancing out the window. "Can't imagine where you got that idea."

After a few more seconds, he finally releases a soft chuckle and nods. "I think I just might have something. Come along." Elijah beckons her with a finger, and she follows dutifully with me in tow.

I stand by the closed changing room door, listening to the soft shuffling sounds of Penny trying on the dress. Eventually the noises stop, and I hear Penny quietly mutter, "I regret everything."

Of course, I knew that bringing Penny to an upscale shop like this would lead to some discomfort. She would no doubt prefer a thrift store or maybe a consignment shop. But as long as we're doing this, I want to really show off. And I'm certain that whatever dress Elijah has given her is bound to be a winner.

"It can't be that bad. Please, let me see."

There's a long pause, and for a moment I wonder if I'm going to have to barge my way into the dressing room. But finally the latch clicks and the door swings open. Penny is still mostly hiding inside, and every inch of her screams with the embarrassment she's feeling.

And that's a tragedy, because she looks absolutely incredible.

For all her dramatizing, it's not as though Penny doesn't wear the dress well. Quite the opposite—it suits that version of herself she showed me in the picture from her brother's gig. The gown has a slightly gothic flair to it, with a high-low skirt that hangs down to her ankles on the back end and rises to just below the knees in front. The upper portion of the bodice and the half sleeves are sheer and lacy, with deep-purple accents running throughout the whole affair. I'm already dreaming up what kinds of accessories we could pair with it to dial this look up to eleven.

"Be real with me. This isn't just some kind of *My Fair Lady* situation, right? You're not trying to get me all gussied up to look good in front of these people? Because I already went through that when I was younger, and I don't particularly want to do it again."

"Not at all. I quite like your…what did you call it? Your 'coal-dusted gremlin' aesthetic. Honestly, this works well with that while still fitting the black-tie atmosphere. I told you, Elijah is a genius." From a nearby rack, I can hear him hum contentedly, clearly listening in on our conversation with pride and amusement.

"Mm." The compliments seem to have been enough to silence some of her worries, without prompting her to dig into my hidden intentions. "And what will you be wearing? Because I'm pretty sure any gown you show up in will make me look frumpy by comparison."

"Good news, I think I'm going to wear a suit instead."

"Oh, come on! We both know you look great in a dress, and I think a suit would be way better for me."

"Probably, but I'm too in love with this look now to change my mind." Closer to the truth, but just veiled enough. I swear, I'm actually starting to get the hang of the Game now. "Now get out here so the genius can start tailoring."

For some reason, I feel compelled to walk Penny all the way down into Copley station. "I'll send you all the details once I hear back from the arts society and get a ride arranged and—Goodness, this really is happening, isn't it?" I can't quite stop my voice from shaking a little. It's just a silly little gala, but for some reason it feels so important in my mind now. Not that I've made it any easier on myself by bringing Penny along, but we're too deep now to back out.

She laughs, and it comes out a little shaky as well, which is comforting in a way. "Yeah, but it's gonna go great, I know it. And even if you don't feel like you earned the accolades or whatever, you're awesome enough that you deserve a little spotlight no matter what. So I say we try to enjoy it." I get the impression she's talking to herself as much as me. This will be nerve-racking for both of us, but perhaps together we can survive it. Hell, we might even have a good time.

"You're right. And…thank you again for agreeing to this. I know it was a bit of a rushed idea."

"Happy to help, honestly."

Without thinking, I wrap my arms around Penny in a tight hug. Aside from planting my head in her lap, this is easily the closest we've gotten, and I find I don't want to let go. She's warm, and soft, and as her arms close around me as well, she holds me with a firmness I didn't realize I'd been missing. "It really does mean the world to me," I say gently.

Penny gives another awkward laugh. "I can tell. But like I said, you're awesome and you deserve good things."

I'm suddenly filled with a very intense fear that I might be taking advantage of this woman. She's being so genuinely nice, and all I can think about is how badly I want this hug to go on forever.

An announcement comes over the PA that the next train is approaching, and we carefully disentangle ourselves before sharing a few rushed goodbyes.

I keep my cool all the way back up to my apartment, but the moment the door is closed I sprawl across my couch dramatically. How much longer, I have to ask, can I convince myself that this is just the Game and not something more? How much longer until I'm hurt again?

STEP THREE: COLOR

CHAPTER TWENTY-ONE

Penny

It was weird enough trying on this getup in the boutique, showing it off to Anthea. But there's something that's even more discordant about putting it on in this ratty little apartment bedroom.

I've managed to cobble together a few accessories from the things I already own, and at least my makeup is on point. That much I can do in my sleep. The lacy choker with the cameo was an acquisition from a lucky thrift store outing, and it fits the dress well. My little crescent moon earrings are equally cheap, but at least they keep the general theme. Still, the combination of all these dark colors with my shiny adornments does make me look like the love child of a raven and a magpie.

I know it's bad form to pair a classy dress with a bunch of trinkets. The kind of people that attend these galas, they're just itching for a chance to point out that kind of shit. But a girl's got to make do. If I'm extremely lucky, no one at this party will even take much notice of me in the first place, and I can avoid any conversations about my "daring" wardrobe choices, or whatever.

More than anything, I know the real reason I'm so uneasy, though, and it's got nothing to do with the dress. I've noticed it during my last few sessions and hangouts with Anthea, ever since her big reveal. It's easier now, more comfortable, and she's dialed up the teasing and playful banter again. There's something between us that's scary and unavoidable—though we've tried our damnedest to ignore it. Or, more accurately, *I've* done *my* damnedest to ignore it. But that can only go on for so long. Sooner or later, the fuse is going to burn up and the bomb will go off. And her taking me out to a fancy-ass gala as "arm candy" really brings it all into sharp relief.

I can't do anything else to waste time, so I finish securing the straps on my black pointy ankle boots with the four-inch heels—some of the only footwear I own that could fit the occasion—and step out of my room.

Kai is waiting out in the living room to see me off. Theo is out at another gig with the band—trying out their coffeehouse set finally—and Meagan is working tonight, but they both demanded pictures. I never should have told any of them about this damn gala. Not that I know how I could have gotten away with that after they saw me walking through the door with a garment bag from a shop on Newbury Street.

Kai wolf-whistles while snapping a few pictures with his phone, and I'd be a liar if I said it wasn't an ego boost. "Damn, Hartwell. You weren't kidding."

"Mm, thank you."

There's a text on my phone from Anthea telling me she's about ten minutes out, so I carefully make my way into the living room to perch on the couch and wait.

Kai pauses his movie and looks over at me a little more seriously. "How are you feeling, anyway?"

"Nervous as hell. Worried that the moment I walk in, I'm going to have flashbacks to when I was sixteen, wearing my little ill-fitting suit and pretending I belong. So I'm mostly just focusing on the fact that there's gonna be free grub. That should carry me at least partway through."

He's clearly unconvinced. "And is that all?"

"Come on, man, out with it. What are you getting at?"

Kai gives me a significant look with his eyebrows raised. "You're all decked out, going to this big party, in a car with a chauffeur, on the arm of a woman who is, by all rights, absolutely stunning. A woman that you have been spending a lot of time with lately. I know that'd make me nervous as hell."

I resist the urge to pick at a thread in the dress. Not wanting to let loose all my worries, I opt to default to the lie I've been telling myself since Anthea and I met. "Sure, I guess. But she's also wildly outside my league, from a totally different world than me." More than even Kai could possibly understand. "I'd feel the same way going to, I don't know, a premiere with Rahul Kohli or something."

"Which would still be a massive deal, mind you, and not something I can imagine you actually being flippant about. Tell me, in this inadequate comparison, have you been hanging out with Rahul Kohli? Have you been regularly painting him in his house, as he lounges nude with nothing but a vase of flowers covering his—"

"It's not a nude portrait, jackass."

"My point still stands. You two have gotten close, right? Do you think maybe she's got ulterior motives for bringing you along?"

"She's not, like, taking advantage of me. Or vice versa. We're… acquaintances. Partners. Borderline friends, maybe."

"Okay, different question, then. Do you *want* her to take advantage of you?"

"Gross way to phrase it," I say, trying to duck the inquisition. But he doesn't let me off that easy, just continuing to level me with a searching gaze. "I don't know! Like, yeah, I would be over the moon if she had any kind of feelings for me. Anthea is amazing— she's witty and warm, intelligent but not egotistical. Not that it matters, because it's so clearly not going to happen. And even if it did, you *know* I've got other issues. You were there when everything went down with Juniper."

"Penny, I say this with love—"

"Those words have literally never preceded anything good."

"You're a neurotic mess. But you're an attractive, talented mess too. And based solely on what you've told me, your chances aren't nearly as slim as you fear. So go enjoy the party and get out of your own head for a while. These things usually have free booze too, so I would recommend taking advantage of that fact. Get a little drunk, do a little dancing, have some actual fun for once in your life. All that other stuff, that's for Future Penny to worry about."

I'm saved by another chime from my phone telling me that my ride is nearly here. Standing up from the couch, I want to be furious with Kai for pushing like that. But he does it with his usual charming ease, and part of me *is* grateful that I'm saying some of this stuff out loud. So I throw my arms around him and hug him tight before rushing out the door to the sound of his laughter.

Unfortunately, I didn't consider the stairwell when choosing my shoes, and it takes me longer than normal to descend all the way to the ground floor. By the time I get outside, I'm regretting my stupid, sexy footwear. But the car is waiting right there, and I don't want to make us unfashionably late or whatever.

The back door on the passenger side opens and out steps Anthea. And she is absolutely killing it—and killing me in the process. True to her word, she's wearing a suit, tailored expertly to show off every single one of her curves. Her hair, usually pinned up carefully, has been left hanging wild and free. Most of her makeup is understated, save for the sharp edges of her eyeliner and the deep-brown lipstick. And I can see that she's wearing small silver earrings in the shape of suns, which I have to try very hard to not overthink.

I can't call it butch, I can't call it femme. But I can definitely call it extremely attractive. And I'm totally fucking sunk.

The only solace I can take in this moment is one small thing, though it feels wildly important. Anthea gives me a once-over, and when our eyes meet, she blushes and self-consciously starts to fiddle with her glimmering obsidian cufflinks. So there's that.

As formal as can be, she stands aside and urges me into the car with a sweeping gesture while holding the door. "Your chariot, milady." Once I'm inside and buckled up, she shuts the door before swiftly moving around to climb in the other side next to me. "Sorry, I just couldn't help myself."

"You'll hear no complaints from me. That was smooth as hell."

She laughs warmly. "Good, because that's about the only move I have for tonight."

"We've got our work cut out for us. Guess we'll just have to make it up as we go." I join her in laughing softly while unconsciously massaging my already-aching legs.

Anthea catches me with a flash of a worried expression. "Are you all right?"

"Didn't really think through my footwear for the evening. Just getting down here was enough to give my calves more of a workout than they've gotten in ages."

Just like that, she's back to looking mostly relieved as she sinks into her seat and the car starts moving. "Once we get to the actual gala, I'll find us a nice corner out of the way where we can sit and not do anything."

"You really know how to sweet-talk a gal." Even as I say it, I realize I mean that sincerely. It's one thing for Anthea to compliment my work or even just to flirt with me. But for her to realize that I want to get somewhere comfortable and safe, and to ensure that she'll find it for me—that fills my belly with butterflies in a way nothing else she's said or done possibly could.

Oh, Penny, you are playing with fire.

I could probably have put at least a little more effort into mentally preparing myself for this. Too little, too late.

After spending nearly a decade in "just trying my best" mode, it's ridiculous how easily all of this stuff still triggers some long-buried anxieties. A parade of fancy cars, a horde of fancy people, a bunch of fancy decorations. It's a lot.

Without much of a concept of how to behave at an event like this as a woman, I think about my mother—something I wish I didn't have to do. I latch onto Anthea's arm the minute we get out of the car and let her take the lead. The good news is that she doesn't seem to mind. Or, if she does, she's not saying anything about it. Though after a few paces, she does gently adjust my grip and loop our arms together with a soft "Here." I'm not too proud to admit how nice it feels.

I'm no longer clinging to her like a scared child, though I do find myself occasionally leaning into her—worrying that at any moment I might trip and send the both of us off-balance and toppling over.

The first half of the proceedings are located in the gorgeous courtyard of the museum, and I say a quick, silent thank-you to whoever or whatever blessed us with such amazing weather. Not so cold that I'm shivering in just my dress, and not so hot that I'm going to end up all gross and sweaty. I know Anthea has explained that she's just a spirit of inspiration or whatever, but the fantastical part of my brain does get carried away wondering if some distant cousin is a weather deity that had something to do with this comfy atmosphere. Perfect temperature, clear skies, a gentle wind. How else could we get so lucky? This early in the spring, you're just as likely to get snow.

Even with the rough gray stone of the walls, there's still greenery everywhere, including the gorgeous ivy that seems to climb its way across every available surface. Add to that the trees just starting to bud and bloom in the encroaching spring, and there's something about the courtyard that feels vibrant and alive. Between the glow from the windows and the fairy lights strung up everywhere, it's all bathed in a gentle golden warmth that pushes back the darkness of the late evening.

The grassy area in the middle has a temporary dance floor, and the stage along one of the walls features the night's entertainment, courtesy of the Worcester Arts Academy jazz ensemble. Along another wall there's an entire series of tables full to bursting with food and drink, and the rest of the space is decorated with standing tables, chairs, and couches.

It's still early enough in the evening that the crowd hasn't fully invaded the space, so Anthea and I have plenty of time to make a beeline for the hors d'oeuvres and libations without having to wait fifteen minutes while someone agonizes over their choices. Before long, we've managed to steal an out-of-the-way couch where I can finally sit and rest.

I pop a quiche into my mouth and chew my way through it before looking around. Most people here really are too busy with their heads up their own asses to pay us much mind, and my various nerves and anxieties are finally unfurling a bit. "Feels like I should apologize. I was supposed to be your emotional support artist tonight, but I'm still trying to adjust to everything myself."

Anthea just shrugs before looking over at me, her lips curling into a fond smile. "Whether it's sympathy or empathy, having you here with me is making me feel better. So let's not worry too much about the mechanics of it."

We spend some time in a comfortable silence, mostly just people-watching while enjoying the high schoolers' musical offerings. I can still viscerally remember the feeling of being an awkward teenager at events just like this one. My heart goes out to the poor kids. But I'll say this much—their rendition of "I Can't Get Started" is stellar.

All the while, I continue to gnaw on my appetizers and drink what is likely an unwise amount of champagne. It's probably not the smartest thing in the world to front-load all these calories and drinks, but I still can't fully shake these stupid nerves. Nor can I decide if they have more to do with the gala, or with Anthea.

Thankfully, someone comes over to our table to provide a momentary reprieve from my worrying. She's got on a slinky black dress with her hair in a professional-looking bun, sporting a pair of cat-eye glasses. "Excuse me, Ms. Corey?"

Anthea tenses up and swiftly puts on a matching tone as she rises from her seat to meet the woman. "Yes?"

"Hi, I'm Bethany, the one you spoke to on the phone last month. I can't tell you how much it means to us that you decided to come."

She extends her hand with a winning smile, and Anthea takes it gracefully, giving it a single firm shake. "I'm sorry for being so evasive before. Obviously it's an honor to be recognized, but I'm not much for crowds or attention. I hope you're not looking for me to make any kind of speech or anything."

Her laugh is just as perfectly manicured as her nails. "No, of course not. We'll be doing some awards and acknowledgments in the auditorium once we've finished out here. All you'll have to do is come on stage when your name is called, we'll give you a small gift, and then you can get right back to your seat. A minute or so, nothing more."

Breathing a long sigh of relief, Anthea nods. "Good. That sounds quite survivable."

"I should hope so." Bethany looks my way next with another professional smile. "And this must be your plus-one. We didn't get a name, I'm afraid."

"Uh. Penny. Penny Hartwell."

"She's a local artist I'm sponsoring. Extremely talented."

I feel like "sponsoring" is putting it mildly, but I understand we have to play our cards close to our chest here. So I'll just let Anthea choose how much we say, and nod along.

Bethany coos. "Goodness, it's not enough to donate to us? That's quite impressive."

"What can I say? It's in my blood," Anthea mumbles with a nervous laugh.

On second thought, maybe I shouldn't leave it up to her to direct this conversation too much. I can see that she's floundering a bit and ready to be left alone. So I quickly drain the last of my champagne before blurting out the first excuse that comes to mind. "Sorry to interrupt, but I actually promised Anthea at least one dance tonight, and I'd prefer to do it while the floor isn't too busy." Why the hell is this the lie I'm going with? Anyone who looks at me must know I'm not much for dancing.

Bethany does momentarily raise an inquisitive eyebrow, but I can't tell if her disbelief is aimed at my fib or at the idea that Anthea is simply my sponsor. But after a beat, she lets the matter drop and shrugs. "Of course. I have about a hundred other elbows to rub. I won't take up any more of your time. Ciao."

"Er, yeah, ciao."

As soon as she walks away, I turn toward Anthea with an apologetic groan. "Sorry, that was lame, but you looked like you needed the breather and I just blurted it out."

To my surprise, she just smiles at me and takes my hand. "I've heard worse excuses. But we'd better get out there if we don't want our cover blown."

Oh, Penny, you are going to get burned.

CHAPTER TWENTY-TWO

Anthea

With the two of us feeling tipsy and warm, I can't deny that this is something I want. It's all just a part of the Game, I tell myself—though that's mostly a convenient lie at this point. A way to ignore what's really going on, the very legitimate feelings that have been igniting within me. I lead Penny out to the temporary dance floor set up beside the ensemble and try to focus on just enjoying the opportunity she's given me.

There are already a handful of others out here, so at least we're not the first ones to do this. The musicians have mostly been playing slow songs thus far, meaning we don't have to break out any impressive dance moves.

Just like in our studio, I can viscerally feel Penny's insecurities, though it's not as if I need our connection to see all the signs. She's glancing around furtively, face flushed, moving hesitantly. "Haven't slow-danced in over a decade, so you'll forgive me if I'm fumbling a bit."

It only makes sense that I take the lead. After all, I'm the one that insisted on wearing the suit. With her left hand still firmly in my right, I bring Penny around to face me and place my free hand against her lower back. After a pause, she brings hers up to rest against my shoulder. Together, we find the beat as the band transitions into a lovely arrangement of "Meditação" and begin swaying in time. After our portrait sessions sharing a metaphorical dance, it's easy enough to do it for real.

"See? Nothing to it."

"You won't be talking so big when I inevitably take a spill and drag you down with me, missy." Her attention is completely focused on her feet, which is detracting from the magic somewhat.

"Eyes up, dear," I say, letting that teasing tone I've been developing drip from my lips. "I'm not going to let you fall. It's all right."

Her blush grows hotter as she finally tears her eyes away from her shoes and up somewhere past my shoulder. "Fine." Her gaze flicks toward me for a split second before focusing on the lights overhead again. When the awkwardness of that position becomes too much to manage, she relents and presses a bit closer to rest her head against my chest.

For a blissful while, we're able to just enjoy the moment, slow-dancing together. For all that I was worried about coming to this gala, I have to admit this is the best-case scenario. If I can maintain this streak of good luck, we just might make it to the end of the night unscathed.

It's not until the song fades out that Penny speaks up softly again. "So, uh…how many of your other artists have you done this kind of thing with?"

"I'm pretty sure it's poor form to talk about exes when you're on a date."

She rolls her eyes, and those nerves of hers evaporate a bit more. Penny even musters up the courage to look my way again, holding eye contact. "I'm serious. Have you ever—?"

"Excuse me, I'm so sorry to interrupt."

Standing on the edge of the dance floor close by is an older man with silver-white hair and a slick tuxedo. I don't recognize him, and it's only when I look toward Penny again and see a glimmer of something in her eye that I realize he's not talking to me.

"Uh, what can I do for you?" She pulls me with her to step off the floor, continuing to hang on my arm. She's putting off a different kind of nervous energy now, and I can't fully tell what the source of it is.

"This might be a bit strange to say, but I felt as though you looked familiar somehow. And when I asked that young woman, Bethany, she mentioned that your name was Hartwell."

"Yeah?" she responds warily.

"You wouldn't happen to be one of the Amherst Hartwells? It's just that I'm an old friend of Christian and Beatrice. My name is Wyatt Reid. I thought I'd met all of their children, but I don't remember you."

"Ah shit," Penny mutters beneath her breath, quiet enough that only I catch it. "I uh—I do kinda remember meeting you, actually. I looked a little…different, back then. Had a few changes since. Name, pronouns, all that."

"Oh," he says softly, then practically gasps as the realization dawns properly. "Oh! God, I'm so sorry. Of course, you're the artist. Well, I must say, it's nice to see you still at it. Heaven knows your parents were always such stick-in-the-muds when it came to art. Far too practical about it."

Penny laughs, clearly relieved that this conversation didn't go in a different direction. "Yeah, you can say that again. It's part of the reason we don't really talk much these days."

"Then perhaps you hadn't heard—"

Any levity she felt dissolves in an instant and she rushes to cut him off. "No, I definitely did. I'd rather not talk about it." Penny's face darkens a bit, and she leans more against me.

"I see, my mistake," he says briskly, trying to pivot gracefully. "I'll leave you to it, then. Have a good evening."

"Yeah, you too," Penny says before bringing all of her attention back to me once he's walked away. "Okay, definitely didn't need that little reminder. I could really use another drink."

I pull her over toward one of the couches near the edge of the courtyard and guide her to sit down. "I'll fetch us something."

One quick trip to the drink station and I'm back in a flash with two glasses of red wine, settling in next to Penny before passing one off to her. "Are you all right?"

"Yeah, just uh…a lot of stuff wrapped up in one brief conversation." She lightly swirls the glass before taking a long sip. "Tell me again that I'm not a horrible person for refusing to engage with all this family bullshit?"

"Hmm. To quote some advice a wise woman gave me recently—fuck those people."

Penny nearly spits up some of her wine as she goes to take another drink, stifling some rather immature giggling. "Holy shit, okay, you win. Thank you."

"They lost the right to make those kinds of demands long ago. And it's their job to apologize and rebuild that bridge, not yours."

She nods but doesn't say anything else. We sit there for a while, finishing off our drinks and letting the buzz of the alcohol settle our nerves. Tonight has certainly been a test of our social skills, but it feels like we're muddling through it together.

To my surprise, Penny looks at me without any prompting, then toward the dance floor. "Wanna get back out there? Y'know, since we kinda got interrupted. One more round before you have to go do this award ceremony thing?"

Standing from the couch, I offer my hand to Penny and smile. "I'd like that."

As we step into place, the ensemble fires up a slightly more upbeat number, "All The Things You Are." While it's hardly the fastest song, we do get to do a bit more enthusiastic swaying, and I even convince Penny to go into a spin that makes her dress flutter pleasantly.

As I pull her in again, I think about what she'd been saying before we were interrupted. "There was something you wanted to ask me earlier, right? About my other artists?"

"Oh, yeah, no. It was nothing. Kinda stupid, honestly."

"Try me."

"Well, I've kinda been getting the impression that you got pretty close—"

"Anthea!"

A decade on and that voice is somehow still etched into my mind. It sends an unpleasant sensation washing over my entire body, my shoulders instantly tensing. The few hors d'oeuvres I had are threatening to rise up amidst a sea of bile. The hand at my shoulder squeezes lightly and Penny catches my eye again, likely seeing the distraught expression on my face. Our dynamic inverts once again, and I swear she's standing just a little taller, looking at me intently for a signal of what to do.

"Anthea Corey, as I live and breathe!"

Dmitri.

He laughs, and it triggers a flood of sense memories. His arm possessively wrapped around me, far too tight, as he chats up a gaggle of fans. The way his breath always smelled like whiskey and pipe smoke. The awful sensation of his stubble against my face as we kissed. I didn't realize just how many things I truly loathed about him until his voice brought it all rushing back in one terrible moment.

Though it pains me to do so, we once again have to break from our dance. I turn toward the source of the voice to greet the most recent inductee to the "pack of assholes." He's still trying to maintain the aging hipster routine. The same glasses, the same ridiculous mustache, just with a few more wrinkles and gray hairs. The flannel has been replaced with a suit, though even that is annoyingly on-brand—right down to the silk pocket square and watch chain.

"Dmitri Ustinov, in Boston? And here I thought you'd made a sacred vow never to be caught dead in this town." In fact, I had rather been counting on that. And him being here, now, feels like a statistical impossibility. "What could possibly make a man as steadfast as you go back on his word?"

He goes for a hug, but I manage to meet him and "fondly" touch his arms, using it as a way to keep him a few inches back. To my dismay, he still opts for an air-kiss, and that stubble is just as unpleasant as I remember. "And here *I* thought *you* were gracefully bowing out of the art world forever. It would seem that both of us have a nasty habit of breaking pledges."

"Forever? Nonsense. Just taking a break to pursue other passions," I reply coolly. "But I didn't want to pull away completely, so I started donating to the society. Hence why I'm here."

"I heard! And I think that's admirable. After all, you…earned all that money," he says, making sure to pause just long enough in his statement to twist the knife a bit. "Best to make sure it goes somewhere meaningful. Anyway, when I heard that my old partner was coming to this gala, I just had to pull a few strings and make an appearance." He's been very purposefully ignoring Penny until now and finally deigns to look her way, the same way someone might gaze on an errant bit of litter. "Though I don't think I'd been told she was bringing a guest. Wherever did you dig her up from?" he asks with a laugh that's meant to be charming but mostly sounds pompous and arrogant.

The bastard is coming out swinging. In just a few sentences, he's implied I'm a gold digger, flexed his myriad connections, and insulted my…

Well, he's being a real prick to Penny. "Precisely, I'm here with a friend. So I'm afraid we won't be able to do much catching up." I reach out to take her hand once more, somewhere between trying to comfort her, and comforting myself. "It would be rude."

Our hands connect, and Penny squeezes tightly for a moment.

"Come now. You're a talented woman, Anthea. Surely you can divide your attention for an evening."

If he's going to insist on this conversation, then I would rather do it away from the dance floor. And preferably with another glass in my hand. "Let's not disturb these people." Dmitri has such a naturally booming voice, he's already drawn the attention of several dancing couples. I walk with Penny toward the nearest caterer and grab almost desperately for whatever they have on their tray and instantly knock back half the contents.

"I really am amazed. You look like you haven't aged a day since I saw you. You must tell us your secret." His eyes flick between me and Penny as he speaks, smiling puckishly.

He's trying to create some kind of suspicion in her, and I'm glad Penny and I have already been through that stage of things. But the fact that he would try to force a human through that revelation is cruel. Dmitri knows firsthand what it's like. "We already had a long conversation about my skincare routine."

"Yeah, I'm in on the big joke, man. No need to play coy or whatever." Penny is still holding herself confidently, and I could swear that she's actually preparing to square up against Dmitri. That comforts me in a way I'm not prepared for.

Dmitri just chuckles, though it's slightly forced. "Okay, all right, just needed to know if we were all on the same page here. So that must make you her new protégée." With this newfound information, he sizes her up a second time, and it would seem that she's still found wanting in his eyes. "I guess you're forced to start in the minor leagues again after all the bridges you burned. You know, I never did figure out what happened. The art world was all you lived for, Anthea. You've sponsored some incredible talents. To be without that? It must have been lonely."

He might be an ass, but he is right. Loneliness, more than anything, has been the most difficult part of breaking away. But I also know that he's fishing, and I don't want to give him the satisfaction of thinking I was suffering without his presence. "I didn't *want* to leave it. I did it because I was being strangled. My very sense of self was being extinguished by *the art world*. And I found plenty of avenues to explore in the interim. Besides, it would seem that *the art world* has chugged along just fine without my presence."

"Chugged along, certainly. But it was dimmed, subdued. There was a void in your wake. And look at you…can you really say that your time away has been valuable? You still have that same desperate look in your eye. Honestly, to see you come sauntering right back in as though it never happened—"

Penny lets out a long, beleaguered groan. I glance over and see that she's also in the process of draining another glass herself. "Oh my god, dude, you've got to learn to read the fucking room." Her voice slurs slightly, and she looks so utterly bored with his behavior. It's shockingly attractive.

"Excuse me?" Dmitri blusters like some kind of genteel landowner.

"Drop this weird Main Character Syndrome thing you've got going on. It's pathetic. Anthea clearly doesn't want to engage with you at the moment. Enjoy the music and the grub. Those little quiche things are incredible."

It takes a second or two of sputtering for him to conjure a retort. "Listen here, Eliza Doolittle. Just because she's turned you into some kind of pet project, don't think you know Anthea half as well as I do."

"I'll tell you what I *do* know. During our sessions together, she's made it abundantly clear that the last person she worked with was a narcissistic asshat and a raging dickhead. I'm racking my brain…do you remember who that would be?"

Penny had really only been irritating him thus far, but now he's properly seething. "If you think I'm going to stand here and get lectured by some impoverished approximation of a woman in a gaudy Halloween dress—"

There's a resounding, sharp noise from somewhere in my vicinity, and it's only as I feel the dull throbbing in my palm that I piece together what has just happened.

If Dmitri wants to lay into me, there's no point in being bothered about it now. I wouldn't get anything out of the experience. But the moment he turned that shitty attitude toward Penny, I lost my composure. And I've done so in the absolute worst way possible, given the setting. He's gripping his reddened cheek, huffing and puffing with useless bluster.

There's some audible gasping and muttering from the nearby groups of attendees. I can already see the way that my actions are rippling out across the courtyard. Soon enough, everyone will want to come see what the commotion is.

As viscerally satisfying as it was to finally give the man what he deserves, I'm just as immediately filled with a sense of deep guilt. This entire event is supposed to be about charity, about putting something beautiful into the world. I never should have come here in the first place, and the best thing I can do now is to get myself the hell away from here.

Still, I can't leave without making sure the point is crystal clear. "If you ever so much as speak to either of us again, I'll do far worse than that." I drop my voice low and lean in close. "You know what I can give. Did it never occur to you that it can also be taken? Try anything, and you'll go the rest of your life haunted by a hollow void where that pathetic mediocrity you call your 'creativity' used to be. Come on, Penny." Setting our drinks down on the nearest available surface, I take her hand and start dragging her away, up the curving staircase that leads back inside.

The smart thing to do would be to get our driver to put several miles between us and this entire affair. But I'm frayed and aimless now that I've managed to escape the immediate problem. From here, I don't know what to do next. So I just stand in the middle of the rotunda, looking around anxiously, while John Singer Sargent's creations stare down passively at the two of us. My breathing is uneven, my body feels simultaneously hot and cold, and I'm probably holding Penny's hand harder than I ought to be. "I'm so sorry. That was incredibly stupid. I don't even know what came over me."

Except she doesn't look upset in the slightest. Shocked, yes, but that's a given. Most notably, I realize she's been giggling, nearly gasping for breath. "Jesus, Anthea, I wish I had known you were going to do that so I could have recorded it for posterity. Seriously, if you hadn't slapped him, I was considering decking him myself."

"He said something so awful, and I couldn't let it stand—"

"Anthea." With her free hand, Penny gently touches my arm and rubs slowly, looking right into my eyes with a smile so warm you'd never guess what we just ran away from. "Thank you. Seriously. I don't think I've ever had anyone defend my honor before."

The comforting helps, but I'm still scrambled. There's something I need, in an almost primal way, and I can feel it calling to me from elsewhere in the museum. I glance nervously at my companion. "Would you be all right doing one more stupid thing with me?"

"I'm down to do as many stupid things as you want right now." Her voice is so full of admiration and affection, there's no way it's just an empty platitude. She means it. I really hope that's true. "Okay?"

"Okay." And I head for the stairwell on the other side of the visitors center with Penny in tow.

CHAPTER TWENTY-THREE

Penny

"I know I talked a big game two seconds ago, but...what do we do if we run into someone?" The two of us are tipsy enough, we can probably play it off one time if a security guard gives us trouble. Say we got lost on our way from the bathroom, or that we just needed to get a moment alone: wink-wink, nudge-nudge, say no more, lads.

But we made a pretty big scene back downstairs. There's a decent chance they might have dispatched someone to fetch us.

Anthea just shakes her head, still moving onward with a determined look in her eye. "If anyone gets too close, I can always give them a gentle push to overlook us."

"With your magic. Got it."

"Not magic."

I chuckle softly, getting a weird thrill out of my obstinate refusal to correct myself. Still, even if it's true she can "push" people away, the two of us having a conversation en route would probably make that more difficult. So I shut my trap and follow along, eager to see just where Anthea needs to go so desperately.

Up on the second floor, I'm pulled ahead and to the right through the nearest hallway. It takes a moment for me to process where we are. Anthea has brought me to the Rabb Gallery. The walls are lined with beautiful Impressionist works—we're surrounded by the likes of Renoir, Monet, Van Gogh, and more. She breathes deep before releasing a satisfied sigh, and I finally see some of that tension fade from her. Which is good, because it really looked like she was carrying a heavy load for doing something so hilarious and cool.

She needs it, this Moment, and I'm happy to let her have it.

After another few seconds of basking, she begins tugging me around the room, taking her time to look longingly at each piece.

There's something about this that feels oddly intimate—in a way that's ineffably different from all the other intimate things we've done. She moves from one painting to the next with a step almost like Degas's dancer statue, who watches us, still and silent, from nearby. Occasionally she gets this faraway look and starts to reach out toward a painting, only to stop herself at the last second. As if there's a desperate need to make physical contact with something from another time, another place. I wonder if she or any of her family inspired something here. Or perhaps the greats got here without such supernatural aid. It doesn't feel right to shatter this delicate atmosphere with an annoying question.

For a solid fifteen minutes, we amble our way along the perimeter of the gallery without a single word. As promised, we're never once approached by a security guard, or an official from the society. It's just us and the masters.

The joy and wonder radiates off Anthea powerfully, and I can't tell if it's her influence or if it's something more mundane than that, but it's infectious. I drink in each work alongside her, marveling at the way these artists can capture little moments in time with sweeping waves of carefully applied blotches of color. To my surprise, I'm not even overcome with the usual sense of inadequacy I usually feel when looking at art from the greats. I just let it be what it is—a moment to admire how much goes into something so precious and meaningful. It doesn't happen easily. Beauty like this takes sleepless nights and intense concentration. A spark will only get you so far.

When we've completed our circuit, Anthea walks me slowly over to one of the cushioned benches to settle in front of Renoir's *Dance at Bougival*. She's still got a firm hold on my hand, and occasionally she brushes her thumb against my skin, sending a wave of goose bumps along my arm. "Thank you for humoring me, Penny. I needed this."

"I'm just happy to tag along." Something in my phrasing seemingly triggers Anthea. Her face falls, and I feel like I did when we first started getting to know each other, so often left in the dark. There are details I'm missing here. "What's going on? I feel like there's more to it than just running into an asshole ex." Initially I say that as a way to continue her joke from before, but I'm realizing too late that's exactly what happened. I never got an answer to my question earlier, but now I don't need it. Dmitri was a lot more than just her artist.

Anthea studies Renoir's dancers for a moment. "I got used to a certain kind of existence with my artists over the last few decades. Big and flashy and loud. As a muse, the biggest charge you can get is from doing what we're made to do—to inspire an artist. And with someone like Dmitri, so confident and self-assured, it can be downright addictive. Worse, that goes both ways. In his mind, it was so obvious that the universe would send him a muse to push him to new heights. He became obsessed, said he couldn't create anymore unless I was there with him. And it just wasn't tenable. My energy is far from boundless. As the well dried up, so to speak, he became more and more unpredictable—sometimes falling into a deep depression, other times flying into fits of rage. Even still, leaving him was one of the hardest things I've done in ages, and it didn't happen all at once. I learned to fight back in fits and starts."

If it wasn't obvious enough already based on his behavior tonight, I can see clearly now that Dmitri was way more than a mere asshole. He put Anthea through hell.

"I've tried, over the past century or so, to find something, anything, that could give me a fraction of what I'd been mainlining with them. SCUBA diving, BASE jumping, ice climbing…I even made an effort to get into flashy cars, like I was going through a midlife crisis. But none of it could compare."

I'm getting progressively more nervous. There's no way in hell that what I do could give Anthea even a fraction of what she needs. I'm not like all those others, given how much work it takes to feel even slightly confident. I can barely keep *myself* afloat half the time, let alone provide her with that kind of intense high. My brain is already concocting several different directions this conversation can go—none of them pleasant.

My only saving grace is that Anthea continues her little monologue, pausing just long enough to give my hand a small squeeze of encouragement. "Slowly, during my decade of quiet, I learned the miracle of small joys. A reliable coffee shop, a delicious meal, a good book, that kind of thing. I realized, much to my embarrassment, that I didn't really know anything about art. The way that muses are…wired, I used to only care about the process of creation. Whether a work was good or bad, whether it ended up in a gallery or in a fire, that never mattered. So I began actually studying art, really *learning* about it after so long spent merely inspiring it. Something about the Impressionists in particular spoke to me. I love the way they can create these amazing images by tricking the mind into blending together so many disparate splotches into a cohesive whole."

"And running into Dmitri kinda messed with some of that zen you've been developing?"

"It reminded me of how I used to be—and made me question how much I've really changed. Maybe, just for a moment, I missed that overwhelming charge I used to get. But then he turned that venom against you, and I remembered why I left in the first place. Because the high isn't worth the crash. This…" she says grandly while gesturing to the room. "This helps remind me to pull back, stop getting caught up worrying about those 'disparate blotches,' focus on the full picture. And I think it's enough to get me to say what I need to say."

If everything else was just preamble, I can't even imagine what she's working herself up to.

"I have felt more fulfilled and content stumbling my way through things with you these last few weeks than I ever did in all the time I've been a muse. And it's not just because of the connection we share or the kind of energy we provide each other. It's you, Penny. For all that you talk about yourself as some kind of struggling creature, I find you to be an endlessly enjoyable companion. And…I hope the two of us can become closer than just partners or friends. I want you to do more than merely 'tag along.'"

So much of my mental real estate lately has been spent constructing a very delicate, very flimsy house of cards predicated on the incontrovertible fact that Anthea and I are simply on two different planes of existence from one another. And here she is busting out the industrial fan. This can't be happening.

The absolute shock I feel must be painted across my face, because she starts to flounder while her grip on my hand tightens a bit more. "I completely understand if you don't feel the same way. And I would rather you be honest and tell me if I'm on the wrong page here—"

The flustered waffling is cute, but I know I need to take pity on her before she combusts. "Anthea! It's okay. I just—I wasn't expecting this."

"Really? And here I thought I was being too obvious."

"Then that's your fault, for underestimating the power of my imperceptivity."

That's enough to loosen her up—including her grip on my hand—and she laughs softly. "Apologies for doubting you."

"It feels almost shitty for me to ask this, but I have to know. You're positive this isn't some kind of residual effect of our connection?"

"No more than any other situation where familiarity breeds affection. But no, there's nothing supernatural about it." She looks at me intently for a moment, as if she's waiting for something specific. But I'm not sure what it is, and finally Anthea voices her thoughts. "So, is this 'okay' as in you're fine with it, or 'okay' as in maybe you feel the same?"

Damn, really thought I'd gotten away with that one. "Truth be told, I was trying to not let myself develop any feelings because I didn't want to end up disappointed. But I'm not very good at stopping myself from feeling things. Like, of course I think you're funny and interesting and absolutely, *achingly* gorgeous. So I hope you'll forgive me if it takes a little while for this to sink in?"

Speaking of things I was trying to not notice, Anthea has been slowly leaning closer while we've been talking. And her face is now mere inches from mine. She gives one of her breathy little chuckles and I can feel it against my lips. "Again, I remind you, some confidence would look good on you."

Even if I could conjure something to say in my defense—I can't—I don't have the chance. With that final reminder to believe in myself, she's leaning down into a kiss with me. Given we're in an off-limits area of a fucking museum, I expect it to just be a chaste peck, a promise of things to come, but it's practically an attack. She's almost launching herself at me, and I have to use my free hand to brace myself against the bench so we don't both go toppling over.

But it's more than just the surprise. When our lips meet, there's a palpable electricity to it. Our feelings might not be the result of her magic, but this almost certainly is. There are fireworks, the way you always hear about in stories, but they're inside my mind and they momentarily deafen my thoughts until all I can think about is this gorgeous woman actually having legitimate feelings for me. One slender hand is resting at the nape of my neck, the other at my hip, urging me closer.

We're getting into dangerous territory for me. The kind of energy she's putting out into this kiss, I get the impression that Anthea is not without her desires. It's taking all of my remaining brain power just to keep up. So when we suddenly hear the sound of someone gently clearing their throat, it takes both of us by surprise and we separate with a collective gasp, but some small part of me feels almost relieved.

Standing in the entryway of the gallery is Bethany. She's shifting her feet uncomfortably and looking anywhere but directly at us while we disentangle ourselves. "I'm sorry to interrupt, ladies," Bethany says self-consciously, pushing her glasses up the bridge of her nose, refusing to make eye contact.

Anthea rises from the bench and idly adjusts her shirt cuffs, trying to play it cool—though that's ruined somewhat by her flushed cheeks and heavy breathing. "No need to apologize. Better you than some angry security guard."

"I actually insisted I be the one to come get you. The truth is, Ms. Corey..." She lightly clears her throat and shuffles a bit more. "I'm the one who approved Mr. Ustinov's appeal to attend the gala. I thought having a well-known artist would be a nice surprise for everyone and never stopped to ask why he wanted to come in the first place. Had I known he would cause trouble, that man would never have made it in the door."

Once I've actually managed to catch my breath, I stand to join them, reaching once again for Anthea's hand. "Kinda thought we'd be the ones accused of making a scene."

"Plenty of attendees overheard what he said to you. I don't think there's any question who the true instigator was tonight." Bethany gives us another once-over, eyes flicking down to our joined hands before looking back toward Anthea. "Is there any way I can convince you to join us for the award ceremony?"

"Perhaps it would be best if we just took our leave. But it really was a lovely party."

"Hmm. Glad to see you got something out of it," she replies briskly, with just a hint of humor. "Let me walk you out, at least."

Not looking to make this poor woman's night any more difficult, we relent and agree to walk back with her down to the exit.

Hell of a way to make my grand return to the arts society, I'll say that much for sure.

Everyone at the gala is still either out in the courtyard or making their way toward the auditorium, so there's no one around to stare at us as we make our walk of shame out of the museum.

Bethany goes to open the door, then pauses and looks us over one last time, lightly gnawing her bottom lip thoughtfully. She reaches into her purse and pulls out a business card. "Ms. Hartwell, Ms. Corey, I feel as though I owe you something for your trouble tonight. Here." She passes the tiny card off to me. "I might be able to help you a bit with networking—put you in touch with a few small galleries that could host some of your art."

I can really only stammer as I shove that down into my purse. This woman has never even seen my art before. For all she knows, I could be a talentless hack. "Wow. Um. Thank you. I'll give you a call if I manage to knock out something worth showing off."

"I look forward to it." She makes her way back toward the courtyard while the two of us head out through the door.

Anthea puts a call in to our driver. I can hear a bit of music and laughter, and figure that maybe he was hanging out with the other chauffeurs to kill time. "Ricky, hello, I'm so sorry about this. But we've decided to take our leave a bit early. Would you be able to come pick us up?"

"Of course, Ms. Corey, I'll be there in a moment."

She hangs up and tucks her phone away before pressing in close to me. A bit of a chill has settled over Boston that wasn't there just an hour ago. I must be shivering slightly, because the next thing I know, Anthea is draping her jacket around my shoulders like a proper gentlewoman, the lingering heat from her body helping to warm me back up.

But that small act of kindness pales in comparison to her next move as she leans in and presses a kiss to the top of my head. "I can't say I expected the evening to take the turn it has. But I'm also not especially disappointed, all things considered. So, I suppose the question is—my place or yours?"

I get it. We're both adults here. Or, well, I'm an adult, and she's an ancient being of inspiration. So it's not like there's any point in dancing around things like awkward teenagers. But…fuck. I'm so not ready. My insecurities about my skills as an artist are nothing compared to That Kind of Thing.

And whether she can see the obvious signs, or she senses something with her muse magic, she quickly starts backpedaling. "I'm sorry, that—Perhaps that was too forward. I'd like to spend more time together tonight, especially since we're cutting our evening here a bit short."

I don't have a good enough excuse prepared, so I'm grateful, and I laugh nervously. "Hah, very smooth. It's all right, I'm still kinda processing the fact that this even happened in the first place.

And it's been a while since I've—Anyway, I guess I'm just a little overwhelmed. Sorry, I hope that's okay."

"Of course. Just know that it's an open invitation."

"Mm. Noted." I don't want her to get the wrong idea here, so I lean over and gently lay my head against her shoulder, and her arms wrap around me affectionately. All is well. No harm done.

Still…I wasn't prepared for Anthea to go there so soon, and I'm already starting to wonder just how long I can delay the inevitable.

CHAPTER TWENTY-FOUR

Anthea

That minor hitch from last night has me worried. All things considered, the gala was quite the unexpected success. But I can't quite fathom why Penny would have turned down the offer to end things on an even more victorious note.

After a good night's sleep, I do manage to untangle my thoughts a bit. As nice as it was to finally clear the air between us, the gala was still a stressful event for myriad reasons. There was that Wyatt Reid man, then everything with Dmitri. And following that up with sneaking around the empty museum before dumping all of my feelings on Penny, it was a lot to throw at the woman in quick succession. It's only natural that she would want to wait for a better moment. She simply wasn't in the mood.

So I resolve to put in the work and do things right. We need a proper date that isn't mired in unnecessary tension.

My first instinct is to go for something classic—a candlelit dinner, perhaps. But that doesn't feel quite right to who Penny is as a person. Putting her through a second night of elaborate clothing and an opulent atmosphere might inadvertently dampen the mood all over again.

I think back fondly to our afternoon at the coffee shop. It was only a few weeks ago, but it feels like ages.

Comparing me to buttered noodles. That's high praise. Yeah, I guess looking at it that way, I am kind of a simple woman.

A simple woman. An easy date. Something basic. There's no reason for me to go over the top with this.

After a bit of brainstorming and Googling, I find the perfect answer and eagerly call Penny.

"Really? Mini golf? Is that the kind of thing you'd be into doing?"

"I'd be happy doing just about anything." Truth be told, as perfect as my plan is, it's not without its pitfalls. I'll be sailing into uncharted waters, moving outside my comfort zone. But for her, it's worth it. "And I thought since you were willing to get all gussied up to go with me to the gala, we might change things up this time around, keep it low-key."

I can practically feel that bashful warmth radiating through the phone. "Hmm, yeah, that actually sounds really cool."

"Wonderful!" We spend some time figuring out when we can go, and before I know it, we've got a plan for our first official date. It might not be anything flashy, but given our collective excitement, I'm quite pleased with myself.

* * *

If only Matilde could see me now. I'm waiting outside an establishment in Cambridge with a name so ridiculous that I had to pick it—Uncle Chuckle's Putt-Putt and Arcade Family Fun-Plex. The massive building looks almost like a barn, with a huge peaked roof and a set of two massive doors. Inside, I can see and hear the beeping of multiple forms of electronic entertainment, and the smell of cheap snack food wafts out, inviting customers to partake of all that grease and sugar to their heart's desire.

I have never once been on a date like this before, and it took me almost an hour to decide what I should even wear. In the end,

I defaulted to just wearing a cute, yellow floral sundress and some strap sandals. Even though this seems casual to me, I still feel a bit overdressed.

But that silly bit of anxiety goes right out the window the moment I see Penny strolling her way toward me. It's not that there's anything particularly different about her. She's wearing one of her usual button-ups—today it's the garish yellow one with the cartoon shark pattern. When she sees me, Penny gives a nervous wave and trots the rest of the distance, unable to suppress her smile.

I'm smiling too, of course. How can I not? "Hello, Penny." Moving to meet her, I wrap her in a hug and press a quick kiss to her lips.

While she may have balked outside the museum at the idea of sleeping together, she seems plenty eager to accept my show of affection. That goes a long way toward soothing any worries I might have been developing. She's clearly still happy to be close. I didn't overstep.

"Hey there. You look amazing, as per usual."

"As do you."

"This old thing?" She giggles and tugs at her shirt self-consciously. "Figured I'd lean into that whole 'golfers dressed terribly' vibe."

"I think it's wonderful."

"You're too kind. Anyway, let's get to it." As we make our way inside to pay for a round, she looks at me curiously. "So, you ever done this before? I can picture you on a real-ass golf course, sure, but what about the deadly world of its miniature counterpart?"

"I actually haven't. It likely doesn't come as much of a shock that the circles I ran in before didn't really go to fun-plexes. Though I did once attend a party in Long Island where the host had a whole collection of vintage pinball machines."

"Ugh, were they all pristine and polished? I bet people weren't even allowed to play them."

"Precisely. So, today will be quite the fresh experience for me."

Once we've paid for our putters and balls, Penny and I head out through the back doors of the main structure and onto the course. The bright green of the Astroturf is overwhelming and I'm starting to have second thoughts about all this. I'm out of place here, I don't really belong. There were a dozen other casual things I could have chosen for our date—why did I have to pick this one?

Penny steps up to the first hole and gives an unnecessary flourish, twirling her putter like a baton. "I hope you're ready to see some extremely mediocre mini-golf skills. Try not to swoon and fall into that pond feature." To my surprise, she looks back at me with a playful wink. She's still working on taking my advice to heart and is attempting some confident preening. I can see it's a tiny bit forced, but that just makes it all the more endearing.

Her banter and flirtation flip a switch in my mind. Perhaps I'm taking all this too seriously. This place is about having fun—it's quite literally in the name—and I should be focusing on that instead of getting distracted by some silly concept of fitting or belonging. Penny is what matters.

As promised, her first putt doesn't even get the ball over the initial hill. It takes five strokes for her to actually get it into the hole, and she looks at me with another grin. "Does that double bogey do anything for you?"

Giggling, I drop my own ball into position and prepare to swing. "Please. I'm almost certain I can get a higher score. Then we'll see who's impressed."

"You do realize the goal is to get a low score, right? Please tell me you understand that."

Throwing my own words from our first meeting back at me. I have to say, I'm impressed.

It only takes me four shots to sink the ball, and I give Penny a sarcastic pout. "Darn. You're already winning."

She laughs and shakes her head. "If you wanna turn this into a contest to see who's worse at the game, then I should warn you that I've had years of practice sucking at lots of stuff."

Eventually the playful banter turns into a more legitimate competition. Neither of us are especially cutthroat, but it's quite enjoyable to play up the rivalry for a little while.

By the time we reach the ninth hole, Penny has really found her stride. I'm trying to line up my first shot while she stands on the sideline and commentates, holding her putter like a microphone. In her best imitation of a soothing English baritone, she narrates the stakes. "It's a beautiful day here at Uncle Chuckle's Putt-Putt and Arcade Family Fun-Plex. Seasoned veteran Anthea Corey has a two-stroke lead over the young upstart Penelope Hartwell. But the notorious ninth hole windmill poses an interesting challenge. Can this daring Don Quixote tilt at the giant victoriously, or will those slothful blades deny her that hard-won lead?"

"Cut that out!" I say through yet more giggling. There's a family just behind us who are no doubt getting exhausted with our antics holding up their own outing. Trying to move things along, I take my hasty shot and predictably end up getting my ball knocked aside by the "slothful blades." I'm forced to take the long journey around the structure and end up going one over par.

"Corey is looking absolutely *gutted*. Let's see if Hartwell can eke out that lead." Expecting her to follow a similar trajectory as myself, I watch in awe as Penny manages to knock her own ball flawlessly through the windmill and straight into its target. Without a shred of dignity, Penny hoots and pumps her fist. "Oh! That's golf, baby! Not spoiling any good walks today."

"It's *mini* golf, and if we don't move this along, those lovely people are going to riot."

But to my surprise, the little girl watching Penny is giggling brightly at her, and even her father is chuckling softly. Still, while they may not mind, I encourage Penny to move it along a bit faster without quite so much screwing around at every opportunity. Even if my blushing cheeks and light laughter make it obvious to everyone how much I'm enjoying her antics.

Despite Penny's self-congratulatory hole in one, I still finish the eighteenth hole a few strokes ahead. But she takes my victory in stride, and we head back inside to explore the rest of the fun-plex. We share some extremely cheap nachos with that signature radioactive yellow cheese before poking around the arcade.

With a stack of tokens in hand, we start checking out the machines. Penny suddenly pulls up short beside one cabinet in particular and gasps excitedly. "Oh, this takes me back."

I tilt my head and inspect it. *Marvel vs. Capcom*. The game promises a mash-up of two titans of pop culture, only one of whom I'm marginally familiar with, duking it out for some inexplicable reason. "Oh?"

"We had a dinky little arcade near our home growing up. Me and Theo would go there sometimes after school and dump our allowance into this exact game." She looks back at me almost like she's that excitable teen again. "Do you mind?"

I hold up my handful of tokens with an encouraging smile. "It's why we're here. Go on, you've got another chance to show off."

With rapid movements that can only come from a life of muscle memory, Penny pops in the requisite tokens and selects her duo of fighters in quick succession. Two robots—a tall one in black-and-gray armor, the other small and blue with a childlike face.

What happens next is more than I can keep up with. It's all just flashing lights and chunky sound effects and the rattling of the buttons. But given the way Penny continuously plays, I at least get the impression she's winning.

Her skill finally hits a wall when she reaches what seems to be the finale, fighting a hulking figure clad in red and purple. Try as she might, Penny can't seem to best him, and the stylish countdown marks her defeat. "Gah. History repeats itself. One day, Onslaught, I will best you."

"It looks like you can put in some more tokens and play again."

"Nah, a girl's gotta know when she's beat. And I wanna see what else they've got around here."

We continue our exploration, choosing machines almost at random. I try my hand at a racing game and lose so spectacularly that I'm certain Penny's respect for me has diminished. "I think I had better luck with the real thing."

She just gives me a pacifying kiss on the top of my head, and I break out in a soft blush. "Oh? What kinda hot rod are we talking about here? Mustang? Bugatti?"

"This was a *while* ago, darling. We're talking an original Aston Martin. Purred like a dream."

"And yet you prefer to hang around with me. You've got strange tastes, Anthea."

"Correction: I have an extremely refined palate. Only a particular sort of woman can satisfy me." Like always, I get that blush I'm hoping for.

We finish things off with a few rounds of Skee-Ball. Neither of us are able to sink many high-point shots, but we at least manage to walk away with two fistfuls of tickets. An acne-riddled teen running the prize counter gestures to the meager collection of prizes available. With surprising enthusiasm, Penny gestures to the bin of plastic rings, plucking one with a butterfly on it.

She holds it out to me as though she were giving me a piece of real jewelry. "For you, my lady."

The foolish offering makes me feel strangely giddy, and with a bit of prying I'm able to fit it over my pinkie. "How romantic." And I truly do mean that. We leave the fun-plex, looking like a pair of giddy teenagers, hanging on one another and giggling brightly. This was exactly the kind of day I was hoping for.

We ride the subway back downtown together, and with each passing stop I can feel my excitement rising. Everything has gone perfectly, and I'm ready to end it with an unforgettable capstone. While we chat quietly, I occasionally brush a finger against the silly little ring and marvel at the way something so small can make me feel so ridiculously happy.

Neither of us is ready to end the day quite yet. Penny scans through three different streaming services looking for just the right movie while I order us some delivery from a marvelous little Indian restaurant. She insists on having some extremely spicy vindaloo, and demolishes half our naan and two glasses of milk just trying to ease her self-imposed suffering.

The movie is a wonderfully sappy gay rom-com that only serves to make me feel that much more romantic and eager. As the credits roll and we bask in the wonderful feelings we're sharing, I decide to go for it. The mood is just right, the two of us nestled together on the couch, my arm around her shoulders. "Penny?"

"Hmm? What's up?" She glances up at me curiously, and I very nearly get distracted just looking into her eyes.

"Would you like to…spend the night here? With me?" To my dismay, her face falls and she starts to sit up. Feeling a bit of panic well up, I rush to try to adjust my proposition. "As I said, it's an open offer, and I don't want you to feel pressured."

Penny sighs softly and takes my hands in her own. She holds them firmly, eventually managing to look me in the eye, with some difficulty. "I'm really sorry. There's just a lot of stuff that I…" She trails off for a moment, seemingly reaching for the right words. "It's complicated, you know? Nothing to do with you. You're incredible."

There are a lot of questions bouncing around in my mind. Is it dysphoria? Does she like to move at a slower pace than I'm used to? Or maybe she's just never had sex before? But I can't think of a way to ask any of them without it sounding judgmental, or like I want to pull her into something that she's not ready for.

She continues, "Today was so fucking good, and I really hate to think I'm ending it on a sour note like this."

"You're right. Today was wonderful, and exactly what I needed. But you're not ruining anything. We have so many days ahead of us. We still have that portrait to finish, and your brother's band performing in the battle. I can be patient, as long as you need."

She breathes a sigh of relief, but there's still something guilty in her face. "Right. Another time. Of course. I'm sorry," she says again.

I go in for another kiss, one that I hope is deep enough and passionate enough to convince her there are no hard feelings here—even if I am feeling a bit disappointed again.

In the end, Penny takes off for her home, and I'm left hoping this is just a speed bump and not a brick wall.

CHAPTER TWENTY-FIVE

Penny

Shit.

Leave it to me to land in the most amazing, perfect situation ever and still find a way to completely ruin it.

You would think that at this point in my life, I'd have found a way to deal with this quickly and easily. But it's not as though I've been exactly swimming in phone numbers and dates lately. My last relationship was with Juniper, and that breakup was what gave me this stupid complex in the first place.

Even though I've just had one of the best dates of my life, I walk away feeling like I screwed it up. Go figure. Story of my life and all that.

I don't feel like going home, so for the first time in my life I decide to drown my sorrows. Which is how I find myself sitting at the bar of The Púca, drinking far too much whiskey, wishing I could be more normal. And that makes me feel like an asshole for thinking that this makes me abnormal when I know full well that's not the case. I know the words, the theory, the discourse, I know it all. I'm a millennial—of course I do. But it turns out when you're there in a woman's apartment, and she's looking at you with those beautiful brown eyes wanting something you can't give, it's incredibly hard to come out with it.

I tap my glass, and Meagan saunters over to give me another. She's been looking progressively more worried with each new drink but has otherwise been giving me space. But it seems like she's decided it's time to do a quick wellness check. "So, uh, everything okay there, Penpen?"

She's never used that nickname for me before. *No one* has, and yet it feels so weirdly natural coming from her. Meagan just exists in that special state of perpetual coolness. I find myself smiling, if only a little. "Not exactly."

"Wanna talk about it?"

"It's…embarrassing. And I don't want anyone here to suffer listening to me going on about my personal life."

Meagan smirks and gestures with a tilt of her chin down the bar toward a guy in his midfifties nursing some kind of sugary, neon-pink concoction. "Johnny there? He likes to come here without his drinking buddies so he can enjoy the 'girly' drinks in peace. Or maybe you're worried about those two," she says, gesturing toward a booth in the back corner where two young bros share a pitcher of beer. They're both smiling ear to ear, faces close, and I catch sight of their feet occasionally brushing together. "A couple'a Boston College boys who just want somewhere they can be themselves. The Púca's a safe space, kiddo. So c'mon, out with it."

I sigh, knowing that this will probably do me some good. "Against all reason, Anthea and me, we started dating."

"And I take it ya hit a rough patch already?" Meagan leans up against the bar and looks at me intently with a sympathetic frown.

"Not really, that's the thing. We went on our first official date today. Like, as a couple. And it was everything I could have wanted. Mini golf and arcade games and shitty nachos. But after both the gala the other night and again today, she invited me to sleep with her. And both times I turned her down."

"Not ready?"

"Not interested." I take a small breath and try to just actually say the words, ones that I don't think I've ever actually spoken aloud despite knowing it for years now. "I'm asexual."

"Oh, fuck, yeah. That'll make things wicked complicated. Did ya tell her?"

"I wanted to, but I was already killing the mood, and dropping something like that means the mood is killed indefinitely. We only just started, and we're already running into trouble."

She props her chin in her upturned hand. "And ya think it'll be that bad?"

"Me not wanting to have sex was what killed my last relationship. So I know it's possible. And she was ready to proposition me within an hour of confessing she had feelings for me in the first place. So I'd just hate it for this amazing thing to be practically dead on arrival."

"Have ya thought of any practical ways around it? Y'know, to get closer without freakin' yerself out?"

I shrug and drain a bit more of my glass, hoping the alcohol will keep me from catastrophizing. It hasn't so far, but you never know. That next sip could be the magic one. "I'm sure there are options. I've read up on it. But I don't know anything for sure without…actually trying it. And the thought of getting as far as the bedroom only to pump the brakes all over again just makes me nervous as hell."

"Well, the good news is that I think I have an idea of what ya need to do. The bad news is that ya probably already know what it is."

"Maybe, but I think I still need to hear it."

"First things first, ya gotta tell her. That's obvious. Do it during a neutral moment, outta the bedroom. See how she takes the news—and if she's really in it for the long haul, then the two a'ya have to figure out what the next step is. Agree to try small things together." It really is bizarre to hear such sage advice through a Boston accent so thick it could star in a Ben Affleck movie. "And if all else fails, make that shit an open relationship, and wish her good luck when she goes out to sleep with someone."

That last suggestion is just brazen enough that I finally crack a little and chuckle softly. "Based on the stories she's told me, Anthea doesn't strike me as the polyamorous type." Then again, I can't say for certain. I still have a lot more to learn about her. "Thanks for pushing me to talk. You really are extremely good at this."

"I take my alcohol therapy seriously. Speaking of my expert advice…" Meagan fills a glass with some ice and water then plants it firmly on the bar in front of me. "Drink that, head home, and sleep on it. See how yer feeling tomorrow."

I do as I'm told and start drinking my water, already feeling a little better. Not a lot. But it's something.

* * *

It takes a little more than one night's sleep for me to gather the necessary courage. But with each passing day, the threat of opening up feels less and less monumental. After a week of sitting on this, I reach the point where I only feel mildly anxious about having this conversation.

Anthea and I have been spending a lot more time together, including a few more sessions working on the portrait. I really only need a couple more hours and I think it will be done.

Charcoal might be my favorite medium—and Anthea's magic birthright or whatever—but I'm glad that we decided on using the pastels too. It's maybe the sappiest thought I've had in a long time, but there's something significant and meaningful there. Working with her, she's got me taking risks and trying things I might otherwise not try. And it's brought color into a world that would otherwise be nothing but shadow.

God, Penny, that's awful. I mean, truly, gag-inducing. But every time I think about it, my heart flutters. So it's complicated.

Since the day at the fun-plex, Anthea hasn't brought up sleeping together. And while I appreciate that, I still can't fully shake the sense of stupid guilt that I've forced her to ignore something she clearly wants.

At the moment, we're sharing a booth in a little hole-in-the-wall bar and grill called Tommy's. This place has become our go-to spot when we finish a session, after stumbling upon it almost by accident. We're currently deep into a plate of wings and a couple beers. Things mostly feel normal now, which I think is about as good an atmosphere as I'm going to get to do this. The rest of the place is dead, so it's not like I'm in danger of having this heart-to-heart with an audience.

I wipe some cheap barbecue sauce from my lips with an equally cheap napkin and clear my throat. "So um. I've been wanting to do a better job of explaining why I was so hesitant about…sleeping at your place." Not sleeping "with you," just "at your place." Jesus, I can barely even say it.

Even though I'm keeping it vague, she still nods in agreement. We're both painfully aware of what's going on. Or rather, what's *not* going on. "Of course." She sits up a bit, giving me her full attention. I'm sure she's been eager to understand.

"It's probably not a huge surprise to say that I was kind of a late bloomer. I grew up repressing a lot of stuff and it took a while for me to really branch out. I didn't have sex for the first time until grad school, and it was the most…*miserable* experience for me."

Anthea gives me a sympathetic look and reaches out for my hand. "The first time is awkward and difficult for a lot of people, no matter how old they are."

"Er, no. I'm talking 'hop off the bed because I'm having a miniature panic attack' kind of miserable."

Her sympathy shifts to confusion. "Were they hurting you or something?"

"No, and it wasn't some kind of dysphoria thing either. Juniper was trans like me and super into the whole sex-positive thing. So when I tapped out, she was perfectly understanding. Once I calmed down and we were able to debrief, she figured out pretty quickly that I was probably asexual, or somewhere on that spectrum at least."

"Did learning that make it easier at least?"

"Yes and no. It was great to put a name to things. But since Junie was all knowledgeable about shit, she also knew that the two of us weren't compatible. Frankly, she reached that conclusion a little too soon and without my input, so while she was all zen about it, I felt like I'd been run over by a truck."

Anthea sighs and gives my hand a small squeeze. "Well. That will certainly do it." She seems to still be processing everything herself. "And you're worried that we're also incompatible." It's not a question this time, but a statement. I'm not exactly being subtle with my fears.

"Not necessarily," I say, maybe a bit too hastily. "I mean, I've had plenty of time to look stuff up, do the research. It's possible there's things that I might still be able to do."

"I wouldn't want you to get hurt or upset just because you want to throw me a bone, Penny." A moment after saying that, she groans softly. "Sorry, that was poor phrasing."

It's a stupid Freudian slip, but it's enough to make me laugh and keep me from feeling totally hopeless. "You clearly like sex. Isn't it kinda messed up to get this far and then pull the rug out from under you?"

"After all the kindness and respect you've shown me, it would be pretty awful of me to not return the favor." She shrugs, and her grip on my hand tightens just a little as she flashes me a warm smile. But it's strained and weird, too. I don't know how to read it, and that makes me nervous. Are both of us just trying too hard for nothing? God, this sucks. "Besides—"

Whatever she's about to say is cut off by a voice that seems to fill the entire restaurant. "Anthea! Darling!"

I feel my body reflexively tighten up. The last time someone enthusiastically called out to her, I had to deal with Dmitri. I'd rather not suffer a similar fate a second time.

Standing at our table is a towering woman with a mane of silky blond hair and shimmering emerald eyes. The moment I look up at her, I hear this song in my head, clear as day. Not one I've ever heard before, and yet infinitely familiar. And I realize slowly who she might be—and *what* she might be.

Anthea looks equally surprised by her visitor but quickly rises to draw the other muse into a tight hug. "Matilde, what in the world are you doing all the way out here?"

She lets out an honest-to-god ojou-sama laugh, complete with the melodic "ohohoh," as the two of them slide their way into the booth across from me. Never in my life did I think I would hear someone unironically giggle like Nanami Kiryuu. "A friend of a client is participating in a musical combat event, and he came out here to cheer them on. I asked if I could tag along. How could I pass up an opportunity to visit you in person, dear sister?"

"You could have at least sent me a text. Unlike some of our siblings, you've never had much trouble with technology."

"Where's the fun in that? The look on your face has made it all worthwhile."

I wonder quietly for a moment how she even hunted us down, hidden away in a place like this. Maybe Matilde found us by sensing Anthea's aura or whatever. But something she said was so baffling that I have to address it, and I raise my hand like I'm in class. "Can we rewind to the 'combat event' thing?"

For the first time, Matilde seems to actually take proper notice of me and gasps excitedly, like she's just seen the world's cutest puppy. "Oh! You must be Penelope." She extends a hand to me, and as soon as I take it, I'm subjected to an incredibly firm, professional handshake. "Matilde de Leòn. I run the Muse Talent Agency out in Los Angeles"

Bold company name. Two points for honesty.

"Anyhow, yes. A local contest for musical performers. I figure, as long as I'm in town, I ought to do some headhunting."

It's a battle of the bands. She has to know what that is. She works in the music industry. If I thought Anthea was a bit weird, then her sister is an outright oddity. "Huh, well, funny story. My brother's band is gonna be there too."

"Are they in need of sponsorship?"

"Sorely. But this might be a minor conflict of interest."

She waves her hand dismissively. "Oh, pishposh. Talent is talent. If they catch my eye, you can be certain I'll give them a fair shake. Let the people cry nepotism all they want."

"Well, seems like I can't stop you. So, uh, thanks." I don't even know how to handle this whirlwind of a woman. It's a fascinating opportunity to finally meet one of Anthea's siblings. If they're all like this, though, then I'm starting to think I might avoid any family reunions. It's not even the way her magic seems to fill my head with random snippets of music or ideas for some lyrical phrase. She fills the space, and I swear it's like she has her own spotlight illuminating her and encouraging everyone to look her way. No offense to the woman, she seems lovely, but I'm feeling overwhelmed and I could use a little breather. "Speaking of, I promised I'd stop by their rehearsal and give them as objective an assessment as I can." Standing from the table, I lean in to give Anthea a quick peck on the lips before smiling at Matilde.

Judging by the look on her face, she didn't realize just how close the two of us are. "I see! Well now I feel a bit bad for intruding."

"No way. I know how important sibling bonding is. You two have fun, and I'll call you soon, Anthea?" I search her face as well, just to make sure she doesn't throw me any signals to stick around.

But she just shakes her head, looking quite happy to have Matilde there. "Of course. Tell them I'm looking forward to the show."

So I leave them as they start gabbing excitedly and head out into the night.

CHAPTER TWENTY-SIX

Anthea

Matilde at least has the grace to wait until Penny has left before nudging me excitedly, shoulder to shoulder, and starting her inquisition. "Gracious, you hadn't told me just how close you two were."

"I guess I got a little wrapped up in everything. I kept meaning to tell you."

"Admittedly, it was more fun to witness it in person, so I think I can overlook the negligence."

The server for my table comes over and looks at Matilde in confusion for a few moments. "Were you always that tall and blond, or am I losing it after too many hours on my feet?"

We both start laughing softly. "No, my date had to take off for the night. This is my sister."

"Oh, thank god. Anything I can get for you, then?"

I tap my glass and smile. "I'll take a refill. And put anything she wants on my tab as well."

"You're too kind, darling," Matilde says while plucking the drink menu to study it for a moment. "Hmm, mostly beer, I see.

Shame. Still, this blackberry cider sounds delightful. One of those, my dear."

Her reaction is similar to just about everyone meeting Matilde for the first time. It always takes a moment to adjust to the sheer force of her personality, but inevitably the charm does its work. "You got it. Back soon."

Once the woman is gone, Matilde swiftly moves around to the other side of the booth so that she can start interrogating me. She's practically bouncing in her seat. "And how have things been with Penelope? I must admit, I'm curious to hear the full story. Please indulge me, love."

Given the revelation from Penny that I'm still struggling with, I decide to keep it surface-level for now. "So much has happened, I don't even remember where we left off."

"It sounded as though she was quite insistent on getting to know you. Which she has apparently done, with aplomb."

"Right. I did my best to keep her at bay. But doing so just made things worse. In the end, the facade was just too much to maintain. I had to let Penny know the truth about me or our partnership was in danger of dying out." It looks like Matilde is about to say something, and I throw up my hands defensively. "I know. It was foolish, but I was desperate. And as you can see, it worked out for the best. Our connection got stronger, and I don't regret doing it."

"Good. Then you learned an important lesson—sister knows best, but that doesn't mean you have to listen to her. You forged your own path." Her smile grows as she glances toward the door, then back at me. "And what about the sudden leap from partners to…something more?"

I flush and tell her about taking Penny to the gala and everything that happened at the museum that night.

At the mention of Dmitri, Matilde's brow furrows. "Honestly, that man. I don't know what you ever saw in him." She's underselling it, of course. When I first told Matilde about everything that he had done, she immediately began plotting all the terrible things she could do to him. And she only put those plans on hold because I asked her to.

"It's not so complicated. He was handsome and capable, and incredibly self-assured. But as you know, that also made him utterly insufferable. Ah, you should have seen the way Penny laid into him. It was a thing of beauty." I continue my story about our escape up to the gallery, my fumbling confession, and our first date.

"I never could have imagined you being wooed by miniature golfing and chicken wings, but here we are. Hmm, one might almost think you're genuinely in love, Anthea." She tries to couch it in teasing, but there's something warning and judgmental in her tone too.

Thankfully, I'm saved from her paranoid notions as our server returns and sets down our drinks. Matilde takes a hesitant sip of her cider, and judging by the happy little wiggle in her shoulders, it must be to her liking.

With the drink meeting her approval, she swiftly swings the spotlight back in my direction. "Now! Let's not gloss over the most important part. If Penelope has gotten this close to you, then the two of you must be having quite a lot of fun, eh? The self-conscious ones always seem to make up for their perceived faults by being especially...*giving* in the bedroom."

And there it is. Try as I might to avoid this, Matilde cuts right through to the heart of the matter. I slump in my seat and take a long gulp of my beer. "You'd think so, wouldn't you?"

"I was hoping to be met with the same level of enthusiasm as the rest of your tale, if this woman is everything you say she is."

Gnawing on my lip, I weigh how much to even say here. Matilde and I have never been shy about discussing our sexual exploits before. And if I balk, she'll catch on immediately. "I don't know if it's my place to say much about the specifics." Even still, I feel like I ought to talk this through with someone.

"A solemn swear, then. You can tell me anything at all and I shan't utter a word of it. Penelope need never know."

That might sound insincere to the untrained ear, but I can tell she means it. "Penny is thoughtful and kind, and she's talented without being narcissistic about it. There's so much about her that I adore. But it turns out that she may not have the same sort of interests that you and I do. Physically speaking. She's...asexual."

"That seems a bit cruel to the poor thing. I know I only just met her properly, and she might be a bit frumpy, but to call her that—"

"No, sweetie. She quite literally doesn't experience sexual attraction the same way that your average human does, and she has little to no interest in sex."

"Oh," she says softly. "I'm sorry, Anthea." Every now and then, she drops the facade, and I always appreciate these moments of earnestness.

"Honestly, it's a disappointment, but I want to believe that this isn't the end of the world."

"Perhaps, but sex is such a delightful activity! All that energy and emotion compressed into such a pure experience. The way humans just *feel* everything and reflect it right back out! I'm not sure I could properly get close to someone who wasn't interested in it."

"Hmm, is it really all that important, though? It's nice, don't get me wrong, but lots of things are nice." Like buttered noodles, I find myself thinking. Like bingeing a show together, or dancing close to the strains of a jazz standard.

Matilde looks at me like I've just said something utterly ridiculous. She doesn't say anything right away, just studies me for a moment. There's something brewing in her head. Another clever scheme. "You know, I think it's worth pointing out that there *are* ways for the two of you to experience a kind of special intimacy that might just suit both your needs. Something that may provide the necessary degree of separation from the act itself."

I gasp and sit up excitedly, feeling like a fool for not thinking of this sooner. "Goodness, do you think? I don't know, I haven't done that in nearly half a century."

"I'll say it again—duck to water, darling! You never really forget. And it's not so different from our normal job, when you get right down to it. You simply have to…adjust your aim slightly." She makes a gun with her right hand and points it at me before suggestively simulating the hammer drop with her thumb. "Bang. And a pleasant time is had by all."

The room feels several degrees hotter than it did just a moment ago. Merely thinking about doing something like that with Penny is leaving me flustered. "Well. I suppose it's worth a try."

We eventually lapse into talking about anything and everything. Even with all our phone calls over the last decade, being in the same space together is a different matter. We share memories, swap stories, and she catches me up on all the latest Hollywood gossip—even though she knows it means almost nothing to me. It's only when the last call goes out that I realize just how many hours have passed us by.

Matilde kisses me fondly on the cheek and gives me a winning smile. "I'd say it's time for me to retire to my accommodations for the evening. Good luck with Penelope, little sister. It sounds like a tricky predicament, but I know you'll be all right."

I truly hope she's right. Penny is the best thing to happen to me in well over a century, and I refuse to lose her.

* * *

After so many weeks to get to this point, there's something almost melancholy about today. Our final session on this portrait— an end to something wonderful. But I was thankfully able to grow close enough to Penny that we doubtless have much more art to make together.

Still, for our first foray, this will always be special to me.

Unlike our usual pattern, Penny refuses to let me actually look at the portrait when she's finished. "No no, I still have to make sure it's properly sealed. And I want to see your reaction when it's actually, really, completely done. Not a moment before." She practically shoves me out of the room before I get a chance to sneak a peek.

So I'm forced to sit on my hands in the living room and let the minutes tick by while she coats the finished canvas in a few layers of fixative. She's just lucky that her dedication to the craft is so endearing.

When Penny calls me in, I'm practically vibrating with excitement. The moment I enter the room, my eyes home in on the canvas instantly.

Of course, my figure takes up the bulk of the image. Penny has managed to capture a kind of easy elegance in my form and a peaceful comfort in my features. The room is warm and cozy, the books on the shelves behind me a sea of colors and tones inviting the viewer to join me in exploring new worlds together.

From the pages of the book in my hands, a kind of blooming effect emerges and fills the air around me. It distorts the space into a hazy, abstract dreamscape of tiny colored blotches. I can make out the shape of four figures traveling together down a yellow road, and a remote English manor flanked by gray specters. At the center of it all is the dim darkness of a lonely cave, illuminated by a glowing bonfire that reveals the shape of someone drawing on the walls with a burnt stick.

The portrait is beautifully evocative, and it gives me some textured insight into how Penny sees me. By simply existing, I bring art to life and give creations dimension. There's a warmth in my chest that I wish I knew how to bottle.

I suddenly realize that she's been waiting on me to say something. "So, um. What do you think?"

"I think it's perfect. Truly. Thank you."

"N-No, thank *you*. We should celebrate, right? I feel like we ought to celebrate."

"I thought that was the whole point of gathering after the battle this weekend. Shining a bright spotlight on the Hartwell twins in honor of their dual artistic accomplishments."

"The vibe's gonna be garbage if they don't win."

"Then I guess Terra Vertebrae had better bring their A game." I gently lean into Penny and smile. "How was their rehearsal the other night?"

"There was some argument about what they'd be playing. I think Theo was rooting for 'Switch-Hitter with a Wrench.' Don't get me wrong, it's a solid song about a bisexual mechanic. But I reminded him that narrative pieces don't tend to wow people as much as something that's a little more universal. So Celeste eventually bullied everyone into agreeing to play 'Shuttle Crash.' Which I think is for the best."

"That's good. I know you've been really hyping that one up, and I'm excited to hear it finally." As nice as it is to chat idly about the future, most of me is still situated very much in the present. I turn to face Penny and take her hands, lightly massaging them while urging her to face me as well. "Still, if you want to do something with just the two of us, I do have an idea. Are your hands tired, or do you think you could handle a bit more drawing tonight?"

She looks understandably confused. I know I'm being obtuse at the moment. "You want to celebrate finishing this behemoth by putting me right back to work?"

I laugh softly and massage her hands a bit more firmly. "I was thinking more about what you told me. About you being asexual, and the two of us learning how to share intimacy in a way you're comfortable with."

"What'd you have in mind?" Some of that confusion has started to shift into suspicion, and I know I need to tread carefully here.

"I believe I mentioned that being captured through art is something of a taboo for my family."

"Oh, um, yeah. Not exactly verboten, but not encouraged either."

"Part of the reason is that acting as the focus of a work can have…unintended side effects."

Her eyes widen slightly and her cheeks go pink. "Oh, god, all this time, have you been getting off while I was working?"

It's obviously a legitimate question, and I know that she needs comfort, but another laugh still bubbles out of me. "No! No, just warm fuzzies, that's all." I give her a moment to breathe a sigh of relief before continuing, "However, that being said? Yes, if I provide my spark in a particular way, under the right circumstances, it can be something akin to a sexual experience. But it's also circuitous and one-sided—a selfish act that I don't normally have the opportunity to indulge in. Given our situation, though, it seems like it might be worth trying something…selfish."

I can still feel the nervous hesitation washing off her. This is a gamble, and we're both taking it on faith that this will work. "I guess we can give it a shot. How does it work?"

"Is it safe to assume you have your sketchbook with you?"

"Never leave home without it," she says with a soft chuckle, bending down to fish it out.

"Then all you need is your instrument of choice, and we can head into my bedroom." I lay it on a bit thicker, allowing a suggestive tone to enter my voice. It feels like we're finally progressing toward an answer to things. And I'm eager to the point of carelessness.

Penny nearly drops her sketchbook before standing and grabbing the nearby case of charcoal. "Well, as long as we're selfishly indulging, I might as well treat myself too."

"That's the spirit," I coo before leaving to sashay dramatically across the hall and into my bedroom.

CHAPTER TWENTY-SEVEN

Penny

I really want this to work. I want to find a way that both of us can be happy. So I go scrambling across the hall after Anthea like the gremlin I am. She's putting on this goddess routine, and then there's dusty little Penny trailing in her wake. But she wants this from me, so I guess I don't look nearly as pathetic as I feel.

It's not lost on me that this is my first time actually entering Anthea's bedroom. I've seen inside it a few times on my way to the bathroom or our little studio. Her bedroom has a similar energy to the rest of the apartment. There's the usual signs of wealth—a large four-post canopy bed, quality sheets, expensive decorations—but it's clearly lived in. The bed isn't made, and a few of her clothes lie on the floor next to the hamper or draping off of it. She has a massive vanity against one wall with a string of lights running across the top, but the contents are spread out haphazardly. The lamp in the corner has some kind of fabric over it that bathes the whole space in a warm glow.

I'm so busy looking around the room and taking it all in that I completely miss the fact that Anthea is turned away from me, sliding her way out of her dress. She makes it look effortless, because of course she does. Unzip, shoulder, shimmy, and then let that bad boy drop. It pools around her feet, and she casually kicks it into the corner to join the clothes on the floor. As she reaches to unclasp her fancy bra, she looks back my way with a coy smile. "I'm not going to be your first nude model or anything, right?"

"Of course not." It's a classic artist thing. You draw so many bodies, you get over the whole nudity thing within a few weeks. You don't gawk, you study. You assess the shapes and curves and break them down into component pieces and shadows and skeletons. By the end of your first year, you don't even blush when the robe goes down.

But we're not in a classroom. We're in her fucking *boudoir*. And this isn't some model being paid twenty bucks an hour. This is Anthea. The energy is completely different. That's not a bad thing, exactly, but it doesn't do anything for my nerves. It's giving me flashbacks to everything with Juniper, and the only thing saving me right now is that I'm clutching a sketchbook and plastic case to my chest. They're my security blanket in this unquestionably sexy scenario. A million artists would kill to be in my position—meanwhile, I'm just focused on remembering to breathe.

But I tell myself that Anthea needs this, just judging by how pleased with herself she looks at the moment. Even if I'm a little uncomfortable, I want to believe that this will be good for both of us.

I'm fully aware of the basic shape of Anthea's body at this point. Even when I'm not working on her portrait, she's worn enough different outfits that I can pretty well tell what she's got going on. Logically, I know what to expect, and I keep it analytical. Golden-beige skin speckled everywhere with deep freckles, strong shoulders, generous hips. I know that her arms are just a touch longer than average for her height. Some part of me can filter all this information quickly and easily in a totally professional way.

Even the "embarrassing" bits, I can appreciate in an aesthetic way. Her breasts are a touch on the small side, but she holds herself so confidently. And while all of her looks classically statuesque already, I can safely say that her butt is particularly sculpted.

But for some reason, more than anything, I find myself lingering for just a moment on her ankles. Like I'm a scandalized Victorian.

She finishes removing her underwear and glides her way onto her bed before finding her pose. Just like always, she slips into it with seamless ease. Her back leg is bent at the knee, the forward one crooked slightly inward as if trying to maintain a shred of dignity. She rests her arms across her belly, staring upward at the ceiling with a thoughtful expression. Even her hair—now unpinned—seems to fall into line, draping across the pillows in a way that is just far too perfect. Whether it's experience or just another part of her super special muse magic, I have no clue.

I grab the plush chair from the vanity and drag it over, but it's heavier than I assumed and makes a kind of squeaky noise as I do so. So there's flawless, sexy Anthea lying on her bed, and then there's awkward, schlubby Penny wrestling with a goddamn chair. She looks infinitely comfortable in her nudity, and I'm struggling to feel human in my tattered hoodie with the hole forming in the elbow.

Whatever, push it down, keep moving.

I lug the chair over until I'm parallel with the bed and plant myself into it. The moment I'm in place with my notebook in my lap and a chunk of coal in my hand, the familiar feeling of her spark washes over me.

She's usually more gentle with it, sending it out in careful waves that ebb and flow in a very natural way. But even I can tell that there's something different about it now. Anthea mentioned that she would have to change up her methods, flex her muscles differently or whatever, but it didn't really occur to me that it would be so…palpable.

The good news is that this immediately pushes me back into the zone. Having something to focus on does keep those worries and anxieties at bay. I lay out the most basic shape for the bed just to give myself something to work with, then get started on Anthea's face and her hair splayed out so perfectly.

For a while, everything goes smoothly enough. I've adjusted to the stronger force of her influence, and my hands are working in concert to create this image. Even with only darkness and shading to play with, I've captured the slight flush in her cheeks and the hazy delight in her eyes.

Then I swoop the charcoal to form her neck, and Anthea lets out a small sigh of pleasure that causes my hand to freeze up. It's only a second, but it's enough to shake me. As much as I tell myself that this is just art on my end of things, the stark reality is that I'm pleasuring her.

That's when she hits me with another wave of inspiration that pushes me to continue, urging me on without saying a word.

But as I start on the curves of her breasts, Anthea's reactions get more pronounced. Those sighs are turning into moans, and she's squirming slightly. Gone is the poised beauty who knows how to hold her posture for a full hour, replaced with someone I almost don't recognize. None of my live nude model classes were like this.

I soldier on, certain that sooner or later I'll finally find the right rhythm here and we'll fall into that easy pattern we always find. It should be so simple. We've done it a dozen times now.

But with each line, she gets more emphatic and passionate. Anthea is barely bothering to suppress her moans, and she occasionally rubs her thighs together or glances over at me with a longing in her features that begs for something I'm not comfortable giving.

Gripping the charcoal with forced intention, I make an honest attempt to get down the curve of her hips. But when Anthea lets loose with a girlish squeak and bucks, I finally have to set down the sketchbook and drop my utensil back into the case on the floor. "I'm sorry, I can't do this."

Anthea pushes herself up to a seated position and self-consciously holds an arm across her chest. "Was that too much? Do you need a break?" Her concern is clear and earnest, but she's still flush with desire that's difficult to look at directly.

So I stare down at the floor and cradle my forehead in my hands, taking a few slow breaths. That's easier said than done with how much I'm shaking. "I don't think a break's gonna cut it. I'm sorry," I repeat unnecessarily as my voice cracks. "You needed

this so much, but it's pretty clear now that I'm just too broken."
There's a stone of guilt in my stomach as soon as I say that word.
This far into my life, I should know better than to confuse a sexual
mismatch with some kind of inherent flaw. But I'm too shaken to
think this through logically. At this point, it's insecurities all the
way down.

I take some time to just focus on my breathing. Anthea busies
herself with something, and after a while she comes over and gets
my attention by lightly putting a hand on each of my cheeks,
drawing me out of my minor anxiety attack. I must have been
down in my hole longer than I realized, because she's already
gotten dressed in some shorts and a T-shirt. "Hey. Look at me."

I sniffle softly and meet her gaze. She hasn't managed to
completely erase that look of arousal, but at least now I can
clearly see the care and concern—which feels like far more than
I deserve. "I'm sorry." Third time's a charm. I have no idea what
else to say here. Anthea has spent so many years being hurt by
the people she's let close to her. And she was so sure that she'd
found someone different, someone who could finally make her
feel worthwhile. And she did, I guess, but maybe I'm *too* different.

"You have nothing to apologize for," she says gently, wiping at
my face where I must have smeared some dust during my panic
attack.

"But—"

Pressing a finger to my lips, Anthea pulls me over to sit with
her on the edge of the bed. With an arm wrapped around me, it
only takes the bare minimum of encouragement for me to lean
against her shoulder, my sniffling threatening to turn into full-on
crying.

After a beat, she speaks again. "If anyone here should be
apologizing, it's me. You were quite clear the other night that
this is a difficult thing for you. But I pushed because I thought it
would be the secret key we needed. A simple answer for a difficult
question. And it's obvious now that I was right about how selfish
it is, albeit in an unintended way."

Goddamn it, why is she being so fucking *nice* about this? It's
all too much, and it finally hits me. One sob manages to wrench
its way out of me, and the dam breaks.

Anthea, despite being an ancient muse, is the normal one here. I'm the outlier, the weirdo, the freak. And when she realizes that we're not going to work—whether that's tonight or in a few weeks—she'll have to break up with me, and she'll be right to do so.

I'm nothing but tears and snot and pathetic whimpering, and when Anthea passes me a gorgeous lacy handkerchief with the intention of me using it…I don't know, that just feels like yet another perfect metaphor for our situation, and it threatens to send me even deeper down the spiral. *Here, hideous mewling creature, take this lovely thing and ruin it with your filth.* Anthea's got coal dust on her hands and I'm about to tarnish this beautiful piece of fabric. Something about me, some core component, has been rubbing off on her, and it's so obvious that we're too different. So obvious that we don't fit together.

She brushes my hair lightly, not saying anything, nor does she prompt me to try to pick the conversation back up. She just holds me for long enough that I lose all track of time.

Only when my horrible noises and disgusting fluids cease does she make an attempt at comforting me again. "Penny, you're not broken. You're the kind of person who feels so guilty over drawing a stranger that you apologize to her the first chance you get. Even realizing how difficult it was to truly know me, you stuck it out. And when I told you about my anxieties over the gala, you were willing to go with me, in spite of your own complicated feelings. You're strong."

This is all very sweet and supportive. But any set of actions can sound good devoid of context. "That wasn't strength. Just a useful confluence of all my character flaws. A shoddily constructed facade built with anxiety and obsession and shit."

I don't expect her to start laughing softly as she squeezes me affectionately. "Honestly, you really deserve to give yourself a bit more credit. And so what if any of that is true? You still did those things, and that means the world to me." She lightly caresses my cheek with her thumb and smiles. "The night isn't ruined. If you like, I'd still be happy to have you stay here. We won't do anything you don't want to do. Just cuddle up together under the covers, and then have ourselves a lazy morning."

That does sound amazing. But as much as I want it, I'm wrestling with way too much, and I just don't have it in me to cuddle her, pretending that everything is okay—that I haven't made things supremely uncomfortable and difficult. So I carefully extract myself from her touch and stand, starting to gather my things. I really thought I'd finally learned to outgrow the Hartwell Twins Special, and yet here I go again. "I uh…I have an early shift tomorrow."

"Penny—" For a moment, it looks like she's going to call me out on my supremely obvious lie. But finally she just gives a resigned sigh and stares down at her lap. "I'll…see you at the battle?"

"Yeah, of course. Saturday."

We share a brief kiss, but it's tentative and full of all the things we're not really saying. And I can't help worrying that it's a portent of our inevitable split. No matter what she says, there's just too many things wrong with me for this to work. Sooner or later, we'll both admit it.

It's cold and raining as I step outside, because of course it fucking is. What other kind of weather would there be in the wake of my absolute failure as a girlfriend? So I pull up the hood of my sweatshirt and start making the journey toward Copley station. In a way, there is something almost comforting about this weather, like the skies are trying to sympathize with me.

Stupid, idiot Penny thought she could have a normal relationship. And it would be one thing if the problem was Anthea being all special and magic. But no, it's me, because of course it fucking is. I'm the abnormal one in the relationship.

I put on my headphones and blast some uncharacteristically aggressive punk rock into my ears to try to drown out the noise of my own mind.

When a train finally does roll through the station, I'm distressed to find it packed to the gills with people. Looking around at all of them, I just feel that much more depressed. There are drunk couples pawing each other in the back corner, and some businessman having an obnoxiously loud conversation on his phone that I can somehow hear despite Johnny Ramone doing his best.

How long do we have before we break, I wonder. Anthea is so goddamn nice sometimes, I'm worried she's going to force herself to stick it out on my account, and that definitely doesn't feel great. I don't want to drag her down just because she's trying to avoid hurting my feelings.

She deserves better than me.

CHAPTER TWENTY-EIGHT

Anthea

I'm woken up by a call from the front desk concierge, though I can't imagine why. Bleary-eyed and yawning, I sit up and grab the receiver. "Yes?"

"Miss Corey, there's a woman here claiming to be your… sister?"

Hell. I forgot I told Matilde to come by and look at the portrait. I think about sending her away. I'm not in the mood for company right now. I want to wallow, dammit. But the woman is a force of nature that will not be deterred. And she'd never let me hear the end of it.

Even though I do my best to wash my face and put my best foot forward, it's obvious the moment I open the door that Matilde knows something is off. But for whatever reason, she doesn't say anything about it, she just breezes past me.

"Well? Let's see it, dear!"

"Right, um, over here." I lead the way over to the spare room and open the door.

Matilde strolls in casually and I follow in her wake, finding myself strangely nervous to see her reaction. She doesn't even say anything right away. The two of us just stand there and study it— or rather, she studies it, and I try to fight the pang of guilt I get from looking at it. The monument to my folly.

When that becomes too much to bear, I look toward my sister instead. Her face, usually so vibrant and expressive, is completely impossible to read. Matilde just taps her index finger against her arm, lips pressed tight together.

And then, just like that, she looks back at me as her face lights up. "I've been meaning to pay a visit to the fabled Boston Aquarium while I'm in town. I hear it's marvelous. The penguins, you understand, I must witness them."

The change in topic is so sudden that I'm experiencing momentary whiplash. "And…what about the portrait?"

"I wanted to see it, and now I've seen it. The woman has talent, and she's captured you expertly. Penelope was worth putting time into. But judging by the state I've found you in, what you need right now is to not think about her for a while. And so, you and I will be enjoying a bit of maritime diversion."

She's not wrong. I can't shake the feeling that things with myself and Penny are becoming untenable. And an afternoon at the aquarium would be far more healthy than moping uselessly around my apartment. Still, I find myself resisting. "The battle—"

"Isn't until tonight, and I promise I will get us both there on time. Now what do you say?"

"Okay. Maritime diversion it is."

True to her word, the moment we're inside the building, Matilde makes a beeline for the penguin exhibit. And I have to admit, they're adorable. Waddling, squawking, swimming.

Penguin things.

For how strange they look on land, it really is a thing of beauty to watch them gracefully slide into the water and go shooting around. I find myself drawn to a rockhopper with an incredibly vibrant yellow brow who does barrel rolls for treats.

Matilde gestures excitedly to one of the South African penguins. "You know, those ones there are sometimes referred to as 'jackass penguins.' Not because they're rude—I believe they're fairly sociable—but because they make a noise similar to a donkey braying."

I had assumed that she was doing me a favor by bringing me here. But now I'm thinking that maybe Matilde had always intended to come here and marvel at these creatures. She seems legitimately enthused by them. This is the sister that I know and love—the one so few people get to see.

We spend nearly fifteen minutes just enjoying the antics of the stylish birds. It really is doing a lot to distract me and keep me from worrying about the world outside this building.

Having apparently had her fill, Matilde eventually turns and starts making her way down a random hallway. We enter a darkened area filled with tanks of jellyfish glowing softly under black lights. Without any prompting, Matilde suddenly says in a conversational tone, "Do you recall our sibling Samius?"

"Please, must we do this?"

"It's important, Anthea."

Of course I remember Samius. They're part of a pantheon that lives in poor Matilde's mind—alongside Erato, Isabella, and many more. If she were of a different disposition, their names would be attached to a corkboard covered in red string and blurry photographs.

So I sigh and nod, and join her in pretending to look at the jellyfish, even though this has obviously turned into something other than a simple museum excursion to clear my head. Instead, she wants to dredge up this madness. "Yes, you were as close to them during the early decades of the first modern millennium as you are to me now. They were your best friend and closest confidant. Until 'that bastard sculptor' Falax captured their heart. Next thing you knew, they were gone."

"Dropped off the face of the Earth itself, dear. Couldn't even sense them anymore, just a gaping void where they once stood. I had my suspicions, ever since Erato went missing after all that business with Sappho. Never did like that woman. But Samius was what clinched it for me, in the end."

Maybe Matilde thinks I've somehow forgotten this during my brief constitutional. As though I could forget one of the greatest mysteries of our kind. It's as rare as a planetary alignment, and it only ever happens to muses that have taken human form. The common assumption was that muses stopped existing when their duty was over. If you inspire enough grand works, you achieve a kind of nirvana.

So when Samius went missing, Matilde's suspicions were properly ignited. After all, Falax was a small-time artist. Talented, but hardly prolific. If Samius's disappearance couldn't be attributed to sparking a work of true significance, then she figured that the problem lay with Falax. And unfortunately, he wasn't alive to answer any probing questions by the time she'd decided he was a suspect.

I try to head all this off, speed things along so she'll get to the point quicker, and we can resume enjoying ourselves. "But you didn't achieve true Prophet Cassandra status until…the War of the Roses, if I recall correctly?"

"I am forever ashamed that I can't even remember the knave's name. All I know is that one day, Isabella is telling me how deeply in love she is, and by war's end, she was gone too. He took her from us. *Love* took her from us."

She says the word like it's a curse. In her mind, that's precisely what love is.

We need to move past this. Like I'm giving a history lecture, I move things toward their conclusion with an appropriately academic tone. "At which point your darling sister Anthea convinced you that perhaps there was no sense in driving yourself mad over some perceived threat that you cannot possibly fight. She stood by you while few others would. And together, the two of you set off on a quest to inspire the best art you could while enjoying all that this world had to offer."

Even this walk down memory lane cannot fully distract me from my interpersonal troubles. After all, Penny and I have this in common, too—a sibling that we chose over family, and a shared dedication to our craft. How am I supposed to recover from what happened if even the most distant topic just makes me think of her all over again?

"Centuries of good times. I was able to let go of my suspicions and find joy again. When you contemplated quitting, I..." Matilde's face contorts, and she once again starts walking without any warning, leading us up the central spiral of the aquarium around the massive, cylindrical tank. "I was terrified that I would lose you too. But I knew that I could handle a decade, so long as I had the promise that you would return. And I was right. I managed well enough. Before I knew it, the last grain of sand had passed through the hourglass, and it was just like old times again."

She's winding up, and I can see now that I am absolutely not going to be free of Penny any time soon. The trajectory of her speech is clear. But still she takes a dramatic pause and watches as a massive turtle goes floating past us, not a care in the world.

"Then, along comes Miss Charcoal. And whatever it is she's done to you, whatever witchcraft she possesses, I find you *glowing*. Like that bloody Citgo eyesore downtown." She says "glowing" the same way she says "love." That carefully crafted mask of hers has finally slipped and revealed some very real hurt underneath. But just as suddenly, it gives way to something even more raw than that, something harder to parse. Guilt, perhaps, or embarrassment. "Normally, this would be the part where I'd feel betrayed, on the precipice of being abandoned yet again."

"Normally? What changed?"

With a sigh, she reaches into her purse and fishes around for a moment before carefully extracting a folded piece of paper. She's looking at it more than at me. "Our brother Isaac...While you were off taking your vacation, I found I could no longer sense him anywhere. But it had happened recently enough that I thought, well, even if he was...gone, then he must still have left some clues behind. And there *have* been quite a few developments in the world of information and technology since the War of the Roses."

"Oh, Matilde, you didn't."

"Without your steadying influence, I went back to my old ways. I spent no small amount of money hiring someone to track him down. And...they did. I had an address and a phone number. But still, I found myself scared to reach out. Can you believe that? All the things I've done in my long life, all that postulating on the nature of our existence, and *that's* what stopped me in my tracks. But when you began telling me about this amazing human you'd met, I finally found the necessary strength to call him. I had to know."

I'm bracing for the impact now. This is a revelation well over a millennium in the making.

"Anthea, he—" She shakes her head slowly in disbelief. "He's alive—and I use that word here very intentionally. He's mortal, Anthea. That's why I could no longer sense him. He has a husband. They raise sheep together in New Zealand. Our siblings, they didn't 'poof.' They chose to abandon their inspiration in exchange for a normal life—to grow old and die with someone."

This is a lot to take in at once, but I'm sure she's well aware of that fact. So Matilde gives me the necessary time to sit with it. I exhale and give a small nod. "Okay."

"Okay?"

"Okay. So…true love really was the answer all this time? Just not in the way you'd thought?"

She smiles, maybe for the first time allowing herself to process the irony of it all. "Essentially. I didn't press him on the specifics. But perhaps, someday, you might want to know more." She passes the small slip of paper to me, pressing it into my hand with pomp and circumstance as though she were giving me the nuclear codes. I suppose, in her mind, that's precisely what she's doing. "You're all I have in this world, Anthea. I hope you know that. Strip it all away, it's just you."

I carefully slip the paper into my pocket, then give Matilde a concerned look. "This is all very sweet, I assure you, and it means more than words can express that I have your blessing. But it doesn't do me much good, considering the way things are between me and Penny right now."

"I had hoped to make it clear you had my blessing when I gave you that precious nugget of an idea the other night. But I also get the impression that things didn't go the way you and I had hoped?"

I shake my head, and we finally resume our ascent up the spiral walkway. "Penny…did not react well at all. She tried, bless her heart, but to no avail. Honestly, I don't even know why I let myself get so worried about her asexuality in the first place."

"I thought it was rather straightforward. Compatibility issues can be quite serious. If there's an incongruence, divisions may form."

"That's the thing, I don't even know if I would call this an 'incongruence,' Matilde. I think some part of me…feels the same way that she does? Yes, I've had plenty of intimate encounters in my life. But I find myself struggling to remember how often I engaged in such things in a truly carnal way. It was a chance for closeness, for intimate give-and-take."

She gives me that look again, as though I'm speaking an entirely different language from her. "I'm afraid I may need you to elaborate for me, dear."

"Take Dmitri, for example."

"I would rather not, but go on," she says, letting a playful grin tug at her lips.

"The more I think back, the more uncertain I am that I ever initiated sex with him because I knew that it would feel good, or because I had some burning need for it. Nine times out of ten, it was just a way to appease him, or to show my gratitude for letting me be his muse." I feel almost ill saying that out loud. It's not a pleasant realization, to come to the conclusion that I used sex— used myself—as a means of ensuring that my artists found me useful and attractive outside of my inspiration.

After some thought, Matilde nods slowly. "I won't pretend to be an expert on the matter, but based on what you've said, perhaps you have more in common with Penelope than you realize."

It's a simple point, but it does feel momentarily eye-opening. Could it be possible? In spite of all my years and lived experience, this is something I never put much thought into. And I find myself wishing Penny were here to help walk me through it. As hard as it was for her to accept something like that about herself, she seems knowledgeable about it.

But even if she were right here with me, that wouldn't be an immediate fix. There's still the thorny matter of how we left things, that gnawing sense of separation developing between us.

"Be that as it may, I can't imagine she wants much to do with me right now."

To my surprise, Matilde just laughs as we reach the top floor of the aquarium, leaning over to peer down into the massive tank below. "Oh, tosh. That woman is in love with you. As you are with her. Or you will be, by summer's end, I would wager."

It's a shock to hear her say that, never mind the fact that she doesn't look like she's going to vomit for once when the word "love" passes her lips. "Wh—How can you be so sure? You didn't see the way she looked at me the other night."

"I suppose I didn't. But you know what I did see, darling? I saw the glow in that portrait, and in you, and the way it's practically suffused itself throughout your entire apartment. You and Penelope share something special. So do me a favor, dear sister, and *talk to the woman*. Because honestly, if one awkward encounter was all it took to ruin a relationship, I would have far fewer conquests in my wake." Matilde gives me a cheeky grin, and I think for just a moment about shoving her into the water. "And if you find yourself balking at the battle tonight, I'll be there to give you the necessary nudge. I promise."

Finally I relent and join her in looking down at the marine life below. Even with all my uncertainty and worries, I find myself starting to smile again. "By summer's end, eh?"

"I'd stake my tune against your spark, confidently. You'll see, love."

CHAPTER TWENTY-NINE

Penny

Even this early in the day, the Lunar Theater is a hive of activity. There are a lot of bands that need to perform tonight, and it takes hard work to keep things moving along steadily.

But it's also one of those hurry-up-and-wait situations. I came over with the band, mostly to act as their volunteer roadie and moral support, as per usual. We unloaded the stuff, and Celeste had to go through some boring paperwork and scheduling nonsense. The whole time, we're constantly dodging the dozen other bands there to compete. It's hardly the biggest venue in town. The Lunar Theater used to show movies back in the fifties, closed down in the sixties, and was bought out in the nineties, revived into what has now become a fixture of the local music scene. But because of its origins, there's only so much room for all these people.

The four of us are left to just sit in the empty back of Cameron's van, in a parking lot full of vehicles with equally anxious bands. It's almost an hour before their sound check, another two hours before curtain, and Terra Vertebrae still has to wait until it's their turn to go on. So the energy is weird. Everyone is tense and eager to go, and we're forced to just chill here and cool our heels.

It doesn't help that I'm being kind of a joy vacuum at the moment. I've spent most of the day in a quiet funk. So much for moral support.

Celeste is actually the one to finally press the subject, to my surprise. "Everything good, Penny?"

"Huh? Yeah, I'm whatever." I don't have the energy to pretend more than that. So it's a paper-thin cover.

"Honestly, 'whatever' seems generous," Cameron says. "Seriously, what's up?"

I brush my fingers through my hair and stare down at the cheap carpet covering the floor of the van. I'm really torn between wanting to talk everything through, and the mortifying ordeal of being known. Today is Terra Vertebrae's big day, and they don't need me shredding their positive energy with my nonsense.

I don't expect Theo to be the one to cut right to the point. "C'mon, out with it. Lemme guess—girl trouble? I thought things were going good with Anthea. Seriously, I haven't seen that look on your face since everything went down with that Juniper girl." It's nice to know that our heart-to-heart has had a positive effect on Theo. He's really been pushing himself to actually talk about stuff lately. It kinda feels like I've got my brother back, more than ever before. And maybe it's because he's putting in the effort that I feel like I should do the same.

"God, am I that easy to read? Yeah. It's a real second-verse situation."

The others look understandably confused, and Celeste sits up a little. "And what did the first verse sound like?"

So yet again, I lay out the details of that incredibly uncomfortable night back in grad school. The only upshot is that it's forcing me to say the words "I'm asexual" a lot. That probably counts for something. "Anyway, so that's kinda happening with Anthea now. And it just feels like it's going to keep on happening forever."

"Yikes." Cameron takes a pull from his weed pen and shakes his head. "That's fucked-up."

He offers the pen to me, and after some contemplation, I cave to the gentle peer pressure and take a few hits to calm my nerves. "I know, I know. It sucks no matter which way you look at it."

"Nah, not that. What Juniper did to you."

I actually do a double take as I pass the vape over to Celeste, who's making grabby hands at me. "How do you figure? She was super nice and reasonable about it."

"I've heard the way you describe your family. You two know firsthand that nice and kind are two different things. Unless you skipped part of the story, she didn't sit down and hash this out with you until you reached a mutual conclusion. She cut you out of the entire process and figured it out herself, then dumped you because *she* decided that was the right thing to do. That's shitty behavior."

Cameron is making a decent point, but I'm not sure I really agree. "She cut and ran. I'd be a massive hypocrite if I judged her for that. Theo knows what I'm talking about."

My brother looks surprised to suddenly be drawn into the equation. "I do?"

"Yeah, man. The Hartwell Twins Special. If things are heading south, get the hell out of there."

I'm positive he'll catch on, but he just keeps looking at me with a quirked eyebrow. "If we have a special move, this is the first I'm hearing of it."

"We cut out the family when their bullshit got to be too much. You dropped out of college. I constantly switched out of classes that were too much work. All the bands you've bounced between. Me waiting so long to start hormones."

Theo snags the vape from Celeste and takes a pull before chuckling softly. "Yeah, emancipating ourselves was a lot of fun, and definitely the easy path. And it's not like I just ran out on the other bands I was in. We fought constantly until we broke up. Terra Vertebrae is the first time I've been in something stable." He looks at the others fondly, then back at me. "Honestly, I'm not even sure that stuff is true for you. It doesn't matter if you took easier classes, you still got a fucking master's. And you haven't quit your shitty job at the station, no matter how much that sucks. Being a girl has made you way happier, but it's been stressful for a lot of different reasons that are much too heavy for this already heavy conversation. Hell, this relationship doesn't sound like a cakewalk, but you've stuck it out presumably because it's worthwhile."

It suddenly feels a little like my world is crashing down around me—yet another earth-shattering revelation in as many weeks. There was no Hartwell Twins Special. Just Penny Making Excuses. I wasn't walking out on things because it's some kind of secret combo attack. I was scared.

"Cool, so I've been buying in to a lie I told myself for years now, and it probably ruined things with my girlfriend. I love that for me."

Cameron chuckles softly as the vape gets back around to him. "Join the fuckin' club. I'm pretty sure that's just life. Anyway, she'll be here tonight, right?"

"Theoretically. But I wouldn't blame her if she decided to skip." Still, I'm almost positive Matilde will be here. And that woman doesn't seem like she'd let Anthea get away with staying home.

"She better not," Celeste says seriously. "She promised to cheer us on, and we need the support."

Still chuckling with raspy amusement, Cameron takes another puff. "C'mon, Celeste, there are more important reasons for her to show."

"I know, I know, because it would give Penny a chance to reconcile, and that's wonderful and beautiful—"

"No, because she's supposed to be throwing the after-party at her place!"

Whether it's the camaraderie or the THC, my spirits have finally begun to lift, and I start laughing at his sense of priorities.

While it may not be much to go off of, the band sounds really fucking good during sound check. I even caught sight of the sound tech bobbing his head along to the music between fiddling with the sliders on his board. Terra Vertebrae has a chance to bring down the house tonight.

With that done, there's not much else going on until the actual show. So we take our collective high over to the nearby McDonald's to fuel up. On the way back inside the theater, I give

Theo and the others a round of tight hugs. "All right, you guys are gonna fucking murder tonight, you hear me? 'Shuttle Crash' is a guaranteed winner, and you've practiced it like a hundred times in just the past week alone. You got this."

Theo squeezes me for an extra few seconds before giving me a quick pat on the head. "Same goes for you. Be honest with her. If you don't wanna lose her, then give it all you've got."

I sigh with resignation and nod. What else can I do in the face of such overwhelming encouragement? "Thanks."

With that done, there's not much else but wait for the show to start. So I push my way through the crowd to hunt down our roommates.

I predictably find them both near the bar. Kai is typing away rapidly at his phone, no doubt still elbow-deep in some argument with the app's project lead. Meagan is chatting up the bartender—I swear she knows half the drink-slingers in Greater Boston.

Once I'm within range, they both turn their attention toward me as Kai sheathes his phone and Meagan spins around on her barstool to ask, "So, what's the good word? How're they looking?"

"I think they're gonna be fine. Theo's a little pissed that they're fifth in the roster."

"Why's that matter?"

"Something about performance order. The acts at the beginning and the end stick out in the audience's mind a little more. So Celeste is making sure they're as hyped as they can be, keeping the energy high and all that."

Someone to my right, way too close to my ear, says, "Well, then, we'd better make sure to scream our lungs out when the time comes."

I gasp and jump, turning to find Anthea standing there with Matilde hovering just behind her. Despite spending half the day feeling anxious about everything between us, the moment I see her face, I'm filled with warmth. If we manage to make it past this bump in the road, I will never take that feeling for granted again. "Anthea! Hi!"

"So, our mysterious benefactor finally shows her face," Kai says with a grin.

Meagan elbows him. "Apologies for this one. What he means is that it's a pleasure to meet ya." Her eyes flick over toward Matilde, eyebrows lifting slightly. "And who's yer Amazonian friend?"

Oh my god, she's flirting.

"Matilde de Leòn. Charmed." She holds out her hand, and Meagan takes it before kissing the middle knuckle softly.

Oh my god, they're *both* flirting. Please let the ground open and swallow me whole.

"Anthea is my sister." She catches a confused look on Kai's face and chuckles breathily. "Adopted."

We continue making introductions until everyone is properly acquainted. My roommates drag Matilde over to the bar to get some drinks, leaving me and Anthea alone—probably intentionally. I lightly clear my throat and rub the back of my neck. "I'll be honest, I wasn't sure if you were going to be coming here tonight."

"Well, I made a promise to support the band," she replies coolly. After a beat, she giggles softly. "Um, sorry. That was a poor attempt at a joke. I wanted to see you, of course."

She's right. Her delivery was a little bit too deadpan. But I'm caught so off guard that I start to laugh softly too. Things are awkward, but they could be much worse. I'll take whatever small victories I can get here. "Is it stupid if I say I missed you?"

"It's not stupid at all." She extends her hand to me, and after a moment's hesitation, I take it. Anthea laces our fingers together, and I really do start to feel like maybe things aren't so bad after all.

The lights slowly dim as a guy in a black B-Cubed T-shirt takes to the stage, illuminated by a bright spotlight. The room erupts in loud cheering.

Anthea has to lean in close until her lips are practically brushing against my earlobe. "I guess it's showtime. Come on." Before I know it, she's pulling me forward through the crowd to find a good spot.

The place is packed, spirits are high, and the competition is fierce. The Agents, Grayscale, Ten Again—it's a lot of big names against Theo's humble little trio.

I fully plan on only giving respectful applause to the other bands as a show of good faith, and nothing more. But the problem is that they're all fucking incredible. Some of them have fun gimmicks and unusual instruments, like Illuminati's horn section featuring a dedicated tuba player. Others, like reigning champs Deviltower Star, groove so well together it's obvious they're just here to have a good time.

The first four acts pass in a blur, and I don't even process what that means until the MC takes the stage again and gestures for the crowd to quiet down. "A'right, settle down folks. We still got a lot more to get through and it's gonna take twice as long if you don't shut your traps." While he goes through his patter, Theo and the others are getting in place behind him. "Up next, three first-timers to the battle scene! You may recognize them from their recent rousing performance at the lavish Park Street Station." Celeste couldn't figure out what she wanted him to say for their intro, so that was my suggestion. It gets a few awkward laughs. When it's clear that the bit has belly-flopped, the MC pivots to get some proper hype building. "Tonight, they're going to be debuting their new song, 'Shuttle Crash.' I caught a little bit during sound check, and it's a fuckin' banger. So please give a warm, *rowdy*, B-Cubed welcome to…Terra Vertebrae!"

While everyone else in the audience applauds—though I am excited to hear a smattering of legitimate cheering—I'm mostly just focused on breathing. And praying that Cameron doesn't try to get flashy like he did at that gig last month and drop his drumsticks in front of this huge crowd.

Thankfully, he doesn't bother. He just bangs the sticks together and counts Celeste in with a rapid-fire, "One-two-three-four, one-two-three-four!"

It's almost like he pulls the rip cord and sends her flying as she fires up the song's absolutely killer opening riff, fingers rattling up and down the frets with passionate precision. After a few bars, she leans in close to the mic and half-sings, half-growls, "I need some fucking air, and you don't even care," at which point Cam and Theo jump into the fray. While Celeste flies high with her angsty vocals and frenetic strumming, they gird her lightning with their thunder—a storm of rock and roll lighting up the spine of the world. "Let's crash this shuttle, just get it over." She slams her foot down on her effect pedal like she's a getaway driver. "Flip those three magic switches, tell me your three magic wishes. Fuck it! Let's slam into Mars and make friends with the rover."

Everyone gets a moment to shine. Cameron's drum work has all the energy of a spacecraft making an emergency landing nose-first into a mountain. And Theo's solo in the middle does an amazing job playing the role of the infuriating copilot, steady and sure and so annoying in the face of impending doom.

"The explosion will be monumental. But I'll miss you..." Celeste sings as the song finally reaches its conclusion, taking a single beat as the boys drop out, leaving her to strum one last painful chord: "being temperamental..."

It's never sounded like this. Celeste may have waited a long time to show "Shuttle Crash" off, but it was all worth it. They fucking nailed it. I'm so proud, and I scream my lungs out when it's over. Everyone else does too. I don't think I've ever heard Anthea so much as raise her voice before, but she's hooting like a drunk sorority girl. When the MC cuts us off, I look over at her, and we're both beaming. I think we've managed to inch closer to some kind of resolution here.

Every time we speak, we have to get good and close to hear one another over the din of the crowd. "Thanks for being here. I don't know if it was quite enough, but I'm glad they had so much support tonight." It's hard to put my finger on why, but the fact that she still supports Terra Vertebrae so earnestly affects me powerfully.

"I meant every throat-shattering holler. I believe in them. The same way I believe in you."

"Present tense?"

"Of course." She glances around, perhaps to see if she can catch sight of her sister. But she's still off being entertained by Kai and Meagan. "Well, we've seen the most important act. Would you like to maybe head outside for a bit and get some air?"

She wants to go somewhere quiet. With me. That must be good news. I'm really hoping it is. "God, yes please."

CHAPTER THIRTY

Anthea

It takes some struggling, but we manage to push past all the spectators, slip through the foyer, and spill out onto the sidewalk. Things are busy, even out here, and we end up having to make our way down the street a bit to find any proper peace and quiet. A handful of enterprising food trucks have set up shop outside the venue, so I buy us a pair of cheap coffees before finding a waist-high concrete planter where Penny and I can sit.

Penny blows on her coffee before taking a slow sip. "Okay, air, check. Even got some sweet caffeine. Was there…anything else you wanted to do? While we're out here?" Her voice has a hopeful lilt to it, which makes me feel hopeful in turn. We're both looking for good news here. I don't know if I have that, exactly, but I'll offer whatever I can.

"I wanted to apologize."

"I'm starting to sense a pattern with us," she mutters softly with a soft chuckle.

"Speaking from experience, this is definitely preferable to the alternative."

"Can't argue with that." Penny sighs and stares up ahead at the dark sky, devoid of any stars thanks to the light pollution. "I'm not sure you have anything to apologize for, really. I mean, I'm the one who went running for the hills because I got scared. If anyone should be apologizing, it's me, right?"

"Perhaps the best thing to do here is both admit that we could have handled the moment better and move forward together?"

She starts to nod, then stops herself with a firm shake of the head instead. "I want to. But a mea culpa—Er, a nos culpa? Whatever, the point is, that just glosses over everything. That's what I've always done, and it hasn't really been the most winning strategy. So I think maybe I need to talk things through."

In truth, I'm not much better at actually working things out as Penny is. I've done a fair bit of glossing myself over the last century. So this will be a challenge for both of us. "All right, then. Where do we start?"

"Uh, so, it has come to my attention that maybe what I thought was a major part of my personality is actually just a bad habit of running away from uncomfortable situations. Also, that the breakup I constantly compare everything against was neither mutual nor healthy. It's got me rethinking a bunch of stuff and… The only thing I really know for sure is that I don't want to run away from you. Never again. If anything, I like knowing that I have a place I can run *to*."

"I like that too," I say before shuffling a bit closer to Penny, grateful that the two of us are finding the courage to be close again, and gently bump my hips against hers. "I want my home to be a safe, welcoming place for you. And I hope I didn't tarnish that by making your first time in my bedroom so…difficult."

"Yeah, that wasn't ideal. But things aren't tarnished, just a little weird. And I definitely want to be comfortable there. Now that I'm not in such an awful headspace, I can safely say that spending a night cuddled up together, followed by a lazy morning? That sounds incredible. So I'm ready to put in the effort here."

"That's good to hear. I was a little worried you might not even want to see me ever again."

"If anything, I was just angry with myself—for being abnormal, for running away, for…a lot of things."

I carefully lean my way over and rest against Penny's shoulder with a soft sigh. "As long as we're discussing shocking revelations of self-discovery, I think I may have figured something out, talking with Matilde today. While it's true that I do enjoy sex, I've always preferred it as an act of affection with someone I care about. I can't actually remember the last time I sought out sex for the sake of sex. And then there were all the times I used it out of…obligation, doing something my partner wanted to so they wouldn't get bored of me." I take a slow sip from my flimsy cup and sigh. "And just like when I couldn't understand why you weren't co-opting all my time, maybe I got worried that you not having any sexual designs for me was a problem—that perhaps there was something wrong with me." Penny doesn't say anything right away, and I look over at her nervously. "Was that too much? I know tonight was supposed to be about the band, not us."

"It's…heavy, for sure. Don't worry, I think I see what you're saying. I'm just letting it all, y'know"—she gestures with her coffee and smiles bashfully—"percolate." Penny takes a drink as well before looking me over more thoughtfully. "Maybe you're gray or demi or something."

I have no idea what that means, of course, and I tilt my head curiously, causing her to laugh.

"Sorry, uh, it's another asexuality thing. There's a lot of different flavors, and they all kinda overlap. None of it is prescriptive, and you're not obligated to actively choose any of them. But it's worth looking into some time."

"Sounds like we've got a few more boot camps ahead of us."

"Drill Instructor Hartwell is happy to oblige." She holds my gaze for a few moments, lips spreading into a wide smile. Penny leans in closer, and I go to meet her in the kiss I've been wanting since I saw her face inside the theater. It's gentle and it's unhurried and it feels like home, the two of us smiling against one another.

But after a few seconds, we're interrupted when her phone suddenly starts buzzing in her pocket. With a bashful chuckle, she pulls it out and glances at the screen. "Oh, shit."

"Is everything all right?"

"Text from Kai. The last act is finishing up, and then it's time for the final verdict, so we should probably get back," she mutters while putting her phone away and drinking down the rest of her coffee.

I stand up from the concrete planter and take our empty cups to a nearby bin to throw away, then grab for Penny's hand eagerly. "This…doesn't count as glossing, does it? I'm excited to see how the band did."

"Neither of us is going anywhere. We've got all the time in the world."

She's right. No need to rush this. What had seemed like a major roadblock has turned out to be little more than a nasty bump, but we're still here, still together. There will be plenty of time to figure these things out. Together.

There's a kind of silence that's been hanging over the band since the end of the battle. As they packed up their instruments and gear into Cameron's van and drove it over to the parking garage near my apartment, none of them said a word. Even now, while I lead the way down the sidewalk, they remain stoic and melancholy.

Theo finally breaks the strange silence just as my apartment building comes into view. "I can't believe we lost," he mutters miserably. He would be getting a good deal more sympathy if he wasn't currently holding their second-place trophy and prize check for three hundred dollars.

Penny looks over at me with a weary smile before looking back over her shoulder at him. "Dude, you beat out some of the biggest names in town at one of the most cutthroat competitions of the year. And look at who got first place! Not Deviltower Star, or even Grayscale. Fucking *Ten Again*. An all-girl punk band with a trans frontwoman. If you have to lose to anyone, you've gotta admit, that's the most rock and roll scenario."

"Hmm. I guess."

We make our way together through the foyer and up the short elevator ride to my floor. I open the door, and for a moment, the tension is defused as Penny's brother and friends all marvel at the place I call home. "You all make yourselves comfortable and figure out where you want to order from, and I'll put some snacks together while we wait."

Things eventually fall into a comfortable lull. The task of choosing delivery has given the band something to focus on, and Penny joins me in the kitchen to help plate up everything else I bought for tonight. Meagan makes herself at home on my sister's lap, the two seemingly having found a kind of kindred spirit in one another. Kai is once more hyperfocused on his phone— something about an app he's helping to develop.

There's a domesticity here that I haven't experienced in quite a long time.

I walk past Penny as she opens a container of gourmet humus, pausing briefly to peck her on the cheek, delighting in the deep blush I receive in return, then start slicing some tomato and mozzarella with a self-satisfied chuckle. She gets her revenge a few minutes later, though, coming up behind me as I plate them up with bruschetta. Silently, Penny wraps her arms around my stomach and hugs me tight. "I'm really glad we talked about stuff. It feels…good."

"It does," I say softly before gently extricating myself from her grasp—though I wish I didn't have to—and place the platter in her hands. "But for now, we've got hosting duties to attend to."

"Fine, fine."

Between the two of us, we're able to get the various dishes out to my coffee table, then one more trip to bring the libations. Seeing the bottle of champagne, Theo's hangdog expression begins to show itself once more. "Hey, come on, there's no need to break out the good stuff on our account. I don't know if we've really earned it."

Matilde just scoffs with a flippant wave of her hand. "Honestly, Theodore, there's no need to act like this is the end of the world. I know a thing or two about talent, and you all absolutely have the 'chops' required to succeed."

Meagan perks up from her lap. "Oh, yeah, yer like a big, fancy talent scout or whatever. Whaddya say? Ya gonna give these three a shot?"

As Penny and I settle onto the couch, Matilde meets my eye and gives me a little knowing smile. "I operate out of Los Angeles. To my understanding, Terra Vertebrae is dead set on staying a Boston fixture. And while it's not impossible to have such a long-distance relationship, so to speak, it's not ideal for a band that is only just finding their place in the world."

Cameron shrugs as he tosses a bit of hummus and pita into his mouth. "I mean, the West Coast wouldn't be the worst." It comes out blatantly unconvinced and unconvincing. They would never be happy there.

"You would need someone local, someone who knows the ins and outs of the venues here." Cool and casual as can be, she plucks a bit of bruschetta and chews it thoughtfully before continuing, "However…that does not mean we are without options."

A look passes between the three band members before Celeste takes the lead, leveling my sister with a look that is equal parts curiosity and trepidation. "Go on?"

While it's fascinating to watch Matilde work, I feel a bit bad letting her drag this out too much, stringing along the poor trio, so I get to the point. "She has plenty of contacts in Boston. And what I believe she is ambling her way toward revealing is that Matilde might be able to put you in touch with some of them."

Celeste's gaze flicks my way now, that mixture of emotions not fully dissipated yet. "Even with a recommendation, that stuff takes time, and it's not a guarantee."

"In the interim, well…Given our circumstances, it hardly seems right for me to stay Penny's patron. But I still believe in supporting artists, and I earnestly agree that Terra Vertebrae is worth it. So, what would you say to a trial partnership? I know you were hoping to win that studio time at the battle. So, I'll sponsor you. And if you happen to make something album-worthy, I might even help with production and distribution."

Granted, the last time I helped anyone put out an album was during the heyday of vinyl records. But I'm a quick study, and I can always call Matilde for some backup.

Now Theo is looking at me suspiciously as well. "What's the catch?"

"I have no intention of dictating your musical direction. But I'd likely be pushing you into a more steady schedule, taking over finding performance opportunities for you. Also, I would strongly recommend that Penny be the one to take care of your visual elements—artwork, merchandise designs, the like."

Penny huffs, though I note that she continues to stay latched on to me. "Putting me to work already. Unbelievable."

For a few moments, the three bandmates quietly stare at one another questioningly, but finally Celeste gives me a firm nod. "Obviously we'll have to hash out all the fiddly details another time. But I think it's worth a shot."

"Hey, that reminds me. Isn't tonight also supposed to be the grand reveal of the portrait that started all this?" Kai asks with a grin. He raises a good point.

And of course, Penny only grows more bashful, practically burying her face in my arm. "No, I'm not ready. We'll show it off another time. Let's say five years from now?"

Kai starts clapping and chanting, "Por-trait! Por-trait!" and soon everyone is joining in.

There's no way I'm letting Penny hide, so I disentangle myself from her and get up from the couch to fetch the canvas in spite of her whining protests. "You have nothing to be embarrassed about. Wait right there, I'll go get it."

When I come back into the room, I'm delighted to hear everyone break out in various noises of appreciation and admiration.

"Holy fuckin' shit, Penpen," I hear Meagan mutter—and make a conscious note to remember that nickname for later.

Celeste somehow manages to make even a wolf-whistle sound particularly melodic. "I knew you were talented, but damn."

Twirling one of his drumsticks almost like it's a fidget toy, Cameron nods enthusiastically while I set the portrait down to lean against the fireplace hearth. "Okay, I am absolutely on board with her doing more art shit for us."

"God knows the T-shirts could use an upgrade," Theo says with a soft chuckle. He moves over to where she is on the couch and flops down next to her, grabbing her roughly, ruffling her hair with brotherly affection. "Seriously, you crushed it. I'm proud of you."

Everyone continues to lavish Penny with more and more praise until she's red as a beet and trying desperately to hide behind me. Before long, she's rescued from her torment by the sound of my door buzzer, and the arrival of our food.

It takes some time, but slowly everyone filters out of my apartment.

Meagan goes first, mentioning that she needs to get to work. Kai goes with her, as does Matilde—saying something about wanting to visit an "authentic Boston pub."

Rather than continue partying, the members of Terra Vertebrae seem ready to sleep. With a loud yawn, Cameron goes first, mentioning that he needs to get the van with all their equipment back home. Theo shares a few parting words with his sister before leaving with Celeste in tow.

Finally, it's just the two of us on my couch. And Penny is warm and drunk and all smiles. Which is when she says the one thing I least expect in that moment. "Can I stay here tonight?"

My face is hot, and I'm sure I'm making some kind of ridiculous expression, because she starts laughing.

"Sorry, sorry. Not like that. I mean it platonically. Or…no. Romantically. But not sexually."

"So…asexually."

"Who taught you that word? Where'd you learn that?"

"From you, okay! I learned it from watching you!" Before long, we're gripping one another tightly, fighting for air through our delirious laughter once again. "Of course you can, Penny. I would be delighted."

I'm careful about the tone that I set from here on out. Even if Penny is the one who requested this, I know it's still the kind of scenario that can be…fraught. So I avoid any lingering looks or suggestive teasing. Holding her hand firmly, I lead her back to my bedroom and provide her with something loose and comfortable she can wear to bed. We change quietly while facing away from each other, and soon we're climbing into bed and nestling together under the covers.

It takes a few minutes for us to each find the right position. But Penny eventually relents and allows me to spoon her. I wrap my arms around her and rest my hands against her soft belly, feeling the warmth of her body against mine. We've slotted together so perfectly, like she was meant to be here.

In that hazy world of darkness and encroaching dreams, she speaks again, and I can feel it reverberate through me as much as I hear it. "I was right, I could definitely get used to this. And you're sure you're okay with not doing any…stuff?" In spite of everything we talked about, the question still comes out timid and afraid. As if I won't be doing everything in my power to keep this woman.

Smiling as I nuzzle into her hair, I give her tummy a gentle squeeze. "Do you remember what I told you at the museum, about the miracle of small joys? Maybe I didn't completely figure it out like I'd thought. Perhaps it will take time. But being with you, it's a good crash course. A simple life. Not everything needs to be blazing infernos and brilliant creations."

"Buttered noodles," she mutters softly.

"Exactly."

EPILOGUE

Penny

It's hard to believe how much can change in just a few months. And it was all so damn subtle, I didn't really notice until I stopped to take a proper look around me.

Things started so simply. Cameron's housemates moved out, so he offered to let Theo and Celeste take their place. Obviously they agreed, happy to share a house and a rehearsal space together.

Then, a friend of Kai's and a coworker at Meagan's bar both needed somewhere to live. Only when I could consider moving in with Anthea a favor to my friends did I feel comfortable with a decision that big. Granted, I was already spending half my time at her apartment anyway, and I'd been progressively leaving more and more of my crap at over there. Clothes, toiletries, art supplies, the like.

Before I knew it, we'd integrated our lives together. The spare room officially became my very own private studio—complete with a spot for my computer and tablet, a shiny new drawing table, and a well-stocked supply of paper, canvas, materials, tools. Everything a girl needs to make art.

I don't even need my shit job at the gas station anymore. I can just do what I love, every day. With Terra Vertebrae's first proper album in the works, a lot of my focus these days is on my new job as their artistic lackey—Cameron's words, not mine. Plus, with August in full swing, I'm grateful to not be working in that horrid place anymore. I can hide away in my studio with the blessed air-conditioning at full blast.

Unkind Gods Don't Let Go is a hell of a name for a first album, and it deserves an incredible image to set the tone. Even though I'll eventually need to do the finished cover artwork on my computer, I find myself drawn to do a version the old-fashioned way. I've got a huge sheet of fine-tooth paper on my table, a stick of charcoal in my hand as I make the finishing touches.

It's a nighttime scene with a sky full of swirling stars and planets. In the foreground, a lonely mountain vista, and in the background, the apocalyptic final days of a dystopian cyberpunk city. Plunged into the frosty ground is a weathered longsword, with a lone robin resting its weary bones on the pommel.

There's a gentle knock at the door before Anthea pokes her head in with a warm smile. "How's it going in here?"

"Really good. I hope they like it as much as I do."

She comes up behind me, wrapping her arms around me and propping her chin on my shoulder. "They're going to love it."

"How was rehearsal?"

"I think they're finally getting used to having someone around playing taskmaster and keeping them on track. And Theo's new song is bound to be quite the sleeper hit." She kisses my shoulder before slowly releasing her grip on me. "I don't want to distract you. I'm going to work on dinner while you finish up."

"Mm, okay. Sounds good." As nice as it is to have her wrapped around me, I know I'll get plenty more of that later. So I turn my attention back to the album cover, brandish my charcoal, and make that night sky really sing. Just as I start to slip back into a state of flow, I hear myself casually toss out a quick, "Love you." As if this isn't the first time either of us has actually said that. As if this isn't a major moment in our relationship.

Anthea's footsteps suddenly stop, and for a brief moment, I worry that maybe I dropped the L-word a little too soon. But just like that, she starts to chuckle to herself. "I love you too, Penny." She puts a strong emphasis on it, still laughing lightly as she leaves the room, muttering to herself, "August. Summer's end. She'll never let me live this down."

No idea why Anthea found that so funny, but I'm just glad she didn't seem to mind.

Anthea

It was, as it has always been with us, the smallest of things.

After putting in several grueling hours on a new, experimental piece, Penny got a text from Liz. Mention of their mother's funeral left Penny in a state of deeply complicated melancholy all evening. She never got that apology, and while she fought to maintain her "fuck those people" attitude, she eventually admitted that a not-insignificant part of her still felt guilty for never going home or saying anything, right up to the bitter end.

To fight off the weighty thoughts, not to mention the biting and cruel Boston winter, I got a proper fire going. Then I forced Penny to take a break with me and cuddle on the couch, encouraging her to put on one of those cartoons she'd been insisting I absolutely had to see.

Fire is a primal thing, as central to humans as it is to my own innate nature. Before long, the glow and the warmth worked their magic, and she unfurled a bit from her introspection. I knew she'd give voice to her thoughts when she was ready. The holidays were on the horizon, and she'd already had plenty on her mind to start with.

For seemingly no reason whatsoever, Penny suddenly grabbed one of her many sketchbooks lying nearby, then got up and went to the fireplace. She took a piece of fresh kindling, sticking one end into the fire. The light flickered in her eyes, a peaceful smile on her lips. When the stick was properly singed, she settled on the floor and began drawing.

Drawing me.

She'd done it dozens of times since that first day in the library. But this was…

I don't even know if I have the right words for it. Cyclical, I suppose? A moment of rebirth for me. The difference here, however, is that I didn't inspire this particular moment of artistic insight. She did it all on her own. I'm not sure if she was reminded of the story of my creation, or if the concept came to her more unconsciously.

All I can say for certain is that I knew in that moment that I had a decision to make.

I pictured a world where I stay a muse. I continue to work with Penny into her twilight years as she grows older, creating until her body can no longer manage it. And all the while I stay the same, unchanging. One day she dies, leaving me to mourn her loss. Perhaps I take another constitutional. Or maybe I find the strength to dust myself off and try again—but who could ever compare to this strange, wonderful, beautiful woman?

That sad, unending story replaced itself with another. A story full of uncertainty and anxiety, but also far more potential and love.

I thought of Isaac and his husband, and their life together, and I knew that it was time. I knew which story I wanted. "Penny?"

"Hmm, what's up?"

"Boston's only going to get colder. Once Terra Vertebrae's album releases in January, we should take a vacation to somewhere warm."

She chuckled and continued to sketch me. "Just like that?"

"Just like that. I was thinking, perhaps…New Zealand. It's supposed to be lovely this time of year."

With a gasp, Penny dropped the kindling and stared at me with wide eyes. She was silent for a full ten seconds before breaking out in a huge smile. "Okay!"

So many seemingly random decisions led us to one another. Her staying in Boston, my leaving Dmitri. The constitutional, the library, the contract, the gala.

And now, here we are, boarding a plane at Logan International, to make the long journey halfway around the world. I'm really looking forward to wherever our winding path takes us next. It's bound to be one hell of a story.

Bella Books
Happy Endings Live Here
P.O. Box 10543
Tallahassee, FL 32302
Phone: (800) 729-4992
BellaBooks.com

More Titles from Bella Books

Jones – Gerri Hill
978-1-64247-598-2 | 260 pages | Mystery
One weekend getaway, six friends, and a deadly secret that will wash away everything they thought they knew.

Merry Weihnachten – E. J. Noyes
978-1-64247-610-1 | 292 pages | Romance
Christmas traditions aren't the only things getting mixed up when these two hearts collide beneath the mistletoe.

Sweet Home Alabarden Park – TJ O'Shea
978-1-64247-570-8 | 362 pages | Romance
She came to restore a royal estate—she never expected to rebuild her heart.

Dr. Margaret Morgan – Christy Hadfield
978-1-64247-628-6 | 286 pages | Romance
Facing the professor on campus everyone hates is terrifying—but falling for her might be even worse.

Overtime – Tracey Richardson
978-1-64247-630-9 | 278 pages | Romance
A charming romance about second chances, found family, and scoring the goal that matters most.

The Big Guilt – Renée J. Lukas
978-1-64247-657-6 | 206 pages | Romance
What if the one who got away became the one you can't have?